Mail
Order Cowboy

Mail Order *Cowboy*

VICTORIA

NEW YORK TIMES BESTSELLING AUTHOR

JAMES

Entangled Publishing, LLC
644 Shrewsbury Commons Ave., STE 181
Shrewsbury, PA 17361
Visit our website at www.entangledpublishing.com.

Amara is an imprint of Entangled Publishing, LLC.

Edited by Alethea Spiridon
Cover design by Elizabeth Turner Stokes
Stock art by simpleman/Shutterstock,
HighKey/Shutterstock
Interior design by Toni Kerr

Print ISBN 978-1-64937-312-0
ebook ISBN 978-1-64937-313-7

Manufactured in the United States of America

First Edition January 2023

AMARA

ALSO BY VICTORIA JAMES

To Megan...thank you for sharing this wild journey with me! Monday morning coffee with you is the best way to start the week! xo

At Entangled, we want our readers to be well-informed. If you would like to know if this book contains any elements that might be of concern for you, please check the back of the book for details.

CHAPTER ONE

Hope Roberts was *not* a cowgirl. Or a rancher. Or even a person who knew how to ride a horse.

She was a single mom to her amazing, smart, adorable, nine-year-old daughter. She was a naturopathic doctor. She was the daughter of two wonderful people. She was also a best friend. A godmother. A widow.

And now, thanks to her late husband's grandparents, she was a ranch owner. Some might see this unexpected inheritance as a sign that her life was finally turning around. She saw it that way too, most of the time, because it was the opportunity of a lifetime to be a homeowner, a landowner. It was the stuff dreams were made of. Except right now, it was more like the stuff nightmares were made of, because she was in way over her head and she didn't want to mess everything up and leave her daughter with nothing one day.

And then there was the fact that she had a whole theory about the way her life worked. Happiness followed by tragedy. So, the last few years, she'd been walking around with an imaginary hard hat on, anticipating when the sky was going to fall.

As she stood outside the legendary River's

Saloon in Wishing River, Montana, peering through the window, taking in the round tables packed with happy people, her gaze resting on her friends, seated at their usual table, panic swelled inside her. They were all there waiting to congratulate her. They were laughing, drinking, enjoying life. She couldn't bring herself to walk in and join them yet. She couldn't go in there and pretend she had it all together. She couldn't be a single parent, run a business, and try to make an abandoned ranch profitable. And yet, she had to. For her daughter Sadie. It was a piece of Sadie's history.

Late-winter icy rain pummeled the rooftop of the covered porch of the old saloon, and she huddled farther into her jacket and tried to psych herself up to go inside. The only person in their friend group who hadn't arrived yet was Dean Stanton and that was just as well. She had enough turmoil swirling in her head, she didn't need her complicated feelings for him making things even worse.

"Uh, Miss Roberts?"

Hope jumped at the sound of the vaguely familiar voice behind her. She turned around to find the young man she'd hired yesterday standing behind her. At least hiring him had been a victory. He was experienced but young and eager, and it would be his first real job. He was willing to do repairs and help her come up with a plan for getting the ranch running again.

Slapping on a smile, she tried to appear as though she were calm and collected. "Hi, Colby. Here for a fun night?" She cringed inwardly. Since when did she sound so old? *A fun night?* Like she was about to drive home and put on flannel pajamas and watch *When Calls the Heart.* Though the idea did appeal to her in a panic-inducing way. She wasn't even thirty. Way too young to be wishing for weekends in flannels with a bowl of popcorn in her lap instead of a glass of wine in her hand and skinny jeans.

He gave her a mangled sort of smile. "Something like that. Bad weather tonight, don't you think?"

She forced herself to make small talk, because this was someone she would be seeing daily. "Well, this time of year is always a bit disappointing. I have to keep reminding myself spring is around the corner."

Judging by his red face and how many times in the last two minutes he'd looked at the ground and shifted from one foot to the other, this conversation wasn't going to be good, and this wasn't about the weather. She slapped on an encouraging smile, like the one she gave to her nine-year-old daughter when she was trying to coax her to admit she'd snuck some cookies.

She took a deep breath and thought positive thoughts. Maybe he needed some advice. Or medical help—they had touched on some strange symptoms he was having lately. She swallowed hard and looked up at him. "Colby, I would love to stay out here and chat, but my friends are all waiting for me inside and I'm already late. Maybe we can talk Monday morning when you come over to my place? You can come a few minutes before you start work. We can have a coffee together and we can resume this conversation then."

He rubbed the back of his neck. "See, uh, the thing is, Hope…"

"Evening."

Hope stifled her groan of irritation at the sound of that unmistakeable, deep voice that she knew belonged to Dean Stanton. She looked over to see Dean stepping onto the porch and walking over to them. The last thing she wanted was Dean listening in on their conversation.

Dean Stanton, doctor, rancher, heir to a ranching empire, was the last man in Montana she needed showing up right now. Despite being born into mega wealth and ranching royalty, he'd also forged his own way and become a doctor. He was loyal to his friends. He didn't ever advertise his wealth and, in fact, sometimes went out of his way to downplay it. But there were things in their past she'd never reconcile. And then there was his father.

She'd given Dean the cold shoulder for

years...even if she'd sort of come to terms with things and had softened her position and felt bad about how she'd accused Dean of being a negligent doctor. They could never be more than they were right now, which was what she'd call reluctant friends. There were so many reasons, some of which everyone knew, one that no one knew. But she knew. Thanks to his father, who'd made it perfectly clear that there was a path forward for Dean and it didn't involve her. Which was fine, because she had no intention of ever trying again for happily-ever-after. But she couldn't deny the undercurrent whenever he was around that threatened to make her forget those reasons they couldn't be together.

The fact that every bone in her body seemed to react when Dean was near was slightly disconcerting, and something she kept to herself. Her friends would be all over that piece of knowledge like sprinkles on a cupcake. And yet she still took a second to appreciate how he looked; his dark brown hair a little longer than usual, blue eyes serious as usual, and tall, athletic frame, perfectly perfect in his button-down navy-and-white checked shirt and worn-in jeans. The man hadn't even bothered to put on a coat from the parking lot to the saloon and he didn't even look cold. Why that should matter was beyond her. And, yet, all impossible to ignore.

Dean had the walk and the look of a man who

knew who he was, what he was made to do. She knew *way* too much about a man she was not supposed to like. As he made his way down the wooden porch that spanned the length of the saloon, her heart skipped a little, in that rhythm that had almost become like a custom ringtone when Dean was around.

What disturbed her the most was that Dean was the only man who'd ever made her this…jittery…or heady. But that shouldn't matter, since they would never be more than frenemies.

He stood beside her and she smiled up at him, even though it felt as though her cheeks were pushing against cement. "Hi Dean. You can go on in. I'll uh, be right there,"

Colby's face lit up and he extended his hand. "Dr. Stanton? Hi, nice to meet you. I'm Colby Cooke."

Dean shook it. "Nice to meet you."

She was about to open the door to usher Dean inside when Colby started speaking again. "So, like I was saying, Hope…I'm really sorry but I won't be able to work for you."

Hope blinked, his words ringing in her ears, rushing through her mind. It was happening again. Catastrophe. The nice young man was quitting before he even started. And worse, Dean was here, silently witnessing her humiliation. She spared Dean a quick glance only to see him staring at Colby with his jaw clenched. Knowing him, he was ready to speak up on her behalf, and that was the last thing she wanted. "What happened, Colby?"

He nodded, his eyes darting nervously between her and Dean. "I…I know, but uh, see, the thing is, I'm at a point in my life that every dollar earned is really important…and I uh, I got an offer where I'm making double what you're offering me."

Hope wished the rickety old porch would just swallow her whole. She forced herself to maintain eye contact and appear calm and collected. "But…but…I mean, I guess I understand. Um, if I were in your position, I would do the same."

"No, you wouldn't. And neither would I. You made a commitment, Colby Cooper, and now you're going back on it a day before you start? Kid, what you need to realize is that your word means everything out here. Your reputation as a cowboy is more important than a résumé," Dean bit out, his voice harsh and unyielding as his stare.

She was about to glare at Dean for speaking on her behalf, but Colby beat her to it. "Uh, it's Cooke, Colby Cooke…and no offense intended, Dr. Stanton, but I'm working at your ranch."

Hope sucked in a breath and Dean swore under his breath. His jaw was clenched so hard that Hope bet she could break a glass against it. But she couldn't think about that now. The rain had picked up and the wind was pushing it onto the porch. Dean's ranch. The Stanton Ranch. Her stomach churned as she tried to come up with something to say but, right now, all she could feel was the sting of hurt and humiliation.

"Who hired you?" Dean asked, his words clipped.

Poor Colby's face went from bright red to white in an instant. "Your...your...father," he stammered.

Dean let out a muffled curse and ran his hand through his hair. "I'll make up the difference in your pay if you stay on at Hope's."

Hope let out a small scream and turned to Dean. "Are you *kidding* me? I let you have your moment of manly cowboy talk wearing your bossy pants, but that was it. Actually thinking that you are going to not only manage an employee, but then offer to pay out of your own pocket without even discussing this with me?"

His eyes were flashing as he looked at her, and she knew she had him over a barrel. There was no way he could deny what she was saying without looking like a total jerk. He ran a hand over his jaw and closed his eyes for half a second. She was going to be satisfied when he apologized in front of Colby. She folded her hands and waited for it.

"Hope, I don't own bossy pants, nor do I even acknowledge them as a real thing."

She gasped and glared up at him. "That's all you got out of what I just said?"

"I'm, uh, going to head inside," Colby said, before whipping open the door and disappearing.

"Coward," Dean called out as the door shut behind Colby.

Hope crossed her arms. "I really want to shove you off this porch right now."

Dean's deep chuckle almost made her shoulders relax slightly. "I don't blame you."

She drew a deep breath. "So you admit you were wrong for speaking for me?"

He gave a noncommittal shrug. "If that moron Cooper—"

"Colby—"

"Whatever, had I said that to either Tyler or Cade, they would have joined me and appreciated my lecture. You could have joined in, too, and you might have even enjoyed yourself. You're…my friend, Hope and friends look out for friends."

Tyler and Cade were Dean's lifelong best friends. They were also married to Hope's best friends. But none of that made her feel better. Neither did the warmth in his voice or the way he'd just smooth-talked himself out of his high-handedness. "I disagree because that doesn't sound like fun at all. What about the fact that you're picking off my employees?"

He winced, taking a step closer to her. She told herself that the only reason her heart was pounding as fast as the rain pummeling around them was because she was angry. The fact that it happened at the same time as him moving close to her was merely a coincidence. "I would never. Which is why I offered to make up the difference in his salary," he said gruffly.

She looked away from his sharp blue gaze. "I could never accept that. I just…I don't know what I'm going to do."

"I'll talk to my father first."

Her heart stopped for a painful beat. "Do not talk to your father."

He frowned. "Why not?"

She fixed her gaze on the parking lot, carefully choosing her words. "I need to do this on my own. I don't need favors. The truth is, I was getting a bargain with Colby. I don't have a big budget but, because this was his first job, he was happy with the money I was able to offer, especially when I said I'd help him with his allergies."

Dean made a sound and she turned her head to him. "What was that?"

"You just happened to notice he had allergies during his interview?"

She lifted her chin. "I'm very intuitive. He was always clearing his throat. Very phlegmy. And then he kept sneezing. And he has quite a bit of acne for someone his age."

Dean smirked and Hope remembered why it was so easy to be irritated by him. "Oh, I'm sure he loved hearing that."

"I didn't comment on the acne. I have a very

good bedside manner. Anyway, I think he might have a dairy allergy."

"Or a cold."

She narrowed her eyes. "Colds don't last nineteen years."

"Okay, fine, we're getting way off topic anyway. Why don't we go inside? Everyone is waiting for us."

"I don't think you understand what this means, Dean. I just lost the one person who responded to the dumb mail-order-cowboy ad my friends helped me place. I never should have let Sarah, who had her own giant fail with cowboy ads, help me with this one. What am I even saying, now I sound like you! I can't blame Sarah for this. This is all on me. This is just my luck," she said, pacing back and forth to ease some of the erratic energy pulsing through her. She barely even felt the cold anymore.

"I'm not following. This has nothing to do with luck. That kid is going after more money, that's all there is to it. And, besides, I don't think Sarah's cowboy ad was a failure, because she ended up marrying Cade."

She crossed her arms over her chest. "So what, I'm supposed to marry Colby?"

Dean's eyes narrowed. "Of course not. That's ridiculous. And you're right. It was ridiculous to put out an ad. Who knows what kind of weirdo could come to your house. But I'm solving that problem for you."

"About the weirdos?"

He gave a short nod. "Yes."

"How exactly?"

He pinched the bridge of his nose. "Hope, I'll be your mail-order cowboy."

She stared at him, the cold wind slapping rain against her overheated face. Dean, the man she had tried desperately to hate.

The man, the doctor, she'd blamed for diagnosing her husband with cancer a year too late for him to survive.

Dean, the man she'd treated with contempt and hostility for five years, the man who was already the hardest working person she knew between the hospital and the family ranch, was now offering his services at her ranch.

But that was a separate issue. She didn't want to be indebted to Dean. She also didn't know why he'd want to do this. He certainly didn't need the money. His family had the kind of money and status most people would never understand, the kind that would make someone like her uncomfortable.

Dean's father had also made it clear to her two years ago that his son was off-limits, and that was something way too humiliating to ever admit to Dean.

She searched for her voice, that one deep inside that spoke the truth without a filter, the one she rarely used when he was around because it always felt like there were so many unspoken feelings between them.

She searched for it, standing here in front of him, in front of the bar they'd been meeting at with their friends for the last five years, and she didn't find it. It was probably hiding with all the other cowardly thoughts inside her mind. So, instead, she gave him the words he was probably already expecting, she gave him the Hope he had come to expect, the one who was cold enough to keep him away.

The one who had to act like she had it all together and was strong.

She cleared her throat and squared her shoulders.

"Over my dead body."

CHAPTER TWO

Over my dead body.

Monday afternoon, as Dean drove the winding dusty backroads of Wishing River to Hope's new house he tried to find the humor in her statement but couldn't. He kept replaying Saturday night on the porch. She was probably praying he wouldn't keep his word.

He wasn't surprised by her reaction; it was the way they communicated. He considered Hope a friend. *Her* best friend Lainey was married to *his* best friend, Tyler. His other best friend, Cade, was married to her other good friend, Sarah. So, they all spent Saturday nights together at River's Saloon.

He was also connected to Hope because her late husband had been one of his patients. She'd never forgiven him for what she thought his role was in Brian's death, and he let her believe that because of the promise he'd made to Brian. Dean felt guilty as hell and it was that guilt that made him want to look out for her. Guilt. Plain and simple.

The minute he'd heard that kid back out of his commitment to help her last Saturday night, Dean had already seen the only path ahead. But when Colby had gone on to reveal that he was

going to be working for Dean's father, it had
sealed the deal. There was no way in hell he'd let
Hope lose out because of his father. So Dean had
resigned himself to the fact that in addition to
being a doctor, and to playing an integral role on
his family ranch, he was going to have to be
Hope's mail-order cowboy. There was no way
around it.

As it was, he barely had any time to himself.
Between his family practice, his rounds at the
hospital, and his involvement with his family
ranch, he was already short for time.

Of course, he knew convincing her to hire
him was going to be harder than birthing a
breech calf in the middle of an open field during
a Montana blizzard. Before they'd walked into
the bar to meet their friends, she'd sworn him to
secrecy. He'd obliged, but it had killed him to see
her putting on an act as everyone toasted her.
He understood her pride, her need to not want
everyone to feel sorry for her. Hell, he even admired it.

Dean eased his foot off the gas as he turned
onto Hope's street. The small log cabin caught his
eye immediately. He'd been down this road a
thousand times, because it was the ranch beside
Tyler's. Not that you could even see Ty's property
from here. The land on some of these ranches was
in the thousands of acres and even though they
were so much smaller than Dean's, there was still

space out here. There was still room to breathe. Maybe more room to breathe because his family name wasn't branded on anything.

As the cab of his truck bumped along the pot-hole-filled driveway, he mentally added that to the enormous to-do list for Hope's place.

The first time he'd had a conversation with Hope she'd been sitting at the counter at Wishing River town landmark, Tilly's Diner, laughing with Lainey, who owned the place. Since everyone knew everyone in a town as small as Wishing River, it had felt like he'd always known Hope. Her dad had been a custodian for a while at the high school when Dean was there, and he did the odd job around different ranches in town.

But Dean remembered the day he'd noticed Hope wasn't a teenager anymore…maybe it was the way she'd tilted her head back and smiled. Maybe it was the way she'd looked at him. Or maybe he'd been imagining that flicker of interest in her deep green eyes. But the next thing he knew she was getting married to a guy Dean would later become all too familiar with. Dean had brushed it all off…his feelings for Hope. He'd been consumed by medical school, anyway, and then when he was working in Wishing River again, he'd taken on her husband as one of his patients. And that had turned into the biggest mistake of his life.

But he'd do it all over again if it meant

keeping Hope from getting hurt. Because during those gruesome years, those years she'd hated him, those years she'd lost her husband, that she'd become a single mom and built her own business, his admiration for her had grown even more. And he could never blame her for hating him, because he had led her to believe that he had failed her husband.

He parked his truck in front of the old ranch house and took in the surroundings. The familiar Montana sky and mountains dominated, even though it was gray and dreary out. But he always thought that no day out here was ever ugly because the sky always held something awe-inspiring. Today, the clouds were fast moving, chased by the wind, angry and turbulent, but so typical for March.

There was something special out here, the mountains and the landscape, the sparkling rivers and the wildlife, the community and the lifestyle. They were all intertwined, incapable of being replicated anywhere else because they were interdependent.

There was no place he'd rather be, and he was fiercely loyal to Wishing River and the life here, even though he'd been offered positions at larger, more urban hospitals. Wishing River was in his blood, for generations, and he'd never walk away from this place, no matter how much he was tempted to because of his father.

His gaze spanned the property before getting out of the truck. There was no doubt about it— Hope had inherited a good piece of land. He knew, since it bordered Ty's property, that this was prime ranching real estate. But he also knew Hope didn't have the kind of money needed to start up a real working ranch. Sure, the land was free and clear, but the kind of capital needed was way beyond a working person's paycheck.

He needed to know exactly how many acres she owned and what her intentions were. He could help her come up with a plan that would be profitable and realistic. But he also was going to mention the idea of selling. Land in Montana had skyrocketed the last decade and selling might be the most prudent option. He knew that probably wasn't what she wanted, but it should be something to consider. But this was still a great opportunity and he'd been thinking up various possibilities. In the meantime, he could help fix up the old house and get that barn up and running. If she did sell, it would make the property only more attractive.

He hopped out of the truck and up the steps just as the front door opened. Hope was standing there, in jeans and a hoodie, her hair in a messy ponytail. She was still the most gorgeous woman he'd ever seen, no matter what she was wearing or regardless of the expression on her face.

Their relationship was complicated at the best

of times. He'd taken the brunt of her anger over the death of her husband gladly and he'd do it all again if it meant keeping his promise and keeping her happy. He'd always look out for her, always make sure she and Sadie were safe.

"You've *got* to be kidding," she said as he approached.

He tipped his hat, choosing his words carefully. "No, ma'am. I told you last Saturday night that I'd be here."

"How are you going to work at the hospital, your family ranch, and…here?"

He crossed his arms over his chest. "Last time I checked, I was a grown man, completely aware of what I can handle. So, consider my schedule my problem."

She placed her hands on her hips and he did his best not to let his gaze travel over her. He already knew everything. Every curve and hollow. And he had no business knowing them. "Well, it'll be my problem if you can't do your job around here. You'll have no energy to keep up with everything. You might even faint from exhaustion and then where will I be? I'm not hiring you."

He couldn't help but laugh at the absurdity of that statement. "I don't faint. It's one of the few things I don't know how to do."

She sucked in a long, drawn-out breath, making it clear what she thought about his knowing almost everything. "I know you may find this hard to believe, but there are other applicants who could be even more qualified than you."

He took a step closer to her, close enough that he could see the lighter flecks of green in her eyes that reminded him of springtime meadows. Close enough that he could almost forget that he was the last thing she needed. Brian had been a family man. Dean was anything but. "Hope, we both know I'm overqualified and there's no cowboy with any kind of experience who will take this job for the money offered. Look at Cooper."

She inhaled sharply. "Colby and that's rude."

"It's a plain and simple fact. Like the fact that I'm the only other cowboy who'd been out here besides him. And I also happen to be a doctor. There's no way you'll find a more qualified cowboy than me."

"How do you know the position hasn't been filled?"

He sighed roughly and made a grand sweeping gesture with his arm. "Okay, Hope. Has it been filled?"

She lifted her chin. "Well, *no*…not technically."

His cleared his throat. "Consider it filled now."

"How am I going to pay you what you deserve? What I'm offering will be a joke to you."

A pang of sympathy hit him in the chest. He respected that pride she clung to. "It's not a joke and I didn't mean to imply it was. Besides, this place is barely liveable. I'm handy and that's what

I think you need around here anyway. If you want to make this into a ranch again, you won't find someone more dedicated and knowledgeable than me. I've got the day off work and that rarely happens. And we're friends. That's what friends do. I thought the whole crew was here last weekend painting. I couldn't help because I was on call, so let me make it up to you."

The high-pitched sound of school bus brakes made him turn around. The sound was familiar. His gaze went to the long expanse of grass that led to the road. The bright yellow bus rumbled at the foot of the gravel driveway and a second later he spotted Sadie bounding down the steps of the bus.

"Sadie's home. I totally lost track of time," Hope said, stepping out onto the porch. Dust kicked up as the bus barreled down the empty rural road and Sadie stopped to open the mailbox at the bottom of the driveway. "She's obsessed with that mailbox and the little flag," she said with a slight laugh.

Dean chuckled. "I guess it's a big change to move out here from town."

Sadie ran up the lengthy driveway, her long brown hair flying behind her, her hand in the air with a stack of mail, her sweet face in a giant smile. "Dr. Dean! What are you doing here?" Sadie said, rounding the corner from the driveway to the front path.

Dean crouched down and Sadie ran into his

arms. She was one of his favorite people even though he'd never considered himself a kid person. But she made it easy. "I was telling your mom I can help her out around here and get this place all fixed up."

Sadie jumped up and down. "That's great! This place needs lots of work. It was my dad's grandparents' house, did you know that?"

He stood up straight and smiled down at Sadie. "I did. It's a pretty cool place. How do you like living out here in the country?"

Sadie smiled back at Dean. "I love it! I might miss city living, but I like the stars out here. I was thinking I might want to be a cowgirl when I grow up. Or an astronaut. Or a doctor. Or drive a pink ice cream truck that shoots sprinkles as it drives."

Sadie stared up at Dean seriously and there was no way in hell he'd laugh about the sprinkle-shooting truck. "Those are all great options. Promise if you get that ice cream truck, you'll stop by my place."

Hope covered her mouth with her hand when Sadie winked at him and pointed to his chest with her index finger. "You got it."

"Maybe your truck can leave extra sprinkles outside Dean's house, Sadie," Hope said, laughter lining her voice.

"Uh, I would hope so," Dean said, shooting her a deadpan stare.

Hope cleared her throat. "Sadie, go inside and

wash up and I'll get you a snack."

"Sure Mom," Sadie said, a happy grin on her face. Hope held the door open for her and they stood in silence, watching her walk into the house.

"She's getting so big. It's been a couple months since I've seen her. You've done a great job with her, Hope," Dean said, turning his gaze from the house to Hope.

"Thank you. She's a great kid. She makes it easy."

He shoved his hands into the front pockets of his jeans, suddenly feeling the urge to leave. "I've got to get going, but I'll be here tomorrow morning at eight if that's okay."

She folded her arms across her chest, her eyes filling with panic. "Dean, seriously, no. What will your father say?"

His heart pounded uncomfortably. This was the second time she'd mentioned his father in two days. "My father? I'm not ten."

Her face turned red. "I just mean that you have your own obligations over there."

"That's my problem. Besides, that roof on the barn is about to cave in. What if Sadie's playing out there? And what about your porch? You know that railing is on its last leg."

"Dean."

He tipped his hat. He knew what needed to be done. "Hope, I'll see you at eight tomorrow morning. And don't be wearing bossy pants."

CHAPTER THREE

The next morning, Dean handed a reluctant Hope a cup of coffee from Tilly's diner. She was standing on the threshold of the front door and staring at him like she was surprised to see him.

"It's not poisoned," he said when she didn't take the cup.

She let out a small laugh. "I didn't think that. Not for more than a second. Thank you. This is very…nice of you. Though you are a doctor and if you wanted to poison someone and then try to cure them, it'd be within your capabilities. But, then again, I'd have to intervene and counter your mocktail of toxic pharmaceuticals with my own remedies."

He tried not to laugh. "Ah, but you might be too busy puking to direct me as to which herbs and potions are the right ones."

Her eyes sparkled. "That's cute and I can't even be offended, since I started this."

He grinned. "True. Because I'm a nice guy, despite what you may think."

Her face turned a lovely shade of pink. "No…I mean, I know you're a nice guy. I guess I'm slightly surprised you're here."

"Oh, so you thought I drove out here yesterday to lie? My word means nothing?"

She took a sip of coffee and averted her gaze. "Of course not. I had a feeling you wouldn't go back on your word. I just thought maybe once you had a chance to review your...other commitments, you'd have realized you can't make this work. Also, I thought you were my parents. They're coming by to pick up Sadie for a sleepover."

Sadie tore out the front door, preventing his retort challenging Hope's statement. She thought he wasn't going to come through for her. He didn't know what that said about him—or her. But Sadie's appearance also gave him an opportunity to distract himself from noticing how beautiful Hope always looked. Even when she wasn't exactly pulled together, she managed to be the most gorgeous woman he'd ever known. Her dark hair was in a ponytail again, errant strands moving gently with the wind and flicking against her fine features. She had on a pink hoodie with a tank top underneath that showed off her creamy skin and a hint of cleavage that made him thankful it wasn't colder out and she could forgo a jacket. Her dark jeans showed off the gentle curve of her hips and slender legs. There probably wasn't an ounce of makeup on her face and she didn't need it, because her skin was flawless and her green eyes were framed with dark lashes.

Sadie dropped her backpack on the porch and

gave him a hug that pulled him away from his thoughts of Hope. Seeing Sadie was always a bright spot in his day. She was this bundle of happiness and she always had something to say that made him laugh. She looked so much like Hope and she had that same clever sparkle in her eyes that kept him on his toes. "Hi, Dr. Dean. I'm going to my grandparents, but I'll be back tomorrow and will help out."

"All right. That might slow us down without you here, but I'm counting on your expertise," he said with a straight face. The sound of tires crunching over gravel and Sadie's frantic waving told him Hope's parents were here.

A few moments later, they were greeting one another on the porch. "Dean's going to help us fix up this old place," Sadie said, grabbing his hand and smiling at him.

Hope's father, Jeff, placed a hand on his shoulder. "I appreciate that, Dean. I know with your experience you can help Hope get this place back to what it should be. I can work right alongside you. Just tell me what you need and I'll be here. And don't go wearing yourself out, son."

Dean held on to her dad's gaze and was surprised at the warmth he felt by that simple statement. It was said as a casual thing, just like the hand clamped on his shoulder, but to him it was more.

Dean cleared his throat, not dwelling on why

the simple gesture touched him. "I'd love your help. As soon as Hope tells me what she wants for the place, we'll come up with a plan. And don't worry, I've always got the time for friends." Even as the statement came out of his mouth, he knew it was a ridiculous lie.

He hadn't exactly figured out how he was going to pull this off. He did have vacation days, but he rarely used them. He enjoyed the work he did at the family ranch when his father wasn't around, at the hospital, at his practice. Maybe he enjoyed it too much, but idleness had never been an option at home. And maybe he'd taken that to an extreme, but as long as he enjoyed what he did, he didn't see it as a problem. He'd never needed much sleep. Had never needed more than one night off a week to meet up with his friends at River's.

Jeff squeezed his shoulder before releasing it. "Well, we're lucky you're here."

"Do be careful, though, Dean. We don't want you wearing yourself out," Hope's mom said with a smile very similar to Hope's.

"I tried telling him it was too much. Don't worry. I won't let him go overboard," Hope said, shooting him a glance he couldn't quite decipher.

"See that you don't. Both of you. You know how proud of you we are, Hope. But remember to take care of yourself."

Hope waved a hand. "I'm fine. Promise. It's

not every day a person inherits a bit of ranchland out here. I will always be grateful to Brian's grandparents."

Dean watched the exchange with avid interest. There was an ease with which they spoke to one another. He didn't sense any undercurrents. It was normal. They were normal parents looking out for their daughter and granddaughter. They were proud of their daughter. Hope was a confident, self-assured woman, and he knew that at least part of that must have come from her parents, the way they raised her and believed in her.

It reminded him of Tyler's father. Martin Donnelly walked around with a grin on his face and pride shining in his eyes brighter than the July sun. Of course, it hadn't always been that way, and when Tyler had taken off for eight years, Dean had been defensive of Martin because he knew what a good guy he was. He'd have given anything for a dad like Martin. Martin didn't have a tenth of the wealth Dean's family did, but he had so much more; he had the *right* things. But because their love for each other was so deep, Tyler and Martin were able to work through their problems and were now rebuilding a successful ranch, side be side. And now Martin was a grandfather, proudly showing anyone and everyone pictures of his granddaughter.

Dean stuffed his hands into the front pockets of his jeans and cleared his throat, trying to get rid of the lump there as he watched Hope's family interact.

"All right then. Sadie, how about we go to Tilly's for breakfast?" Hope's dad said.

"Yes, I'm starving! Bye!" Sadie said, turning to give Hope a hug and then him one.

They laughed as Sadie ran over to the truck. "No one can resist breakfast at Tilly's," he said as he watched her.

"Some things never change," Hope's mom said over her shoulder as they walked back to the truck.

But some things did change. As he stood there with Hope watching her parents and Sadie drive away, he was aware how things changed. How life changed. "You have great parents, Hope."

She nodded, her gaze fixed on the truck pulling out onto the road. "I do. I hit the jackpot with them. I know I wouldn't be here, in one piece, if it wasn't for them…"

"I think you could probably handle just about anything thrown your way."

She crossed her arms over her chest and stared into the distance. "Well, I'm glad that's the image I give off."

"I think it's the truth."

"So, um, do you want me to show you around?"

He gave her a nod, her shift in conversation typical. She'd never let him close. Even when he thought that maybe she'd started to thaw toward him, or forgive him for what she thought he did, she'd pulled back. But that was for the best. Hope deserved a man who knew how to love.

They started walking toward the barn. She pulled her sweater closer, shuddering as the wind hit them. "Definitely. Maybe it'll give us some ideas of what to do. What was this land used for? I don't remember anything much being out here."

"Not much. Brian's grandparents didn't live here for years. I think at one time there was a small family ranch, but Brian barely remembered it. His grandfather had chronic health issues and couldn't run it. It wasn't large enough or profitable enough for them to continue to pay anyone."

They'd stopped outside the barn, and he was eyeing the broken and weathered wood. The roof looked as though it was ready to cave in at any point. Basically, she'd inherited a money pit. He glanced over at her, realizing she was probably waiting for him to say something. She was staring at him with such expectancy and trust, he didn't have the heart to tell her what he really thought. And it didn't matter. What mattered was that he'd make it right for her. "It's a beautiful piece of land. The rest is fixable. This barn is fixable. You just need to know what you want to do with it. For now, maybe I can concentrate on making it safe so if Sadie wants to come out here, or sneaks out here, we don't have to worry about her getting hurt." The minute he said "we" he could've kicked himself.

But she didn't seem to react to that. Her head was tilted back and she was looking up at the weathered gray structure. "I'm so glad you said that. I was worried I'd inherited some kind of money pit."

Hope was a realist if anything. Maybe too much so. He pulled his hat a bit lower on his head. "It'll be fine. One step at a time. I'll get the barn repaired, and maybe some of the stalls so Sadie can get her horse."

Hope let out a laugh. "Don't you dare give in, Dean. The last thing I need is a horse to care for, too. We don't know the first thing about horses."

He smiled, wanting to tell her he could do that for them, but didn't. He had no idea where he and Hope would be six months from now. Hopefully, still speaking. "Don't worry. We'll get it set up… just in case."

Her smile fell and she crossed her arms and looked at the ground. "Dean, I've been thinking about all this. I can't let you give up your weekend and what little spare time you have to help out. I have no idea what I'm going to do with this place. It's not fair to you. Especially…with how things have been between us."

When her voice trailed off, drifting away with the cold wind, she stared up at him. It took everything for him to not reach out and touch her. Dark, glossy hair had escaped her ponytail and danced around her face, every now and then catching on her lips. He'd memorized her face years ago, had seen it in his dreams, but rarely were they alone like this. They were usually surrounded by their friends on a Saturday night at River's. The two of them would usually exchange some tense words or get in a few digs, but when it was just them they retreated to silence.

It was the heaviest silence he'd ever experienced with anyone. He'd had no idea, before Hope, how silence could be filled with so many unspoken truths.

He cleared his throat, hoping to keep things neutral. "How have things been between us?"

Her mouth dropped open slightly. "I… I've made assumptions about you. Accusations. And you've…made assumptions about me being a naturopath."

He almost laughed except he hated the idea that his teasing might have hurt her feelings. "I only ever bugged you about being a naturopath because you made clear what you thought about my abilities as a doctor."

She looked at the ground and kicked the gravel with the front of her sneaker. "I'm sorry. I was petty and immature. It took me a long time to figure out that sometimes life just happens. I was so wrong to blame you. I like to think I've matured since then."

An unfamiliar ache formed in his chest. He

hated thinking back to those days. They'd come a long way. He didn't want to remember when she hated him for Brian's death, when he'd let her believe it was true. He'd given her every reason to hate him. Too much time had passed and he'd made a promise to Brian and he was taking it to the grave. "Well, me too. And for the record, you weren't petty. You had every reason to question me and to…be angry with me."

She looked up sharply. "No, I didn't. I'm sorry, Dean. And I can't help but wonder if you're doing this to try to make it up to me. Like you really think that what happened to Brian was your fault. It's not true and I'm so sorry for everything I said to you."

He broke her gaze, his jaw clenching as he attempted to hold on to the words he really wanted to say. She was forgiving him, even though she didn't know the truth. He couldn't process what that meant. Dean didn't screw up. Dean had never made mistakes. He couldn't. The tiniest mistake growing up would mean weeks of ridicule, but he was forced to keep his promise to her husband. He didn't break promises, not for anyone.

Instead, he focused on the battered barn. "Don't apologize. I'm not doing this out of guilt. I'm helping a friend. Let's consider this a fresh start, a truce." He held out his hand.

Hope shook his hand firmly and that jolt of

electricity every time his body made any kind of contact with her, ran through him. They stared at each other, the cold morning air swirling around them, and despite all the reasons they couldn't ever be together, there was that spark that refused to be carried away with the wind. He gave her a nod.

"All right. To fresh starts."

• • •

Three days later, Hope filled a travel mug with hot coffee and grabbed two of the blueberry muffins she'd baked and a freshly made ham sandwich. Guilt was pricking at her conscience as the wind howled around the small house.

Dean had been in the barn all day, and she knew he'd worked at the hospital the night before. As much as she needed his help, she couldn't accept it if he was going to run himself into the ground.

She quickly put on her chunky wool sweater and picked up the muffins and coffee and opened the door. A stack of mail blew off the front table with the gust of wind and she quickly shut the door, putting the food and coffee down while she gathered the mail.

She paused, one letter standing out. It was from the property management company she rented her office from. But it was part of the

Stanton family properties, even though she and Dean had never discussed it. He probably wasn't even aware how many properties his family owned, since the management company took care of everything. She opened the envelope and quickly scanned it, her heart pounding as she came to the end. Her rent was doubling, effective next month.

How was this even possible? She stared at the letter, mentally calculating what she'd made last month, already knowing this wasn't going to be good.

She stuffed the letter back in the envelope and tried not to panic, but her stomach was churning and she fought for control over her emotions. Glancing out the window in the direction of the barn, she decided not to tell Dean.

She picked up the food and opened the door. Wincing against the strong wind, she quickly walked toward the barn. The sky loomed large and ominous, dark clouds swirling through the mountains, teasing at impending rain. She wasn't going to give up. The rent increase could not break her business. Well, it actually could, but she'd find a way.

She would spend tonight getting the house in order and going over her numbers for the rent increase. She would be able to make it, but it'd be tight. Giving up her Fridays off was a last resort. Right now, Fridays were essential for her sanity as a single parent. But if she had to take on more appointments to make rent, she would.

She took a deep breath and forced herself to push all those thoughts aside or Dean would know something was wrong. Even though she'd grown up in Wishing River, living on this much land would take some getting used to. It was slightly intimidating and she wasn't used to that. The house was small and perfect for just her and Sadie and she felt secure inside. But doubt crept in every time she stepped onto the porch and realized how much land they were on, how isolated they were.

She opened the barn door to find Dean hammering something on one of the stalls. The barn smelled musty and it was dirty, old hay in corners and cobwebs dangling here and there.

She took a moment to appreciate the work he'd done…and him. His jacket was hanging by the door and he was wearing a Henley and jeans and boots. He moved with a confidence and purpose that she'd always associated with him. She cleared her throat, not allowing herself to admire him any longer. "Hi, sorry to interrupt. I thought you could use some food. It's hours past lunchtime."

He paused his hammering and looked over at her. "Oh, thanks. You don't have to feed me." He walked over to her and she met him halfway. She refused to stare at him, or how good he looked even though he must be exhausted. The Henley stretched tight over his broad shoulders and chest and was loose around his narrow waist. His jeans were worn and fit his strong body in a way that made her regret ever looking.

"I can't have you getting malnourished and tired out. I was making lunch and baking anyway," she said, placing the food on a sturdy looking shelf on the back wall.

"I appreciate it. Is that coffee?"

She smiled at his obvious happiness. "Freshly brewed. I'll get out of your hair and let you eat."

He took a sip from the cup and sighed. "This is great. Join me?"

She shook her head, crossing her arms over her chest. It was the perfect time to leave, before she started worrying about her rent increase and have him notice something was wrong. "It's freezing in here, and I don't want to intrude."

He picked up one half of the sandwich and held it out for her. "Are you sure you don't want some?"

She waved her hand. "Absolutely. That's for you. Eat."

He gave her a salute and proceeded to consume half the sandwich in two bites. "This is delicious."

"Good. I knew you were starving. How long do you think you'll be able to keep up this pace? I don't think it's healthy, Dean. I can find someone. Or, I've been thinking maybe I should slow down with getting this place up and running. It's not like I can run a large ranch. Or I can help you. I may not know a lot about ranching, but I can handle small tasks. It could speed up your work."

He polished off the rest of the sandwich and took a long drink of coffee. "You have enough on your plate, too. You're not wasting my time. You could be sitting on a really profitable business. Are those blueberry muffins?"

She almost laughed at the abrupt change in conversation and the way he was gazing at the muffins. "Yes."

He took a large bite, chewed, and then held out the muffin as though examining it. "Really good."

She narrowed her eyes on him. "You say that with surprise."

He grinned sheepishly while popping the rest of the muffin top into his mouth. "I assumed this would be some kind of horrid gluten-free, sugar-free, everything-that-tastes-good-free kind of muffin."

She lifted her chin. "I'll try not to be offended."

He flashed her a smile before taking a sip of coffee. "I wasn't trying to be offensive."

Her gaze was drawn to the red on his knuckles as he lifted the mug. She didn't want to stare, but from where she was standing it looked like eczema. "Are your hands dry? Do you want some lotion?"

He choked. "I don't use lotion."

She rolled her eyes. "They look painful."

He lifted a shoulder. "I get the occasional eczema flare-up. I have some prescription steroid to put on it when I get around to it."

She rolled her lips inward in an attempt to hold back her opinion. "Sure."

He let out a ragged sigh. "Why don't you tell me what you're thinking and save us some time."

She shrugged. "Do you have any food allergies?"

He rolled back on his heels. "Nope."

"Have you been tested?"

He opened his mouth and she could swear there was a sarcastic remark coming but then he shut it and just shook his head.

"Well, I could order some for you. For food sensitivities."

"I appreciate the thought, but I'm fine. I'm not sensitive."

She rolled her eyes. "Sure, you are perfectly fine."

He frowned. "I am."

"But if it's tests you have a problem with, you could try removing some of the biggest problematic foods."

"And those would be?"

"Dairy, gluten, sugar…"

"I don't hate myself, Hope."

She burst out laughing. "I've helped a lot of people, Dean. Even Lainey. She's been off dairy for years and is doing great."

"Lainey? I always catch her scarfing down lasagna on lasagna night at the diner."

This was true. Lainey wasn't exactly the spokesmodel for sticking with an alternative diet. "Well, it doesn't need to be one hundred percent of the time once the inflammation is under control. I've helped Sarah with her migraines by identifying some problematic foods and introducing some new supplements. Leaky gut can cause a lot of problems in people."

He choked on his coffee again. "Leaky gut? I don't have leaky anything."

She rolled her eyes. "I'd have expected a certain amount of maturity coming from a medical doctor."

The corners of his lips twitched, and she tried to remain unaffected by it. The truth was that he was pretty funny and completely gorgeous, even when he was trying to get her riled up. "Clearly. And you should've known my level of maturity based on my best friends."

This time she laughed out loud and her stomach fluttered a few times when he grinned back at her. "So aside from your potential gut issues, how are things going out here?"

He leaned against a post. "Not bad. I'll feel better once the major hazards are dealt with. Then we can move forward with whatever you plan. Maybe one night after work I can stop by your office and we can go out for dinner and hash out some details."

Her stomach dropped. Was that like, a date request? The image of his father sprang to mind and she took a step back from him. "That's okay. My evenings are pretty short, and I need to focus on Sadie."

He tilted his head, that blue gaze serious on hers. "What is it? Why do I feel like one minute we get each other and we're having a good time and the next you shut down?"

Hope glanced away guiltily. He was right. She was used to handling her own problems. This sudden rent increase was a big deal. But she'd signed a lease with his father's property management company, not him. Tattling to him about the rent increase seemed petty, and she didn't want any special treatment because of their friendship. He was staring at her with that intensity she found impossible to ignore. Dean was someone who'd been clear about what was right and wrong, and she was keeping something from him.

Then there was that warning his father had given her   it was all embarrassing. She was struck by the image of his father telling her that Dean was off-limits. While Hope had never felt ashamed of her family's lack of money, or her dad's jobs, Dean's father made her feel inadequate. And he made her feel…uncomfortable. He stood a little too close, his gaze lingered a little too long, just a creepy vibe that made her want to never be alone with him again. And the way he'd reached out to touch her arm…he'd held her upper arm and his thumb had stroked it. But none of that made sense, because he'd been warning her about staying away from Dean at the same time. She hadn't shared that day with anyone, preferring to think she'd been imagining things.

What did she really know about Dean's personal life? Other than the few times they'd been alone together, they mostly always had been surrounded, buffered by their friends. And the only times they'd really been alone together were when her whole world had fallen apart and he'd been there to keep her standing and when he'd driven her home two years ago after Lainey's party. Thank goodness his father had set her straight the next day about why she'd never be good enough for Dean, that there was someone else waiting for him. It was better she knew that, better she didn't let her mind get carried away in some kind of fantasy about what the two of them could be one day.

She crossed her arms and looked up at him. "That's not true, but life has gotten complicated, and I have a lot on my plate. That's all. The way

I'm feeling has nothing to do with you."

He took a step closer, and her body reacted as though he'd touched her, as though he'd just sucked all the air out of the room and she couldn't find a breath deep enough. "Then why don't you share? Why are you keeping it all to yourself? If we're friends, tell me."

She swallowed hard, looking up at him. "Friends shouldn't be a burden."

He frowned. "Burden. God, you're the furthest thing from a burden to me."

That gruffness in his voice, the tenderness in his eyes, was enough to make her wish she could take back every snarky remark that had ever come out of her mouth. He made her wish for things that were long forgotten. He made her wish for a future she'd given up on. He made her feel in a new way. He made her feel new, like she was a different version of herself, or that she could be this different version of herself. He made her want to trust him. "Dean...I..."

He reached out and took her hand in his, and it should have been a casual touch. A gesture offering comfort, encouragement. Instead, it made her heady. Her mouth went dry and her gaze went from his to their joined hands. His larger, tanned, rough hand gently holding hers made her feel safe. Protected. *Alive.*

Had she not been living until now? Was that possible? How could Dean holding her hand, talking to her in that deep, comforting voice, make her want to throw all caution to the wind and…"Hope. Tell me. Trust me. I will always help you."

She swallowed hard and tried to focus on what he was asking her and not how it felt to have her hand wrapped in his. It had been so long. So long since a man had held her hand. But she knew this response wasn't because a man was touching her, it was because *Dean* was touching her. And maybe on some subconscious level she'd known she would react this way. He was…intense, intimidating, hard, in a way that didn't make her afraid.

She pulled her hand out of his and tucked a strand of hair behind her ear. She blurted out the first thing that came to her mind, hoping it would pacify him. "It's a financial issue with my office. Not a big deal. That's why I was thinking it'd be great to bring my practice home. It would be more cost-effective and I'd never have to worry about not being home for Sadie after school."

The warmth that had been in his eyes a few moments ago had disappeared. "What financial issue with your office?"

She waved a hand. "It's nothing. Just a small rent increase."

His brows snapped together. "Do you have a lease?"

"Yeah…well, I did. But we've been going month to month the last year. My fault. I thought, since I'd been there so long, things would be the same. Really, Dean, this is on me."

He ran a hand over his jaw. "That's one of my family's properties."

She glanced away guiltily as she remembered what happened the day after he'd driven her home from Lainey's party. It wasn't his fault and she didn't want his dad to know she was talking about him. It didn't matter anyway, because she wasn't interested in a relationship with anyone. "Oh, right. But don't worry about it."

He stared at her. "There's more, isn't there?"

She twirled a piece of hair between her fingers, wishing the floor would open up or a gust of wind would blow her away. "No. Maybe. Look, I don't want to get involved in any family issues. I'm sure it's all business."

His jaw clenched. "Hope…how would you be getting involved in family issues?"

She held her breath but didn't say anything.

"Hope."

She squeezed her eyes shut to avoid that blue stare.

"Hope, come on."

She slowly opened her eyes and met his gaze. "Ugh. Dean, I…do you remember that night you drove me home from Lainey's party because Sadie wasn't feeling well?"

He nodded tersely. "That was two years ago, but yeah."

She took a deep breath and decided she had to rid herself of this secret. "The next day your dad paid me a visit in my office. He said…" She stopped speaking for a moment and tried to push aside her embarrassment, but it was there, holding on to her words.

"He said what?"

She cringed at the anger in his voice. This wasn't good. "Give me a second, I'm trying to remember," she said, stalling for time. Should she soften what his dad had said? Should she just blurt it out?

"Hope, you're seriously killing me. What did he say?"

She kicked at the dirt floor and kept her eyes downcast. "Okay, okay…he said I shouldn't get my hopes up, that you and I would never be anything…something about your family having to uphold certain standards…that I couldn't meet."

His face had turned ashen and his jaw was clenching and unclenching. For a second, she thought he was going to do something in anger, like smash his fist through a post. Or storm out of the barn. But when his eyes finally landed on hers, they were shiny, the emotion in them capturing all the breath in her body. "That's garbage. He's an ass, Hope. He's a pig. I'm sorry. God, I'm so sorry. It's bullshit, and I'd never think that. Certain standards, hell, you are above everyone in my dad's social circles. He had no right to talk to you. To put it into perspective, I don't meet my father's standards, and I'm his son."

Her throat tightened, and she chose to focus on him and not the part about what he'd said about her because she didn't know how to handle that. "I didn't know things were like that between you."

"Please don't tell me you think I'm like him."

She stared into his eyes, seeing the hurt there, knowing instinctively who he was. She wasn't going to let her own fear for him force her to say something she didn't believe to protect herself. "Of course not. You've never made me feel lesser than."

He lifted his hand, reaching out to frame the side of her face with his hand. She stopped breathing the moment his rough hand gently touched her face, his eyes filled with a longing she knew was echoed in hers. But this could never happen. She didn't want this. She didn't want a relationship again, especially not with Dean. His father made it clear there were big plans for Dean, and she wasn't about to get involved or between him and his father.

They also had their past that hadn't been resolved. It was painful to bring up, but she knew she would one day, because she would hate to think he still thought she blamed him for Brian's death. It was wrong of her. She was ashamed for how she'd acted. And then there was his dad and the way he'd touched her. She couldn't quite bring herself to tell Dean, not because she didn't trust him, but because she was embarrassed. Maybe his dad was like that with everyone.

"Hope," he said in a voice she'd heard a hundred times in her dreams. It was deep and rough and tender all at the same time, and it made her toes curl and made her want to forget every dumb insecurity she had and lean into what he was offering, lean into him. So, naturally, she took a step back. He dropped his hand and stood his ground.

"I…I'm sorry, Dean, it's just that…"

He held up his hand. "No explanation needed. Never has been. I'll see you tomorrow."

Her mouth hung open, the words on the tip of her tongue. She wanted to ask him in for a drink. She wanted to cover his hand with hers. She wanted to take that last step between them so she could feel what it would be like to be wrapped up in Dean. Deep down, under all the layers and walls she'd constructed around herself to protect herself from feeling, she was afraid that being kissed by Dean would be unlike anything she'd experienced. Because the truth was that no one, no man, had ever made her feel so alive, so aware of herself, as him.

Dean did. He made her feel things she'd never imagined.

She watched, motionless, as he walked back to

his truck. The tall, powerful lines of his body were already memorized in her mind, but she stood there anyway, wishing that things could be different. But the past was sewn together with delicate threads, and if she pulled at them too much, some of her best moments would never have happened. She would never wish away the life she'd lived, but that also meant she had to protect herself from ever experiencing that kind of pain again. That there could actually be a future for them.

CHAPTER FOUR

"…certain standards…that I couldn't meet."

Dean stood in the foyer of his father's house, Hope's voice on replay. Each time he heard her voice and saw her face, it stopped him in his tracks. Of all the times in his life when Dean had been hurt by his father's actions, nothing cut as deep as hearing the embarrassment and insecurity in Hope's voice. For that, for his father's interference in his life, in Hope's life, and for his callous and cutting remarks to her, this had to end.

The night that kid had told them he'd been hired by his father, Dean had wanted to dismiss it as a coincidence. It seemed too small a thing for his father to be involved with. Now…well, now none of this could be deemed a coincidence. He'd known from a young age there was something wrong with his father. He'd been cold and unapproachable. When he was a kid, he'd try to impress his father. He had taken the criticism to heart, thinking all he needed to do was try harder and then his father wouldn't think he was a failure or lazy. But then he'd started noticing that he spoke like that to everyone, including Dean's mom and brother.

Morgan had a chip on his shoulder the size of the Grand Canyon, his father used to say. While Dean had tried to impress their father, Morgan had tried to piss him off. Their mother had been a silent enabler—when he ripped into his sons, and when he cheated on her. His father was a serial cheater. Most people in their circles pretended not to notice and maintained polite relationships. Then there were others who enjoyed that about his father, who played their own part in it.

When Morgan was twenty-two and ready to propose to his girlfriend of one year, at their family's annual Christmas party, all hell broke loose. It was the last night Morgan had ever spent in their home. It was the last night Dean had spoken to his brother.

The sound of Morgan's roar from his father's office was something Dean would never forget. The memory of it still had the ability to make him stop in his tracks, to make his stomach clench, to make him forget the present moment. Dean had run into the office and stopped, assessing the situation, not actually believing that what he was seeing was real. Morgan's girlfriend, Patricia was getting dressed, her face red and not looking at any of them. Their dad was half dressed and pinned against the wall, Morgan's hand on his throat.

Thinking the worst, Dean ran to Patricia, helping her get dressed and gently asking her what had happened. But it wasn't what he'd thought. Patricia admitted to a secret relationship she'd been having with their father for the last few months. Dean managed to wrestle Morgan off their father and pull him out of the room. But the damage had been done. There was no going back. There was no pretending their father had any redeeming qualities.

Morgan marched up to his room, Dean following on his heels.

Morgan had turned to him. "I've never wanted to kill him until tonight. I would have, if you hadn't come in."

"He's not worth going to jail for," Dean said.

"I've always hated him. But tonight... Dean, I'm leaving. If you ever need me, call me. But I can't stay here anymore. He's sick and twisted and I don't want to be his son anymore. I can't even tell Grandpa what he's done. He'd have a damn heart attack."

Morgan slammed his suitcase shut, everything about his movements jerky and rigid and fraught with a tension that was begging for release. "What kind of person does that to their own son, Dean? And where is he now? He couldn't care less. He looked...happy. When I had him pinned against the wall, I swear, he looked smug."

Dean frantically tried to come up with something that could keep him there. The panic stormed through him, making it almost impossible to think straight. "Morgan, stay. We can start out on our own."

"You know we can't do that. He'll never let us. He'll have any ranch we try to start destroyed. We don't have any significant money. He would never give us our inheritance if we walk out and would sabotage our efforts at making a living here. At least if I leave town, I can start a new life and pay my way. Mom is gone, and it was a life of misery and humiliation for her. I'm not going to be one of his lackeys. You stay here. You're too young to leave. Stay with Grandpa. Be a doctor and then leave. Get out before it's too late, before he ruins your life."

"That's it?"

"What would you do, Dean?"

Dean had stared at him, desperation making him want to leave, but duty keeping him still. "What about Grandpa? He wouldn't recover if you left."

Morgan had run his hands down his face. "I don't know. I don't know what to say, except I think he'd understand."

"What about a job?"

Morgan shrugged. "I'll find something. You know I've been playing around with crypto currency. Maybe I'll get into that."

"Morgan, that's a big gamble."

Morgan had been a math whiz, never studying for anything and understanding everything. He was brilliant but he wouldn't have a penny to his name. "Well, that's all I've got right now."

"Just so you know, I'll always be here for you. No matter what. If you need money. Anything. I'm never going to be like him, Morgan."

"I know. You couldn't."

That was the last time he'd ever seen his brother.

Dean stood outside his father's office door, remembering the look on Morgan's face when he'd walked out of here that night. And, now, he remembered Hope's face, the red in her cheeks when she told him about his dad's conversation with her.

Dean had been a fool. He'd stayed too long. His grandfather's request hadn't seemed too un-reasonable at the time and he owed them. His father didn't deserve this ranch anymore. He knew his grandparents had worked themselves to the bone to build this family legacy, but asking him to stay here and put up with his dad so he could one day inherit it was starting to eat away at him.

The anger that had coiled in his stomach spread throughout his body. Morgan's words about their father sabotaging their lives were like a warning. He was interfering in Dean's life, and he'd crossed a line when he'd approached Hope. "We need to talk," Dean said.

His father looked up from his desk. There

wasn't a hair out of place, not a wrinkle in his white shirt, not a hint of happiness in seeing Dean in his doorway. "Hello, Dean. It's not Sunday."

"Did you talk to Hope privately about me two years ago?"

His father leaned back in his leather chair, not looking the least bit contrite or worried. "I like being upfront with people. I think you should, too. She's a good tenant, I'd hate to see her get her hopes up, latching herself on to someone with your kind of wealth."

Every image of Hope in the last few years, those times he caught a smile in his direction, a softening...had been ruined by his father. "You have no right to think about her, about me. You have no right to approach her about me or anything. There's so much wrong with what you did and what you just said. Let me make something perfectly clear. You have no authority over my life, what I do, who I'm with, any of it. You overstepped. Worry about your own life, your own mistakes, and see if you can be a better man than the one you were for Mom or Morgan."

His father's lips formed a thin line. "Watch your tone."

"No. I'm not a five-year-old. I'm a grown man and as far as I can see, the only family you have left. You treated Mom like shitty property and you screwed Morgan's girlfriend just to prove to him you could. You know nothing about family loyalty."

"Get out of my office, Dean, before you say something you'll regret."

Dean stood there, trying to keep his head clear. "Stay away from her."

"I'm a father looking out for a son."

"You're looking out for you and your image. Nothing else."

"I was just speaking with Celeste's father—"

"I made it clear. I'm not marrying anyone just to increase your ego."

"You're an idiot."

Dean clenched his fists, determined to keep his temper in check long enough to get the answers he needed. "Did you raise Hope's rent?"

His father shuffled some papers on his desk. "Do you really think I have time to go around raising rent on some piddly properties we inherited from your grandfather? I have better things to do."

"Did anyone else's rent go up?"

"I don't know, Dean. Like I said, I don't bother with that. The property management company does it all."

Dean walked forward and placed his hands on his father's desk, leaning forward and staring at him. "Bull. So, you raised rent on a single mother just to hurt her. Why? You must be proud of yourself."

"You're taking her word against mine. Why did it take her so long to tell you we had a conversation?"

"She was embarrassed."

"So, she has something to be embarrassed about?"

Dean's muscles coiled as he stared into his father's smug face. "No, but you do. Did you also hire a young cowboy just to spite her?"

His father laughed. "This is sounding delusional. What? I'm obsessed with that woman and out to ruin her life? You can tell her not to flatter herself."

Dean stared at him, the statement sending off a warning bell. "How is that flattering herself?"

He waved a hand. "Dean, I'm tired of this. Go ahead and play the gallant hero with the poor little single mother. You could have had Celeste if you hadn't ruined it. That was a real match. I don't get your love of trash—Cade, Tyler, Hope, the list goes on and on. And stop making yourself out to be better than me. How many tramps have you gone home with from River's? You think you're so different? You think you can stay with one woman for the rest of your life? Why don't you hook up with that woman and then get her out of your system and move on?"

Dean physically stepped back from the desk, rage pummeling through him. His grandfather's face, the feel of his hand pressing in the keys to his cabin, tugged at him, reminding him of the promise he'd made. "It's amazing to me that the man who screwed his son's fiancée, who repeatedly cheated on his wife, is going to call Hope and my friends trash. Grandma and Grandpa were so ashamed of you. You already lost one son. I don't think you want to lose another. What will that say about your image? Because, unlike Morgan, I won't leave town. I'll be here, I'll be in your circles, I will be a thorn in your side until the day you die. You know nothing about me, about who I'm with, about what I want. Don't put your sick tastes onto me. And don't ever talk about Hope again."

His father leaned forward, placing his elbows on the desk, not a show of any emotion. "You think being a doctor is such an accomplishment? You were handed everything. Big deal, you got into med school."

Dean straightened his shoulders. "You had everything I did and you couldn't get in. A whole line of doctors. Even your mother, when there were a handful of women doctors, was one. But not you. I guess that must still sting. So, in case I need to repeat myself to make it easier on you, stay out of my life, stay away from Hope."

"Don't squander all the opportunities you've been given. Watch who you keep company with."

Dean bristled. This wasn't the first time he'd heard this. He was sure it wouldn't be the last, even though part of him wished it could be. His father kept company with nearly half the women in town.

He wanted to tell him that maybe his mother would still be here if his dad wasn't such an ass and had broken her heart repeatedly with his infidelity. But there was no point. He'd learned long ago the best way to deal with his father was not to deal at all. To let his comments just roll off. There was no winning; there was just getting sucked further and further into the pit of resentment. That had been his strategy since he was young, and it had served him well. Almost. He'd lost a brother in the process, but he couldn't go back and change the past. He was here for one reason only, the promise he'd made to his grandfather. Dean had never broken a promise, his word was everything.

Being left behind meant developing a thick skin. When he'd engaged with his father, it just became a long, drawn-out battle that went nowhere. They'd never see eye to eye, and he was grateful for that. They'd never have that father-son relationship like in the movies and, frankly, he didn't want that. Being friends with his father meant not having a backbone, not having an opinion, and turning a blind eye to the lives his father wrecked. "I'm not a child and there's nothing wrong with any of the people I associate with. If this is about Celeste, again, I already gave you my answer. Not happening. We've always just been friends. I understand that puts a wrench in your plans to unite two ranching empires, but I'm sure you'll survive."

His father crossed his arms over his chest. "No need to get so defensive all the time. If you and Celeste want to throw away the opportunity for a solid future, that's your fault."

Dean held his father's stare. It was no surprise that he'd wanted Dean to pursue a relationship with Celeste. They'd been pushed together by their respective families since they were kids. While they liked each other, they were both completely uninterested in being set up by their parents. They'd often laughed about that and had made a pact to never even entertain the idea. Celeste was like a sister to him. "I'm sure we'll manage just fine."

"I'm not always the bad guy. I'm just a father looking out for his son. I know you're working nights this week. I don't want you to wear yourself down, but you're an adult. You're free to do whatever or whomever you please. If you want to waste your time with Hope Roberts, that's your business."

Dean's muscles coiled until it was painful, heat pulsing through his body. Now this, him mentioning Hope, was something he couldn't ignore. There were lines that could never be crossed, truths that could never be shared. Hope was that line, his feelings for her, that truth. He didn't like his father even mentioning Hope's name. "What the hell is that supposed to mean?"

"It means I know you've been eyeing that opportunistic single mother since her husband was buried."

Dean held up his hand, forcing himself to take a step back, toward his truck and away from him instead of giving in to the rush of anger pummeling him. He was able to control it enough to concentrate on the warning bells ringing in his ears. "Don't talk about her like that. Don't talk about her, don't think about her, don't approach her. You know nothing about Hope. You know nothing about me."

Dean had the perverse satisfaction of seeing red rise from is father's shirt collar all the way up to the tips of his ears. "You can look down on me all you want, but we are the same. Even how you want to avenge your grandfather and Morgan— that's exactly what I would have done. Your grandfather and Morgan didn't have a vengeful bone in their bodies. Morgan left. But you're here. Out of greed. Just like me. And you're not married; just like me. Because you are not a family man. You're not the man to stick it out with one woman, and we both know it. You're incapable of love, just like I've always known."

The blood that rushed to Dean's ears seemed to pulse through his entire body. It took all his reserves, all his years of experience in dealing with his father, not to let his words get into his head and let him have the last word. "You know nothing. Nothing about me."

"I know you have no relationship with the brother you claim to love. I'm pretty sure if you loved him as deeply as you claim, you would have gone after him. Or at least have some kind of relationship. But he's not in your life. Just like all the other women you've screwed. Where are they? Nowhere around you. So get your damn high horse out of my office. Son."

Dean stared at him, his words leaving bullet holes throughout his body. But he refused to give him an ounce of satisfaction. "Gladly." He walked out of the house, his chin held high as he strode to his truck. He had to keep his head in the game and not surrender to the anger ready to burst from him.

He needed to get the hell out of here. If he could have gotten into his truck and driven away, right now, and never look back, he would. If he could take the Stanton name branded on everything around this ostentatious ranch, and delete it, he would. And if he could wipe that smug smirk from his father's mouth with his fist, he would do it in a heartbeat.

But he couldn't. Because of his promise to his grandfather. And maybe because of spite. Maybe he was like his father. Maybe that's what got under his skin the most. He wanted to watch his father sign everything over to him one day, with grim satisfaction. If Dean was the only one left here, then it better have been for a damn good reason. Bringing this ranch back to its roots was a good reason.

Dean stared at the wide expanse of perfectly manicured lawn. Fountains and empty flower beds that a few months from now would be filled with an abundance that was an embarrassment in these parts. He could still remember the frown of disapproval on his grandfather's face when they were being installed.

His grandfather had been humble, hard-working, and Dean and Morgan had spent countless hours at his side learning ranching. Those days were long gone, and he knew better than to wish for family like that again. That was once-in-a-lifetime stuff. Long days in the pasture, coming home to the smell of freshly baked apple pie and homemade stew and biscuits, his grandmother a comforting presence at the door. He and Morgan would prefer to go to their grandparents' old cabin at the foot of the mountains and have a peaceful dinner as much as they could.

When their parents were entertaining, though, both boys were expected to be home. Somewhere along the way, his grandparents had stopped attending dinners at the main house. Maybe it was when his father kept adding extensions onto it, inviting people who weren't from the community anymore, and their old housekeeper was replaced by a full staff. The house became unrecognizable, and his grandparents preferred the simplicity of their old home. Dean also suspected it was the only way his grandparents could keep the peace with his father, by staying away as much as possible.

He started his truck and took the narrow ranch roads toward the mountains, trying to calm down, trying to process emotions he didn't know how to deal with. There was one place he needed to see, to ground himself. He'd become a master at compartmentalizing. It was survival instinct in many ways. His father was the king of manipulations and innuendos. The only thing was that most times, it meant nothing. Today, it had meant something. It had hit too close to home. Too much talk about the past—about the people who were no longer here.

If it hadn't been for their grandparents, Dean didn't think he and Morgan would have ever turned out normal. Dean wished there hadn't been a rift between them. Their four-year age difference had seemed like a lifetime back then, and Dean hadn't been willing to accept the harsh truth that Morgan had accepted from a much younger age. Dean didn't know what that said about himself, but right now it made him think he was a sentimental fool for giving his father the benefit of the doubt when he was a kid.

If he were the sentimental sort, he'd think about those days fixing broken fences with his grandfather, absorbing everything he was being shown. Watching the ways his strong, weathered hands had deftly worked the wire, all the while telling Dean tales of old cattle drives he'd gone on with his own grandfather, back when Wishing River was just a village with a dirt road. Dean would imagine it was like the old black-and-white Westerns his grandfather would watch on Sunday afternoons in his favorite recliner. He could still see the deep grooves in his tanned, leathery face. Lines of laughter. Lines from days in the sun. Lines from a life well-lived. A life he'd built with the love of his wife.

Dean wanted those lines one day. The kind that told stories of the decades he'd lived. Lines from working hard, from worrying about children, from loving hard. His grandfather would tell him that Dean needed to find a love bigger than the Montana sky, because that's how much he loved Dean's grandmother. And a love that big could outlast everything.

Dean cleared his throat past the lump there. Thinking about his grandparents always brought a hefty dose of emotion, the kind he tried to keep at bay. He focused on the road ahead. The familiar sights, the rambling wood fences, the mountains in the distance, flickered across the windshield as he sped along the empty rural roads. The openness had always been comforting, maybe a subconscious reminder that though the family ranch was vast, his father's influence without bounds, there was enough land out there for him to make a new start.

It was also a reminder of how alone he was. There was no one he could take this shit to. While Tyler and Cade were his best friends in the world, there was no way he was going to be the poor rich boy complaining about his daddy problems. He didn't have it that bad. It's not like he'd been physically abused. He had every material thing he could ever want. So, who was he to complain about a father who put him down or made a remark or two? Everyone had their own shit to deal with and his best friends were no exception, except they didn't have the wealth he'd grown up with and that changed everything. It was an unspoken truth.

Being wealthy in Wishing River had always been awkward. He didn't like being known as the rich kid among his classmates. He'd tried to downplay it as much as he could, just wanting to be like everyone else. It made it impossible to ever confide in his best friends about what his home life was really like. When you were this wealthy, no one wanted to hear your sob story. There was only one person who really got it, Morgan, his brother, but he wasn't around anymore.

When he was out with his friends, he was sure
to drive the pickup truck, to leave the flashy
watches and designer clothes and BMW at home.
He'd always been more comfortable in jeans and
T-shirts over suits. Or hospital scrubs and sneak-
ers. He loved ranching and he loved being a
doctor. The doctor part had been born out of a
need to follow his own dreams, create his own
success, to pursue his own interests…and to have
another career in case there came a day he would
put an end to the bullshit that went along with
working for his father. Morgan had gotten out
years ago after a disgusting betrayal from their
father and hadn't spoken to any of them in almost
a decade.

Dean barely felt the bitter March wind as he
parked his truck and got out at the base of the
mountains. Low-hanging clouds hugged the
mountains in the distance, and he took a half
second to admire the view. It was the same one
since he'd been a kid, but without his grandparents around, all the gray seemed bleaker. When
his grandparents had been alive and he'd visit
them in their cabin at the foothills of the mountain, he'd imagine all sorts of things. Disappearing
into the clouds. Climbing the mountain. Running
away.

But now this little cabin was his. It was the
part of his past that he clung to. The part that reminded him he could be a good person, like he'd

been when his grandparents were alive, when Morgan had been here.

Clearly, his father didn't know him. He wasn't in love with Hope. He wasn't in love with anyone. He wasn't like Morgan or his grandfather. Again…maybe it was another unsettling trait he had in common with his father. Dean wasn't wired that way. He loved women, he just had never been in love with one. Not like his grandfather had, or the way Morgan had. It had come easily to them, and that's the way love was supposed to be; if his grandparents' relationship had demonstrated anything, it was that. He could still see the love emanating from his grandfather's eyes as he'd stared at his grandmother. It had been palpable. And Morgan…well, Morgan had left everything because of love. Dean would never leave this place; his desire for revenge was greater than his desire for love. And Hope deserved love. A family man. A man who came from a good family, like hers. Someone who knew how to be a father, someone who could give Sadie another set of grandparents—not a monster like his father.

He took a deep breath and pulled out his cell phone. Enough thinking about things that would never get him anywhere. He needed to deal with the facts. He called the property management company his father used. While he wasn't in touch with them regularly, it was small-town business and they knew it wouldn't be unusual for Dean to be calling on his father's behalf. A few minutes later, he had the answer he'd already suspected. Hope's office was the only property who'd received a rent increase. Bastard.

Now what was he going to do? He couldn't let Hope lose her office or get gouged with the rent. He could pay it, without her knowing. He could pay the difference and tell her his dad had changed his mind. But Hope would see through his lie and he hated lying. Dammit.

Hope didn't have money to spare, and it gutted him to think he was responsible for her added problems. The only reason his dad would raise rent was to send a message to Dean.

But the other thing that was bothering him was the way his father referred to Hope. The flattering herself was an odd remark for a man solely interested in raising her rent. Dean pushed that thought aside and knew he had to find a way to help Hope out of this mess. His only solution was to call the property manager and ask him to inform Hope that rent would go back to normal.

Dean would pay the difference and she'd never find out. He'd help her build up her ranch and then they'd just go back to seeing each other on Saturday nights at River's. She'd find some great guy to marry, and he'd be a great dad to Sadie.

It was the perfect plan. And he'd be fine being Dr. Dean for the rest of his life. He'd be fine with just that moment in the barn when he'd touched her. When he had to force himself to move away from her. When he wanted to kiss her more than he wanted to kiss anyone, ever.

But she deserved more than what he had to offer. She deserved the real deal. A man to love her with all his heart.

Except the thought of all that, of that man not being him…hell, it hurt.

• • •

Hope frowned as another email cancellation came in from one of her patients. That was the third one this week. Clicking open the email and reading it, doubt scurried down her spine. The patient was not only cancelling the appointment, but not moving forward with any more treatments.

Trying not to let panic get the best of her, she quickly looked up that patient's chart, almost positive she'd been successfully working through a protocol that required a follow-up. Sure enough.

What was happening? No one who'd cancelled had rescheduled their appointments.

She put her elbows on the table, resting her chin on them. She was sitting at the kitchen table, her planner, a plethora of notepads, and pens strewn about. Since it was dreary out, she'd lit a vanilla-scented, clean-burning candle one of her patients had gifted her. Looking around the small space and all her notes and to-do lists, she worried that maybe she wasn't going to be able to make this work.

Even the best and most organized to-do list couldn't solve the problem of a dwindling practice. She just didn't get it. Everything had been going so well.

Glancing out the window, she looked for any sign of Lainey. Her best friend was going to be walking over with Ellie, and Hope couldn't wait to see them. She was going to shake off her worry, because the last thing she wanted to do was burden Lainey with her problems.

She was happy Dean was working at the hospital today. It gave her a chance to relax a little from having him around. Ever since their conversation in the barn, she hadn't been able to shake the feeling she had unintentionally set things off in a different direction. She'd replayed that conversation, the look on his face, and as much as part of her was relieved he'd known nothing about what his father had been up to, another part of her was slightly worried that she had caused him problems with his father.

And then there was the fact that she couldn't stop thinking about what it felt like to touch him. How she'd wanted to lean into him. She couldn't even think about him without her pulse racing. But that terrified her. This wasn't high school anymore. She was a grown woman. A mother. She owned a house, a business. And yet Dean had the ability to make her weak in the knees and forget how to breathe.

She was a mess. Her business was failing as her rent was increasing and she was sitting here fantasizing about Dean kissing her. This visit with Lainey was the perfect distraction. Between being a new mom and Hope inheriting this house, it felt like they barely had time to see each other.

Excitement swelled in Hope's chest as she spotted the bright red stroller down the street. Hope jumped up from the table, turned her already-prepped coffeemaker on, and grabbed her sweater before bounding out the door. She ran down the steps and driveway to meet them. Lainey was waving and then holding her finger to her lips. They gave each other a big hug and were careful not to be loud.

Hope peeked in the stroller to see the adorable sleeping baby. She was all bundled up with a pink knit hat and matching blanket. Hope's eyes stung with emotion as she looped her arm through Lainey's and they walked up to the house. "She is so sweet, so perfect, Lainey."

Lainey smiled. "Thanks. I feel the same. I kind of knew being a parent would change me…and Tyler, but I couldn't ever imagine how much. Part of me feels like the same old Lainey, of course, but then there's this other part of me that I feel like I'm just getting to know. We don't have it all figured out yet and we barely sleep, but Hope, I'd do anything for this little girl. Anything to keep her safe and happy."

"I know. Kind of amazing how that happens, isn't it? I remember watching Sadie when she was sleeping, thinking how, a few weeks before, there was a world without her in it and then all of a sudden, she was the most important person in the world."

"Exactly. She is. And Martin and Mrs. Busby dote on her constantly. It's so sweet. She is surrounded by so many people who love her."

Hope leaned down to carry one end of the stroller while Lainey grabbed the other and they made it up the porch steps without waking little Ellie. She fought the waves of emotions and memories crashing through her. All her memories of when Sadie was young also held the imprint of Brian, Brian healthy, Brian sick, Brian dying.

Then it was just her and Sadie. And what no one knew was how she'd watch Sadie sleeping, not because she was so beautiful and peaceful when she slept, but because Hope was worried she would never wake up. Those lonely nights Hope would lie curled beside her little girl's side, the moonlight keeping her company, thinking of all the things that could go wrong, and then thinking of all the ways she could prevent sickness. And she knew deep down that her obsession with clean eating, clean everything, stemmed from a deep-rooted fear that she would lose Sadie. If she could control everything they ate, then maybe she could control their health.

The sun rose and set with Sadie and as long as she was happy and safe and loved, then Hope had no right asking for anything else. Because if she dared wish on a star on one of those lonely nights, it would be to let Sadie live a long and happy life. She wouldn't waste a wish on herself. All her prayers were for Sadie.

Hope pushed aside those thoughts and grabbed the diaper bag from the bottom of the stroller and they made their way into the house. She'd rather focus on Lainey and not on the past. And there was no way she'd confide any of this morbid stuff to a new mother. All her friends had been there for her, she wasn't going to burden them even further. "Definitely. I'm so happy for you and I know I keep saying that but it's true. Okay, make yourself at home. I made coffee and fresh banana bread."

"It does. Oh, Hope, I really love this house. You've already done such a great job in here. You've made it so homey and welcoming," she said, standing in the open living room and looking around.

Hope walked into the kitchen and started filling their mugs with coffee. "Thanks. It's starting to feel like home. And Sadie loves it here, especially how much room there is to run around outside."

Lainey smiled, rubbing Ellie's back and gently bouncing from one foot to another. She already looked like a pro. "I'm sure. Is her room all decorated?"

Hope nodded, picking up the mugs. "You know Sadie. She had it all planned out before we even moved in. Here, let's go sit on the couches. I have the banana bread on the coffee table."

Lainey sat down on one of the couches, balancing the baby in her arms. "Perfect. Oh, this is exactly what I needed. I missed you so much."

"I know. I missed you, too. It's been so busy. Here, why don't I hold Ellie and you sit back and enjoy your coffee?" Hope said, reaching out for the baby.

Lainey nodded, placing her in Hope's arms. "Thanks."

"I think I could hold her all day long," Hope whispered, looking down at her porcelain skin and feeling the precious weight in her arms. A lump formed in her throat.

She'd always loved babies. So many of Sadie's early childhood memories were tied with Brian's sickness, and sometimes she felt guilty about that. Sometimes she felt angry about it, that they'd been robbed of enjoying their child's first years with carefree joy. She knew on a logical level they weren't the only people out there who'd had tragedy strike during childhood, but it made her feel guilty. Like, maybe she hadn't been a great parent to Sadie. She had been so distracted, so preoccupied. Some days she'd been on autopilot. Had she given her enough of herself?

Had Sadie noticed when Hope stopped laughing? Had she noticed her smiles were all forced? And then after, had Hope given Sadie the emotional support she had needed? Lainey and Tyler were so happy. Could Sadie sense Hope hadn't been always happy?

"Sometimes, Ty and I sit and watch her sleep."

Hope settled back in the couch and forced herself to concentrate on what her friend was saying and not on the memories and insecurities it all triggered. "I remember those days. How are you guys doing? Tyler?"

Lainey smiled before taking a sip of her coffee. "I don't think I've ever been happier. Tyler too. He's crazy overworked, has goals for what he wants the ranch to be, and you know his dad is supporting that vision. Long days. Long nights now with a baby."

"I'm really happy for them and that Martin is doing so well. Have you had any time for your art?"

Lainey shook her head. "Not much, but I manage to sneak in a few hours on Sundays when Ty is home all day. And I do have some exciting news. Another gallery bought a few more of my pieces. So, I can't complain."

"Lainey, that's fantastic! You know I'm home with Sadie on weekends. Bring the baby over and we'll watch her. You know Sadie would love that. It'll give you some time to paint. Seriously."

Lainey nodded, her eyes sparkling as she stared at Hope over the rim of her mug. "Thanks. I will totally take you up on that, especially when I take on my hours at the diner. We also have Martin and Mrs. Busby, so we're doing okay. So... how are things going around here? Dean...?"

Hope fidgeted with the edges of the pink blanket. "Good. I...can't get over the guilt because he's working way too hard. Way too many hours and I don't even know what I'm going to do with this place. I've dumped a lot on his plate."

Lainey put down her banana bread and leaned forward. "You know he's here because of how he feels about you."

Hope took a deep breath, forcing herself to deal with her emotions instead of denying everything. "I don't think it's as simple as that. I feel like there're so many things left unsaid between me and Dean. I... I want to have that conversation but part of me doesn't want to. It's like he's holding onto things that he's keeping from me."

Lainey tilted her head. "Why? What do you mean?"

"I don't know. It's a hunch. Maybe we're the same. Afraid to let each other in. I'm scared to let him in."

"Do you want to let him in? I know there is no timeline on loss and how hard all of it has been on you, but is there part of you that is ready to move on?"

Hope let out a shaky sigh. She and Lainey had been through everything together and she was a sister to her really. Lainey would never judge her, yet it was still hard to talk about all of it. "It's complicated and it doesn't have to do with Brian anymore. Directly. I don't know that I want any kind of relationship again. And Dean is…kind of more than I want to handle. He's intimidating, his background, his accomplishments, his wealth. He's the opposite of Brian. I know Brian was young and a hard worker and responsible, but he was uncomplicated. I was in charge of most things at home, in our marriage. He got sick so early on I couldn't lean on him. I had to always be in control, and I'm not sure I know how to let someone else in. Dean feels like he's layers of complicated, not that I'm not. And then there's Dean's family… Have you met his dad?"

Lainey made a face and nodded. "They're nothing alike. From what Tyler tells me, he's pretty cold. He said Dean doesn't talk about him and never has, and they project that they are a happy family, but his dad has a reputation. He cheated quite a few times on Dean's mom when she was alive. Everyone knew. His older brother Morgan left for reasons Dean refuses to talk about. His father has come into the diner only a handful of times and he gives off a slimy vibe."

Hope's heart was pounding with this new information. Dean never spoke of his family, and when she mentioned his father's visit, he'd been livid. "Yeah. I know. He's my landlord and he raised rent on me without any notice. And he approached me after Dean drove me home from your party and implied, well, I don't know. I thought at the time I was reading too much into it but now, based on what you're telling me, maybe I was right. He was weird. He touched my arm."

"What do you mean? Like, brushed against it? Or…creepy touched your arm?"

Hope swallowed. "Creepy. It was a touch, with a little stroke of a thumb. But maybe I'm imagining things. You know, some people are touchy-feely by nature. Except…he's not exactly the warm and cuddly type."

Lainey's eyes widened comically. "What? Why didn't you say anything?"

"You were just home and hadn't seen Tyler in so long, I wasn't going to bombard you with my drama. Nothing ever happened so I let it go and nothing happened since."

"Did you tell Dean?"

Hope shook her head. "I ended up telling him about the rent and that he approached me about staying away from Dean. I was relieved he knew nothing about it. But the rest is awkward. And I needed to be sure I wasn't reading too much into it. Anyway, it doesn't matter because that was a long time ago."

"Uh, I'd mention it to him, Hope."

"If this were ever to go anywhere, then fine. I don't want to come between him and his dad."

"From his dad's behavior I don't think they're close. He never forgave him for driving his brother away. Tyler said the only reason Dean didn't leave was because of some loyalty to his grandparents. But I also don't think you can decide any of that on behalf of Dean. He wouldn't be here if he's worried about what his dad thinks."

Hope had a hard time not feeling bad for Dean based on this new information. What kind of a father would act that way? There was so much about him she didn't know. While Dean could be hard and aloof, there was never any doubt in her mind that he was a good man. He was so sweet and kind to Sadie. Every single patient they shared had nothing but good things to say about him. Everyone loved Dean. "You're right."

"Okay, so where does that leave you and Dean?"

Hope leaned her head back on the couch and groaned. "Lainey, you don't give up, do you?"

"I want you to be happy. You deserve it more than anyone I know. And I've gotten to know Dean really well the last couple years. He's a great guy."

"You don't have to tell me. I know."

"So then don't let his dad push you away. Dean is here because he cares about you and Sadie. There's not a lot of men who would take on this place in addition to their already demanding career."

Hope winced. "I feel so guilty and I worry he's taking on too much. But Dean is more stubborn than I am. This house was supposed to have solved a lot of my problems but in some ways, it feels like things have become more complicated. I'm now involving Dean in my problems; I'm also worried because rent is going up and my appointment bookings have been going down drastically. I've had a few cancellations already for next week and that never happens."

"Do you think it's the new naturopath in town?"

Hope's stomach churned as she stared at Lainey. "What new naturopath?"

Lainey's brows knit together. "I thought you knew. They opened up outside of the downtown, in one of the old houses. It's all renovated and they have a big sign out front."

Hope's stomach dropped. "What? I… I don't know anything about this. They?"

"There's two of them. And they're going to be offering other holistic services like Reiki, massages, an organic spa…"

When Lainey's voice trailed off, Hope knew it was even worse than she originally thought. Her mind raced, her stomach rolling around like a never-ending roller coaster. "Lainey, this is bad. I can't compete with that. It was hard enough starting a business like mine in a rural community. It took me years to get the client base needed to make a decent living to support myself and Sadie. Even with this house being paid for, it's a ranch, a lot of land, and if I need to turn it into something, I'll have to have money to invest in it. I can't do that if my business is in jeopardy."

Lainey put down her coffee mug, her brows knit together. "Of course. Okay, I think you're getting ahead of yourself. They're offering different services. We don't know if that's why people are cancelling. It could be a coincidence."

Hope shook her head, tearing her gaze from her friend's worried expression and going to the landscape outside the picture window. Why was it the minute things were going right for her they took a nosedive? She inherited a house. A dream come true. And then everything started falling apart. Again.

She held Ellie close, watching as rain streamed down the windowpanes. "I've never had that many cancellations at once. And these are established relationships. The timing of all this is the worst. I've scrimped and saved and I still can't afford to put Sadie in all the extra-curricular activities she wants. I still can't afford to get her that American Girl doll she's been begging for forever. I should have been able to earn more. But now, if I'm losing patients, there's no way I can make this work."

"Hey, stop being hard on yourself. Sadie isn't a child who's lacking. Do you really think she's the only kid in her class who doesn't have one of those dolls?"

"Of course not. She's such a good kid. She's been through so much. I want more for her, more than generations of struggling. I feel like a failure."

"Failure? Are you kidding, Hope? I look up to you. The kind of mom you are. I've been taking notes. I want all this, all you've created. The warmth in here, the love, I felt it the minute I walked through the door. It's in the little things. Sure, luxuries are nice, but that's not the stuff that lasts. It's the memories. It's the way Sadie feels when she comes home from a day at school knowing she is loved and cherished. Knowing she has a soft place to fall at the end of a crappy day out there in the world. That's what you've created. That's what I hope to create for Ellie and our future kids. Stop being so hard on yourself."

Hope blinked back tears as Lainey's words sunk in. "Lainey, thank you for saying that. I guess sometimes I get so caught up in what I can't do for Sadie. I have a lot of guilt from when Brian was sick. I… I wanted to give her everything but I couldn't. You're right. I'm going to take your advice and stop beating myself up."

"Good. As for your business and this ranch... maybe Dean can help find a way to make this place profitable," Lainey said softly.

Hope shut her eyes briefly, the image of him working in the barn overwhelming her. "How much more can he do for me? This was destined to fail from the beginning. The man is a doctor and he's out here working for pennies. Am I going to repay him with gluten-free muffins? I... I may have to tell him this is over."

CHAPTER FIVE

"I don't know what the hell I'm supposed to tell Hope. There isn't enough money for more than fixing up that old barn and a chicken coop for Sadie. My dad is the biggest ass because he's raising her rent and she only just told me this. How can all of this be happening at the same time? How much more is she going to have to deal with? Hell," Dean said, taking off his hat and running his hands through his hair.

He, Tyler, and Cade were on horseback, deep in the foothills of the mountains. The horses were Tyler's and they had spent the last few hours on Hope's land. He had wanted their opinions before presenting to Hope some options.

"I didn't know things were that tight. I thought maybe there was some extra money there from the grandparents," Cade said.

Dean shook his head. "This place was all they had. It was never much of anything. The value is in the land, that's for sure."

"I could talk to my dad. We've done well this past year. Do you think Hope would be open to selling some acres? That might generate some money to build," Tyler said.

"Yeah, as much as I'm sure she'd appreciate

the offer, that would also prevent her from ever making it a ranch. There's land, but not enough to parcel off. I think that's the last thing she would want. She wants Sadie to have something of Brian's. I will tell her, though," Dean said as they started back toward Tyler's. The sun was setting, tucking away behind the mountains, stealing with it what little warmth there had been in the March air.

He could get used to this part of Wishing River. There was a simplicity out here. The opposite of his family estate. Here, the sky seemed bigger, the fences not so constricting, the air lighter. In the distance, he could just make out the tumbling of smoke from the chimney at Hope's house. And something stirred in him. A longing to belong here. To Hope. To Sadie. He felt it every day, even though he tried to deny it. But he could. He could deny himself if it meant protecting Hope in the long run.

He glanced over at his friends, knowing they had that. They had their wives to go home to. Tyler, a baby waiting for him at home, a future that was more than work. Their lives were full because of the women in them, not because of the money in their accounts or the name in their signature.

After he'd cooled down from his argument with his father, he'd thrown himself into work. That had always been his way to deal with things.

The harder he worked, the less he had to deal with his feelings. But he did know that no matter what, he wasn't going to let her lose this place, or her practice. There was no way he was going to let his father hurt her. He just needed to find a way to keep his promise to his grandfather and pursue a relationship with Hope.

This land she'd inherited was way out of her comfort zone, but not his. They needed to sit down and hash out some options that went beyond fixing up the old barn. He stopped suddenly, remembering something. He glanced over at Tyler. "Remember when Lainey rented your place out for that ranching vacation?"

Tyler chuckled, his eyes sparkling. "Can't forget."

Dean didn't care to hear what wonderful memory he'd brought up between Tyler and his wife. "Was it profitable?"

Tyler nodded. "It was a ridiculous amount of money for what we were offering. But it's a real thing. People want an escape from their everyday lives and they want exposure to what life is really like out here. They want the mountains, the horseback riding, the air. And they're willing to pay big money for it. If I liked people more, I'd consider it a great way to earn extra money."

Dean's head was spinning, and by the time they made it back to the barn at Tyler's he was itching to get over to Hope's place. Maybe there was a way to make this work. Between the rent she'd save and his new idea, he felt like maybe there was a chance. "I'm going to head over to her place with an idea."

"So, you and Hope seem to be getting along. I thought she'd have kicked you to the curb by now," Cade said while Tyler laughed.

"You're funny. Actually, Hope and I are getting along just fine."

"Yeah, and how are you juggling everything? You look kind of shitty," Tyler said while Cade nodded.

"You look like shit, too, and I had enough manners to keep it to myself," Dean snapped. Did he look that bad? Okay, maybe he needed a shave, but he still showered daily. He made a mental note to look in the mirror longer than the two minutes while he brushed his teeth.

"No need to get so defensive. I'm the best looking of the three of us," Cade said.

"According to who? Sarah when she loses her vision before a migraine?"

Tyler almost fell off his horse laughing and Cade was ready to lunge at Dean, but he was ready for him, and he was really itching for his fist to make contact with someone. Even if it was all for fun. But a figure in the distance by their trucks made him pause. "I think that's Aiden."

"Speaking of good-looking. I don't know what it is about that guy that all the women see in him," Tyler said, shaking his head. It was a long-known truth that Aiden Rivers had been the most sought-after bachelor in Wishing River by any woman who walked into that saloon. None of them had figured out why.

Dean shrugged. "Me neither."

"I think it's the dimples," Cade said under his breath.

"It's the hair," Tyler countered.

Dean shook his head. "Eyes."

"I don't want to talk about this anymore," Cade said.

"Me neither. And be quiet now, because he's walking toward us," Dean said. He had always liked Aiden, and what his friends didn't know was how he owed Aiden one. Aiden had been there for him one night when Dean had been pretty sure his entire world was falling apart and would never get better.

"Hey, guys. Lainey told me you were out here. I might have what you're looking for, Dean," he said.

"What are you looking for, Dean?" Tyler asked. Dean could feel both he and Cade staring at him as though he were sitting under a microscope.

"A pony."

Cade burst out laughing.

"For Sadie," Dean snapped.

"Obviously," Cade said, looking slightly

disappointed, as though he actually thought Dean wanted a pony for himself.

The four of them stood around their trucks ironing out the details and making small talk. Aiden not ever really hanging out with them was something he still needed to deal with. He'd been too damn busy, and making friends wasn't something on his list of priorities.

After a while, he became aware of the time, and they all went their separate ways. There was no way he could tell Hope he was looking at ponies. Besides that surprise that he was going to shelve for later, he was dying to get over to Hope's to explain his idea. This could be the thing that would change everything for her.

When he arrived at Hope's, he found her on the porch with a worried look on her face.

She smoothed her hair and he took a quick moment to let his gaze flicker over her. His heart slammed into his chest at the idea there might be something really wrong. Sadie. "Hey, everything okay?"

She was wearing that giant wool sweater that covered all his favorite curves, but she still managed to look gorgeous. She smiled, but it didn't quite reach her green eyes. "Totally fine. I was waving Lainey off. You look like you're ready to burst."

He grinned, relieved that there was nothing serious. "Kind of. I have good news. I think I have a plan to save this place."

Her mouth dropped open and she blinked rapidly. "I could use some good news. Come in. Do you want a coffee?"

He nodded and followed her into the house. The fire was crackling and the smell of banana bread filled his nostrils. Even though the house was simple, Hope had managed to create a cozy and inviting environment. Every time he walked in here, there were some new touches. New boxes she'd unpacked. A new way to make it feel more like home.

It felt like a home he'd known once. It felt like a warmth he'd experienced at one time in his life. This little house, with its quirks and imperfections, was the most perfect place he'd been in since his grandparents were alive. If he were one for wishing, he'd wish this was his home, he'd wish that the one he'd grown up in had never existed. And he'd wish that Hope was the woman he was coming home to every night.

Two white couches flanked the stone fireplace, and a coffee table ottoman with a wicker tray holding books and a flickering candle sat in the middle. There was a basket beside one of the couches filled with throw blankets and some of Sadie's coloring books. The small kitchen table was on the other side of the open space. The kitchen was all white and sparkling despite its age. There was another candle in a jar flickering on the counter and he could smell the rich aroma of whatever she was cooking.

His eyes went to the wall of pictures beside the coatrack. They looked like Sadie's school pictures. He couldn't help his smile. "These are really cute. Amazing how kids change from year to year. God, she looks like a baby in that first one," he said, a lump in his throat forming. That must have been preschool. That was the year Brian died. He cleared his throat and turned away from the pictures, from the memories they evoked.

Hope glanced over from the kitchen where she was pouring coffees. "I know. Sometimes I look at her and search hard for that baby girl. She'll always be my baby, I think," she said with a soft laugh.

"She has an infectious smile. Your smile," he said, crossing the room to the couches.

Hope sloshed coffee over the rim of the mug and made a sound under her breath. He wondered if it had anything to do with his comment. "Thank you." She placed a mug in front of him on the white coffee table. He sat opposite her, on one of the white slipcovered sofas. He took a sip of the piping hot coffee, glad for the warmth. "This is good."

"Help yourself to the banana bread. It's gluten free."

He pulled back his hand like he'd been scorched, as he'd been about to pick up a slice. He wasn't willing to admit defeat in that department yet. But better than having to pretend something was good and be forced to eat it. "I'm good."

She laughed before taking a sip of her coffee. "You're stubborn. And you did like those blueberry muffins."

He let out a short laugh. "Yeah, but I don't want to take my chances."

She shook her head. "Whatever. I'll drop it because you came here with the best intentions. So, tell me. What have you come up with? I'm willing to entertain almost anything after what I just found out from Lainey."

He eyed the banana bread again as his stomach growled. Hell, he'd give just about anything for a plate of bacon and eggs and home fries right now. He hadn't been eating or sleeping enough, and he knew he was going to have to make more time for that if he was going to keep up with everything. He ran his hands through his hair, remembering how his friends told him he looked like shit. Maybe he did need to eat more. "What did you find out from Lainey?" Her words finally registered and permeated his cloud of hunger.

"Eat the stupid bread, Dean. I can hear your stomach growling from here. I promise you'll love it."

He reluctantly picked up a piece of the loaf and took a bite, not expecting much. He was pleasantly surprised by the texture and taste. He stretched his legs out, the sweetness of the bread and the carbs, coupled with the coffee, making his muscles relax. "I don't know how you do it, Hope, but this is amazing. Probably the best banana bread I've ever had."

She sat a little straighter and smiled at him, and he was pretty sure he'd eat even the crappiest health food she offered from now on, just to see that smile. God, he was a glutton for punishment.

"I'm glad you like it. Grain, dairy, and sugar free."

He reached for another piece. "Stop trying to make this sound so bad. You really need to work on your marketing."

She laughed and he found himself smiling as he polished off another piece. "Noted. So, I've had a bunch of patient cancellations in the last few days. That's very unusual for me. Most often, I can't work enough to fill my appointments, since I take Fridays off. Anyway, then Lainey tells me there's a new clinic. I looked them up and it's like a whole holistic center. They have a spa and everything. We've never had anything like this in town. Very high-end but not high-end prices. I think that's why I'm getting all the cancellations."

A knot formed in the pit of his stomach, killing the rest of his appetite more effectively than the mention of how healthy the banana bread was. His father couldn't be behind an entire new business opening in town, could he? That would be a bit much even for him. But what were the odds? This wasn't exactly the center for that kind of thing. Their population was so low they'd have to rely on out-of-towners coming, too. He tried to keep his expression and voice neutral. "What building is it in?"

When she told him the address, he had his answer. It was one of his grandfather's old places his father now owned. This wasn't a coincidence anymore. His father had probably offered them drastically reduced rent or even free rent depending on how important putting Hope out of business was. It didn't add up, though. It's not like putting Hope out of business would make Dean stay away from her. There had to be more to make him want to destroy her practice. He wished Morgan was still here. He'd understand this.

Dean sat back in the sofa and ran his hands down his face. "I'm sorry, Hope. That doesn't seem fair at all. You do have a loyal patient base, though."

She nodded, but the worry didn't leave her eyes. "I know. But I can't afford to lose anyone, especially now. And I can't work that extra day without it impacting my time with Sadie. I love working but I love having that day to catch up on things around here so I can spend time with her on the weekends. Between this and rent—"

"Don't worry about rent," he said harshly.

"Why not?" she whispered, her gaze focused on him.

"I've dealt with it."

She sat up a little straighter. "Dean, what did you do?"

He shrugged, trying to look casual, when in fact he felt like he was about to explode. His father was crossing so many lines. "It was a mistake and now it's been corrected."

She leaned forward and looked him squarely in the eyes. "I can't have you going around town fighting my battles for me."

He met her stare, refusing to back down from her even if it meant telling her only the half of it. "I'm not. But you can't also be paying more rent because my father is trying to control my life. So, consider the problem fixed. Moving on, I think I have a plan for this place. I was talking with Ty and Cade and was reminded of the time Tyler rented out his cabins for the weekend—"

"Wait. You're trying to change the subject. How did you fix my rent problem?"

He shrugged. "I spoke with the property management company. No big deal."

She tilted her head, her gaze steady. "I'm serious when I say I can handle my own problems, and I don't want to cause a rift between you and your dad."

"The rift began the moment I was born, so don't worry about it. Has nothing to do with you."

She tucked one foot under her on the couch, her eyes softening. "I'm sorry you're not close."

He took a sip of coffee, ignoring the sympathy she was offering. Soft Hope was entirely too tempting. Soft Hope made him want to join her on the couch. Made him want to kiss her the way he had no business to as friends. Made him want so many damn things. But he didn't talk about his family with anyone. "Don't worry about it. Anyway, back to my idea. Maybe you could do something here like Ty did."

She sat back in the sofa, her eyes not leaving his. But he caught the sparkle in them. That worry was finally gone and was being replaced by something that looked like hope. "Omigosh, Dean. That's perfect. In the future I'd want to work from home, but this house is too small for that. But what if I somehow made it work and, instead of cabins for people who want a taste of Montana, what if I made it like a holistic retreat? Where I bring in some other people? Then it's like a wellness vacation."

He put his mug of coffee down. "Hell, that's a great idea. I love it. It's perfect for you, for this land. And that leaves the option open of selling land to Tyler and his dad to help with some of the initial capital. Then you could apply for a bank loan, but you'd still keep the house, so Sadie will have part of Brian's family."

She was nodding and taking notes on her

phone. "I wonder if I could use this front room of the house for my clinic. It's not ideal but I'd save a lot of money. And my appointments all happen when Sadie is at school anyway. I wouldn't have to pay rent. That money could be used toward the business."

"Maybe in the future you could use the house for your business and then build a home for you and Sadie, farther back on the property. You'd keep your work and family life separate. This house is small but would be perfect for a business. You could use the bedrooms for appointment rooms or massage or whatever," he said with a cough. He was getting way ahead of himself and talking about stuff he had no idea about. His mind also ran away with the idea of building a home out here for Hope and Sadie. It was stupid to be this invested. He stood up abruptly, needing space and fresh air. He owed Hope. Too much time around here, wishing for things like a kid, was going to get him nowhere.

"Wait, where are you going? Dean, your ideas are amazing," Hope said, following him to the door. The softness in her voice and eyes made him want to sit his ass back down on the couch and spend the rest of the day here.

He placed his hand on the doorknob, itching to leave. What the hell was he even doing? He was running from the feeling in this house. From her. He wasn't the man she thought he was. He was closer to the man his father had accused him of being. So, he was going to have to get his head back in the friend zone. "I'm glad I could help. I have to get to work though."

"Work. Which job?" she asked, looking up at him with concern.

"I'm in the ER tonight."

She frowned. "How are you going to stay awake? Well, promise me you won't come here tomorrow—you need a day off."

If he let himself, he'd be touched by her concern. But he'd rather tell himself that it was just the way she was. Hope would have been just as concerned for Tyler or Cade. "I'll be fine. I'm used to it. I'm glad we have a starting point for your business, though."

She smiled up at him. "Me too. Thank you for everything. After Sadie is in bed tonight, I'm going to do some research and get going on a business plan. I'll need that for the bank, and I don't want to wait too long."

He nodded. "Good to hear. Well, good night, Hope."

He stepped out into the cold March night and strode to his truck. Anger toward his father came shooting back as he remembered the excitement in Hope's eyes as she thought of her business. He hadn't the heart to tell her that if his father was determined to put her out of business, no matter how good her plan, how good her services, she wouldn't survive.

So now it was up to him to deal with his father and find a way to make this right for Hope and not fall for her.

CHAPTER SIX

Two days later, Dean knocked on Hope's front door, tired and chilled to the bone. He'd put in a full day's work around the ranch, but the weather had turned nasty and daylight was gone. He wanted to let her know he was leaving.

It's not like he was looking for an excuse to see her again because he missed her.

A moment later, the door opened and she stood there looking like all his dreams come true. Her dark hair tumbled over her shoulders, and she was wearing that oversized cardigan sweater again with leggings and a fitted tank that showed off her flawless skin and a hint of cleavage. She didn't have any makeup on, and her lips were full and red and her green eyes bright. And for half a second, he imagined kissing her, coming home to her after a day like this. "Oh my gosh, Dean. I didn't know you were still here. Come in, it's freezing out there."

He shrugged. "That's okay. I'm sure Sadie will be home soon. I just wanted to let you know the barn is coming along fine. I think the most dangerous things have been fixed. I'll get going."

"Wait. Come in. You look soaked, and the roads can't be that great. It looks like freezing rain out there," she said, her eyes filled with concern. For him.

"I don't want to intrude," he said, pulling the brim of his hat lower in an attempt to ward off some of the chill.

She opened the door wider. "Oh, please. Sadie would love it if you were here."

"Well, in that case, maybe for a little while." He stepped into the small entryway. Immediately, he felt enveloped by a warmth that had nothing to do with the roaring fire. Hope had transformed the run-down home into a small sanctuary.

"Can I get you a coffee? Dinner's not quite ready yet."

"If it's not a bother," he said, taking off his jacket and hanging it on the iron coatrack beside the door.

She was already pouring him a cup. "Not at all. I made a fresh pot."

He accepted the big mug of coffee, noticing she'd set it on the counter instead of handing it to him directly. "Thank you. Every time I come in here, it looks better than the last. It looks like you've been living here for years."

She leaned against the counter and picked up her mug of coffee. "I've never owned my own house, so I think I got a little excited."

He didn't know how to respond to that without sounding like a snob. This was one of those times when he became self-conscious because he couldn't relate to any of his friends. Hope was a single mother who had been struggling. She worried about bills. About providing for Sadie. He'd never had to worry about money. He cleared his throat. "Well, it's very…comforting in here. A good place to escape from the rest of the world."

Her features brightened. "That's exactly what I wanted. I always want Sadie to feel like home is her safe place, you know? Like, whatever is happening out there can stay out there. But when she's home, she's cared for and loved. I think that's why I cling to my Fridays as a work-from-home day. It lets me get ahead on house stuff. Throw in some laundry in between emails or get dinner started early or…wow, this is a boring conversation, isn't it?"

He shook his head. He loved hearing her speak about her home and Sadie. It was a side of her he hadn't been privy to before. But all around was her heart. It was in the candles and the fire and the dinner simmering away. It was in the little things she did; they had a big impact. In all his years growing up, he'd never had a homecoming like this. They had big rooms and formal dinners, echoing hallways and empty greetings. Never had his home felt like a sanctuary. Home was a whole new battle and not a place you could let your guard down, which was why he and Morgan had gravitated to their grandparents' cabin. This was what he'd felt in their cabin. "This isn't boring conversation at all. Sadie's a lucky little girl to have a mom like you."

Her cheeks turned pink and she quickly turned from him and stirred something on the stove. "She makes it easy. I worry a lot about her, and I know I shouldn't, but I worry I'm not enough sometimes."

"Enough? You're larger than life with everything you manage to do. You're the best role model she could ever have. You're smart and beautiful and fearless." What. The. Hell. Why had he just said that? He sounded like some commercial for a teenage pep talk. The shock on her face was enough to make him want to leave. Of all the stupid things.

Hell. It was this place. This little cabin in the woods with its promises of rainbows and unicorns or something. Or it was bringing out some of his own unfulfilled childhood wishes. Whatever it was, it was damned embarrassing, and he'd think twice about speaking whatever came to his mind in this cabin. His friends would have a field day with this one.

"I'm not sure that's all true, but I'll take it. Sadie's been having a rough time with one of her friends lately, so I thought I'd make her favorite beef stew and biscuits and apple pie."

"That sounds delicious." He didn't know why this was making him long for everything domestic but it was. He'd never had a parent want to help soothe him after a rough day. Not that he would have even confided in either parent if he'd had a rough day. Or that either parent would even know what his favorite meal was. And besides, they'd changed cooks so often in the house, that a favorite dinner had never been established. But his grandmother had known their favorites. When she died, his grandfather cooked, but he always grumbled that he'd never be as good a cook as Grandmother. But Dean had figured it was probably because no meal would ever taste as good to his grandfather without his grandmother.

Her phone vibrated against the counter and she frowned, picking it up. "Oh, it's my parents. They're going to wait until the freezing rain ends before bringing Sadie back. So…it's just you and me for dinner. I hope you have an appetite."

"Starving. I'll go wash up."

She pointed down the hall. "First door on the right."

"Thanks." He left the kitchen very aware that Sadie wasn't here to be the icebreaker; he had no idea how Hope was going to respond to him. If she'd let her guard down or not. There had been a softening and he felt it in her, but he had no idea the extent of it. Once he had splashed some water on his face and washed his hands, he joined Hope in the kitchen again.

She was spooning a thick, steaming hot stew into a shallow white bowl. "Here you go. Biscuits are on the table."

"This looks and smells fantastic," he said as they walked over to the small table together.

He pulled out her chair for her and she gave him a startled glance.

"Habit. Don't mean to be weird," he said, sitting down opposite her.

She picked up her fork and gave him a questioning stare. "You hold a lot of chairs for women, Dean?"

He held her gaze, straight on. "Just the right ones."

She paused, her fork halfway to her mouth. He scooped up a large forkful of the tender meat and potatoes and thought he'd died and gone to heaven. "This is fantastic," he said, when his mouth was finally empty.

She smiled. "I'm glad you like it. Old family recipe. And I can't take credit for all of it. Grass-fed local beef is the other secret."

"No shortage of that around here," he said, breaking off a piece of the fluffy biscuit. It had an unusual taste and texture but was delicious nonetheless. Icy rain rattled against the windows, and every now and then he could feel a draft come through. He eyed the windows, noting how old they were. "I could probably apply some caulking around the windows in the house if you aren't going to be replacing them soon."

She waved a hand. "You have enough to do.

I'm not about to add anything else."

"It's no big deal. Consider it done."

She placed her fork down and stared at her plate for a moment. "Dean…"

"Yes?"

"Do you want dessert?"

• • •

Hope had no idea how Dean, just one man, had managed to swallow up the rest of her home. His presence took her small house and made it a tiny house. He was everywhere. His smile, his laugh, those blue eyes that seemed to hold so many more secrets than she had ever noticed. She wanted him to leave as much as she wanted him to stay.

They'd finished washing the dishes and were now sitting by the fire and she was desperately fighting a battle with herself to ask him more about himself. There were times when she caught an inkling that there was more to his family life than he let on. She barely knew anything about his brother who'd left years ago. "Did you enjoy a lot of home-cooked meals growing up?"

He let out a short laugh. "Unless you consider dinner from a live-in chef home-cooked. It was great, though. Fine dining every night at my parents' house. I can't complain. I was close to my grandparents and would go to their place as often as I could."

Hope took in the stiffness in his posture. A few years ago, she might have inwardly scoffed at the idea that a live-in chef wasn't a dream come true. But now she knew more about him and she was getting a very different picture of Dean. She'd horribly misjudged him. He had seemed genuinely delighted by her simple dinner and had eaten seconds. This was probably the first mention of his grandparents, too. There was so much hidden in everything he was telling her. "So... neither of your parents were into cooking?"

He ran a hand through his hair and her gaze followed the gesture. Dean had great hair. Then again, Dean had great everything. There was no doubt that he was a good-looking man, even though there was so much more to him. She found herself noticing things, like the roped muscles in his forearms when he reached for more biscuits. Or the way his shoulders filled out his shirt. Or how much she loved the stubble on his face, and had even let herself imagine running her hands over it. The way his rumpled jeans fit his strong body. It was getting a little ridiculous, and she found herself wishing for Sadie to get home soon so she could focus her attention on her daughter rather than Dean and all his attributes.

"No. They had more important things to do."

"Oh. But that's nice you were close to your grandparents," she said, desperately searching for something positive to say to draw him out.

He gave her a nod, shifting on the couch. "They were good people. I meant it when I said Sadie was a lucky girl. What you're building here, the way you put her first, that's not as common as it should be, Hope."

Emotion tickled the back of her throat, and instead of brushing off the compliment she opened up to him. "It hasn't been easy. Sometimes, I've been lost and haven't felt like myself. Sadie's happiness...her being whole and safe and strong are the most important things in the world to me. I would do anything for her. It can get overwhelming but, in some ways, I love the simplicity of this. Like, making a bowl of stew or a homemade dessert is an easy way to show someone how much you love them. I always want Sadie to know even though Brian isn't here, I have enough love for both of us."

"I don't think there's any doubt she knows that. She's bursting with confidence."

She gave a short laugh. "She does have confidence, that's for sure. Hey, so I wanted to tell you I'm moving forward with the plan to bring my business home. I haven't handed in my notice, but it should be fine, since I'm not breaking a lease."

His jaw clenched. "Okay. I can let the property management company know."

"Thanks, but I already did."

He cleared his plate and the mood suddenly

changed as he put his dishes in the sink. "Did you hear back?"

"No," she said coming over to stand beside him.

She placed her hand over his when he went to pick up the dish soap. When he turned to her, her hand fell from his and she realized how close they were standing. How small the kitchen was. How silent the house. How far they were from each other, even though they were standing within inches. "I'll do the dishes later. Why do I get the feeling you're mad at me?"

"I'm not mad. I just don't want you dealing with them. Or my father."

She tilted her head to the side, watching the expression in his eyes, looking for that warmth that was there earlier. "I appreciate that, but since I made the deal, I need to be the one to break it."

"Did my father contact you again?"

She shook her head.

"Good," he said, his posture stiff.

"Dean…this is my problem."

He walked to the door. "It's not. Don't worry about it. Well, I'd better head out. You uh, sure you're okay out here?"

She nodded as a barrage of ice pellets hit the windows, and tried not to act as disappointed or confused as she felt. "Of course. Besides, I keep reminding myself that Lainey and Tyler are next door."

He stood there, looking like he wanted to say something, and she wanted to avoid anything awkward between them. "They are. And if you ever need anything, I'm a phone call away."

She folded her arms, looking up at him. "I know. I appreciate it, Dean."

He gave her a nod. "Good night, Hope."

"Good night. Drive safely."

Hope let out a sigh when she closed and locked the door behind him. She looked around her small house, seeing him here, everywhere. Without him, it felt empty and lonely. How had she gone so many years keeping him at a distance? The image of his father, his uncomfortable vibe, his warning reminding her that Dean was off-limits. She didn't need to bring any kind of turmoil into Sadie's life. She couldn't risk this new truce, this friendship they were building. She couldn't risk falling in love with him and losing him. There were no guarantees, and all she wanted were guarantees from now on.

CHAPTER SEVEN

Hope stared at the closet filled with cleaning supplies. Her vacuum, mop, duster, and all the various bottles were taking up the entire back door closet. Storage was at a premium in this small house and would be even worse once she brought her business home, so giving this up for a vacuum wasn't going to work.

She was confident in her new plan, to make the nasty, unfinished, spider-and-perhaps-rodent-filled basement slightly more palatable. She'd also come to the difficult decision to give up her bedroom for her business. Since it was right off the back entrance, patients would be able to come through there and then enter the bedroom—which would become an exam room. Giving up the front room wasn't practical for her family life. Sadie needed a place to spread out and just be a kid. It was also open to the kitchen, so that would mean there would never be a separation between home and work life, and she didn't want that for Sadie. So, really this was the only option. But that also meant she needed to make the basement function as a storage room.

She'd been in the basement exactly three times; when she'd first moved in and thought she'd just walked onto the set of a horror movie, then when the electrician had come in and shown the electrical panel to her, and yesterday when she'd come up with the idea of using it for storage.

Her plan was to paint the dingy and dusty wood staircase a calming, soothing blue...something to encourage her to keep walking into the abyss of creepiness. Then, she was going to lay down some rubber tiles she'd purchased on Amazon at the bottom of the stairs. They were the kind that clicked together like an oversized puzzle. Lastly, she was going to place a folding table on the tiles to house her cleaning equipment and bring in the bookshelves she had in her office. Having everything elevated should discourage any critters. It was a sound plan. She glanced over at the door to the basement and shuddered. She'd already painted the door, so she had left it ajar, not wanting the paint to stick. She was dreading the work involved. But it was a Friday, and Fridays meant tackling the house stuff because her parents would be bringing Sadie home after dinner.

She would've thought that keeping busy would keep her mind off Dean, whom she hadn't seen in a few days. It was probably for the best. He'd already shared his hospital schedule with her. Their dinner together that night had been strange. There were too many things left unsaid between them and she couldn't afford to ever get hurt again. Just the idea of being happy with someone...Dean...would mean she'd always be looking over her shoulder and waiting for something bad to happen. So this, this life of painting creepy stairs to the basement and being a single parent forever, was more than fine. They were great. She was great.

Picking up her can of paint she placed the doorstop under the thick basement door to prevent it from closing and then began painting. She let herself get lost in the methodical stroking of the brush. She'd completed four steps from the bottom when there was a knock at the door. Not expecting anyone and assuming it was a delivery, she resumed painting. The knocking grew louder. Putting her brush down with a sigh she jogged up the rickety steps and was surprised to see Dean standing outside.

She ignored the way her heart raced as though it knew she was in for a treat. Pulling open the door, she smiled, resisting the urge to smooth her hair. Actually, she had no idea what she looked like at the moment and tried not to get preoccupied by the idea she might have paint on her face. "Hi."

He took off his hat and stepped inside when she held the door open wider. As usual, the man seemed to swallow up the small space and transform it from boring single mom's fixer-upper to excitement central. "You have paint on your face."

She frowned at the observation and the flat way he said it. "Thank you, you look wonderful yourself. I'm so glad you stopped by unannounced."

His lips twitched. "Sorry. You're beautiful as always, Hope. I was remarking on the blue paint on your cheek."

Her face flushed and she crossed her arms. "I wasn't looking for a compliment."

He shrugged. "Sure. I was driving on my way home from the hospital—"

"Wait a minute," she interrupted. "I wasn't looking for a compliment. That's true."

He pinched the bridge of his nose and then looked at her again. He did look tired. And according to his schedule, which she'd all but memorized, he had just finished a twelve-hour shift. So maybe she would ease up on pushing his buttons. And maybe she was looking for some kind of reassurance. Or compliment. That was horrifying and mortifying. Did his opinion of her matter so much? "Anyway, I've been thinking about your business plans and I'm not sure bringing your business home is the right thing to do."

She toyed with a strand of her hair as she stared at him. "You were thinking about my business?"

He gave her a quick nod. "It's important to

me. You and Sadie are important to me."

She tore her gaze from his, looking over at the open basement door. "Uh, well, of course. We're all good friends. I was painting the stairs and you're welcome to talk while I continue. I want to use this time while Sadie is out."

"Uh, sure," he said, following her to the basement.

She marched down the stairs like she wasn't afraid of anything down here while he sat on the top step. "Okay, so tell me what you're thinking," she said, resuming her position and picking up her paintbrush.

There was a pause. "Ah hell, Hope. I'm not going to sit here and talk while you paint. Do you have another brush?"

She looked up at him sharply. "And I'm not going to let you get another brush and help me when you're already overworked. Stop trying to show off."

"I don't need to show off."

He was right. Not that she'd let him know that. "You're not helping."

"I'd rather be a show-off than lazy."

"I can think of a lot of adjectives for you, but lazy isn't one of them."

A slow grin spread across his face and her heart raced as if on autopilot. "I wouldn't mind hearing the other ones."

She almost laughed. "You seem quite confident that they are flattering."

He let out a low chuckle. "I can't say I suffer from lack of self-confidence. Now, before you manage to think of something unflattering to say, where are the brushes?"

She smirked. "Not telling."

He gave her a deadpan stare and marched down the stairs where the other brushes and second tin of paint were. She was careful to sidle up one side of the stairs so there would be no contact. "It's much faster if you agree with me," he said, picking up the can and paintbrush. When he was settled at the top of the stairs, she resumed working at the bottom.

She slathered too much paint on one of the steps. Irritated with herself for being distracted by his presence, she worked quickly so there wouldn't be any globs of paint on the step. "Okay, so are you finally going to tell me what issues you have come up with about my plan?"

"Yes, I am, as soon as I get this shut so I don't get any paint on the hardwood upstairs."

It took her a moment for his words to register, followed by the dreaded sound of the heavy door shutting for his actions to sink in. She paused, stood, paint dripping from her brush, and stared in horror at the closed door. "No! Omigosh, Dean! What have you done?"

He frowned at her and held up the paintbrush. "Uh, tried to protect the hardwood upstairs. How quickly you've gone from not needing help to wearing the bossy pants again. I know how to paint, Hope."

She dropped her brush and ran up the steps, trying the old knob. Sure enough, it wouldn't budge. She slowly turned to him, only then realizing how close they were on the narrow staircase, how much she had to lean back to look up at him. He was too...everything. Large. Strong. Smart. Right now, she didn't know if her heart was racing because she was one steady breath from her body contacting his, or if it was because he'd just locked them in her dungeon basement. "I just painted that door. It's stuck. We're stuck. It's not going to open."

A flicker of doubt shadowed his eyes, but then that arrogance came back. "It's not stuck. I'll open it."

She rolled her eyes and made a sweeping gesture with her hands. "By all means, Dr. Cowboy."

He frowned and then tried the knob. "I'm not Dr. Cowboy."

"I just tried the knob. It's not going to magically open because you're trying it."

He ignored her and rattled the knob again. Then he shoved his shoulder into the door and tried turning it at the same time.

She tapped him on the shoulder.

He ignored her.

She watched with rising panic as he continued

the same maneuver only to have the doorknob fall off and into his hand. He cursed softly under his breath and turned to face her. She lifted her chin, feeling only slightly redeemed. "I'm too polite to say I told you so. But I told you so."

"I thought you said you were too polite to say it."

"True, but I really felt it was justified. So great. Can you perform some kind of emergency operation to get the door open?"

He gave her a deadpan stare. "Do you have tools or anything down here that might help?"

She turned around with a sigh. The basement was empty except for the few things she'd brought down. The lighting was also bad because there was only one lightbulb dangling creepily at the bottom of the stairs. "It does feel like a basement where an ax murderer could have hidden at one time, so there's a slight chance you might find an ax."

He let out a choked laugh and bounded down the steps as though her warning meant nothing. Standing at the bottom of the stairs, he ran a hand through his hair and surveyed the area. "We can't stay down here all night. Hell, you don't even have a window open," he said, starting to walk off the rubber tiles.

"Stop!" she yelled, cringing, because her voice sounded slightly panicked.

He turned, waiting.

"You should know that's a dirt floor."

He shrugged. "I would've expected as much."

Her eyes widened. "Really? I never in my wildest dreams expected that."

"Okay, so are you trying to tell me something?"

"Yes, a friendly warning that there may be carcasses from rodents and God knows what else. That's why there isn't a window open."

"Let me get this straight, you're inhaling paint fumes for hours because you don't want to venture off some rubber tiles because there might be dead bodies from an ax murderer down here?"

She crossed her arms and lifted her chin. "Not funny. And it's nontoxic paint but that's fine. Go look around, just don't say I didn't warn you."

She stood in the middle of the staircase on one of the dry steps and watched as he turned on his phone's flashlight and wandered around the small basement. At one point, she couldn't see him at all when he'd reached the other side of the dark room. She shuddered. It really was a creepy basement. But a few minutes later he was visible again and his face was grim. "What did you find? Rodents?"

He scowled. "I found nothing and your windows don't open."

She groaned. "This is a disaster."

"When is Sadie coming home?"

She groaned, running her fingers through her

hair. "Not for another four hours."

"How's cell reception? Maybe I can get Ty over here," he said, holding up his phone.

She winced and just let him hold his phone in different spots, already knowing the outcome. "Um, I should tell you that there is no cell reception at the best of times out here. Also, I don't have wifi."

He ran a hand over his jaw. "Why?"

She crossed her arms over her chest. "Well... I'm not sure about all the radiation so I'm hardwired."

He blinked. "Of course. Hardwired."

She nodded. "Yep. It's a thing."

"Sure, if you're from the past. Okay, so, we're stuck in the basement. We can sit on the stairs."

She eyed him as he jumped past the first few steps to sit down halfway up the stairs. She decided to join him, inching as close to the wall without touching it as she could, but also managing to keep an inch or so from him. It wasn't a distance that was going to be maintained for long. "You're taking this reasonably well."

"Why wouldn't I? Are you cold?"

"Nope," she answered, noticing he had his jacket on. She wasn't cold while she was painting but now sitting here, it was getting a bit damp. But he was warm enough, so hopefully that would do.

He rummaged in his pocket and pulled out

two Snickers bars. He handed one to her. She waved her hand. "No thank you."

He let out a rough sigh before dropping one on her lap and ripping open the wrapper on the other. "Your loss."

She glanced over at him while he was chewing. "I think that has gluten in it. And if you eat those on a regular basis, that might be why you have eczema. Not to mention the sugar, glucose, fructose, corn syrups, and hydrogenated oils, all highly inflammatory."

"You know what else is highly inflammatory? You dissecting my candy bar. First, I don't have eczema. Second, of course it has gluten. That's part of the reason it tastes so good. Third, I can see you drooling and maybe if you weren't so hell-bent on being perfect, you could actually be sitting here enjoying yourself."

She inhaled sharply and fought the flood of tears she felt coming on, which in and of itself was ludicrous, because she didn't cry every time someone made a comment about her strict dietary rules. But coming from Dean...that he thought of her as this rigid, uptight, perfectionist?

Standing because she needed space suddenly, she marched down the stairs and stopped on the tiles. She wasn't going any farther because...she did have some common sense. She turned around and extended her hand. "Give me the chocolate."

An odd expression crossed his face. "Hope...

maybe I was a bit harsh. I'm sorry. It's been a long day and I'm hungry."

She shook her head, being sure to keep her shoulders back and head lifted. "No, no, you were right. I don't know how to enjoy myself and I'm a perfectionist, so clearly eating junk food will make me a fun person with flaws and, since that's the only type of person worth being, I should eat it."

He rubbed the back of his neck. "Hope…"

She jetted her hand toward him. "The chocolate, please."

"I wouldn't have expected you'd be one to cave to peer pressure."

She rolled her eyes. "No, not at all. I would hate to think that one of my closest friends thinks so lowly of me. Here I was, just trying to live a healthy lifestyle and preserve my arteries and keep my immune system strong because my daughter has only one parent left and my parents are old and she has no other family so if I keep myself as healthy as possible, then I can be there for her. At least until she's an adult. And if something happens to me…" She stopped speaking when her voice cracked.

"Nothing's going to happen to you," he said, his voice raw and harsh.

"You don't know the future, no one does, especially now that I'm eating genetically modified corn syrup and…" She stopped speaking as her throat clogged with emotion.

His jaw clenched and his eyes glittered. She hadn't wanted to reveal all that, not to him. But it was something she never admitted to anyone. It was one of those fears that kept her up late at night. It had woven itself into every decision she made. And she wasn't perfect. She did allow herself a weekend night at River's, but even then she supposed she'd made it healthier because Aiden ordered organic wine for them and she knew that he used local, grass-fed beef in his burgers. But, still, she did allow herself the fries. And the ketchup. See, she knew how to have fun.

"Nothing will happen to you."

She nodded, trying to infuse some lightness again to the conversation. "Of course. It's fine. I don't even know why I told you all that. I'm just paranoid. Chocolate please."

He didn't move. "Hope…"

She held his gaze. "Chocolate. So I can be fun like you."

He stood and slowly walked down the stairs toward her. When he reached the small landing, she was tempted to take a step back from him but couldn't because of the tiles, so she was forced to look up to meet his gaze. What she saw there made her stomach drop and her heart race. He cleared his throat.

"You're fun and I let my frustration get the better of me. You're an amazing mother and person and you set a wonderful example for Sadie. You're the most interesting and strongest person I know. Just to set the record straight. And your world won't fall apart if you let yourself have some fun. You're not alone."

Tears stung her eyes and she didn't know what to do. She didn't know how to process that from him. He was standing so close to her, and there was nothing she wanted more than to take that last step in to him and feel his arms around her. She wanted to rest her head on his strong chest and she wanted to kiss him. She wanted a relationship with him, one that went beyond this friendship they'd established. She wanted to tell him what she really thought of him as well, but didn't.

They'd get too close. She would get her heart broken one way or another. Or his father would force Dean to make a choice, and she didn't want to come between him and his father. She cleared her throat. "That's really nice of you to say, but I think I'll still have the Snickers."

He slowly dug into his pocket and handed her the bar. She tore the wrapper off and shoved a piece of chocolate into her mouth, not expecting the taste to do anything for her, especially in her current state. But when the chocolate melted in her mouth along with the nuts and sugar, she closed her eyes and held onto the railing. Except it wasn't the railing, it was Dean's arm. "Oh wow.

This is the best thing I've tasted in a long time."

He let out a muffled laugh. "I'm sorry I've tempted you to join the dark side."

She clenched his arm, trying not to pay attention to how good he felt, the strength of his bicep. And then she noticed how delicious he smelled. Fresh and crisp like he'd just showered. So, she did the only thing she could and continued to eat the chocolate like it was the last time she would ever eat. When she was done, she licked her fingers and carefully put the wrapper in the front pocket of her jeans, because she was not about to leave any morsel of food down here and attract any kind of critter. "I'm about to admit something that must never go beyond this basement."

He gave her a terse nod.

"You were right."

CHAPTER EIGHT

Dean stared at Hope and couldn't feel any sort of vindication because he hadn't wanted to be right. That wasn't the point. He was kicking himself for blurting out what he'd said. But there was this wall that was always up with her, and it had been a moment of weakness. "I wasn't going for right," he said finally.

She lifted her eyebrows and gave him an adorable smirk. "Weren't you, though?"

What he was going for was beyond him. But what he wanted right now was to lower his head and kiss her until the smirk vanished, along with all the other cobwebs between them. He wished they could start over. He wished he came from a normal family. He wished he was nothing like his father. Or he wished he'd never made that promise to Brian, because maybe it was too great to overcome. If he told Hope the truth, she might never speak to him again for hiding something from her for so long, or she might hate him for agreeing to keep that secret for Brian in the first place. But he'd also be betraying Brian and breaking an oath, so he knew it couldn't happen.

And the downside of keeping the truth from Hope was that she might never forgive him for something he never actually did. "I wasn't. I wanted you to have a damn chocolate bar. Sometimes it feels like you have the weight of the entire world on your shoulders, and I want you to know you don't. You have me, all your friends. It doesn't have to just be you and Sadie."

Her mouth dropped open and he jammed his hands in the front pockets of his jeans so he wouldn't reach out to touch her. She glanced away, then back up at him. "Thank you. I... I know that. I didn't mean to imply I didn't know you guys are always there for me. I know what you're sacrificing by putting in so many hours here."

"I'm not sacrificing anything."

She shook her head. "You are. And now we're being way too polite. I think I liked it better when you were egging me on to eat that junk food masterpiece."

He chuckled. "True. All right, so what are we going to do now that we're stuck down here. Want to sit down?"

She nodded, crossing her arms and he caught the shiver as she walked by him. "Sure."

"Okay, but you have to wear my jacket."

She rolled her eyes but didn't argue when he put it around her shoulders and sat down beside her. Their legs were touching and with anyone else platonic, innocent touching wouldn't have elicited a response. But his denim-clad leg against hers, the woman he'd wanted for years, had an entirely different effect on him. "Thank you," she said, her voice soft and breathy. Almost breathy enough to make him wonder if she was feeling the same.

"You're welcome. I guess we better settle in for a few hours. How's your project going down here?" he asked, in an effort to get his mind off how good it felt to be this close to her.

"Meh. It's going. Not ideal, but I'm trying to make a storage space and free up some room upstairs."

"So, you're determined to bring the business home?"

She nodded. "I know it sounds extreme, but in some ways my life will be a lot easier. I won't have to worry about driving into town in the winter. I'll be home for Sadie and never have to worry about having my parents pick her up. It'll be easy to stay on top of work and not have to be at the office. And I'm going to be saving a ton of money."

He didn't say anything for a moment, carefully weighing his words. It was a sound plan in some ways but it also meant bringing people into her home, and it was hard to trust people. He'd seen a lot in the ER and, while there were so many nice people out there, all it took was one angry and unbalanced person to change everything. They were so isolated out here. Plus, he hated that she had to make these choices, that she was on her own with no one to help her financially. He tempered his response. "That money will go a long way for sure. But how well do you know your patients? And if you take on new patients, they would be strangers, and you'd essentially be inviting them into your home."

She shrugged. "It's not like this is a big town or anything. Maybe I can do phone appointments for my first-time patients. I know what you're saying and I know I probably sound really naïve; it's something I've thought of. But when it comes to the money, I can't beat this idea. It will give me breathing room, and right now I have none. No rainy-day money. This place takes so much money to run and I don't want to give it up because I want Sadie to have it."

He nodded. "Yeah. Ideally, it'd be nice to build a place on the property; you have enough land that you could use this whole house for your business."

She let out a soft laugh. "You've read my mind. That's the dream. Who knows, if that other business in town flops and I can pick up more patients, then maybe that will be in my future. At least I won't be sinking further in debt by paying rent at my office anymore."

If they were together, they could build a house. He could give her all the things she deserved, but she wouldn't want to hear that and he had no business saying it at this point. As for how she ran her business, all he could do was offer his opinion, and whether or not she took his advice was up to her. But he couldn't help but be slightly worried about the idea of her being alone out here. "What about doing more online appointments? You could broaden your client base right from home. It could really bring in more people. I'm sure there are lots of people in rural locations who wouldn't want to drive all the way in for an appointment."

She was silent for a moment. "That's a good idea. I don't know anything about online marketing. Any marketing actually. My patient list was very much word of mouth. But I could look into it… How long do you think we've been down here?"

He shrugged and pulled out his phone. "An hour. When did you say your parents are bringing Sadie home?"

She groaned. "At least another three hours. Now what are we going to do?"

Life was a cruel joke sometimes. They were alone. In the dark. And yet nothing could ever happen between them. "We could finish painting the stairs."

"That's boring and now I'm crashing from all that sugar. My body isn't used to the pollutants."

He smiled at the laughter in her voice. "Mine is and I'm not crashing. You can take a nap if you want."

"On the stairs?"

He looked out into the dark basement. "Is there anything else down here?"

She scoffed. "I don't know. A rodent carcass?"

He choked out a laugh. "Probably."

She inhaled sharply. "You think?"

He frowned. "It's a dirt floor."

She rubbed her temples, his jacket falling with the motion. He lifted it back over her shoulders, his fingers brushing against her silky hair. He needed some kind of medal of honor for sitting here and not giving in to the attraction between them. It was like some kind of test and, so far, he was acing the test while losing the woman and it wasn't damn fair. "I'm going to get my dad to look around here tomorrow with a light to see if that's true. I can't be using this area if I'm sharing it with creatures that spread disease."

"I can have a look."

She placed her elbow on her knee and rested her chin on her hand, letting out a forlorn sigh. Dramatic, forlorn sighs were not sounds he'd ever associate with Hope. "Sure. Thank you."

"So, what's with the sigh?"

"I've admitted I have an aversion to rodents."

"You have an aversion to a lot of things, adding one more to the list shouldn't be traumatizing at this point." The minute the words were out of his mouth he regretted them. He'd meant to tease gently but it came out as more of a criticism, and he didn't know what the hell was wrong with him.

She shot off the step and grabbed his phone, turning on the flashlight. "I'm not afraid, Dean, and I'll wander this entire basement right now by myself. You sit."

He cursed as quietly as he could manage before standing. "Hope, it's okay to be afraid of something."

"I never should have let my guard down around you. I'm not afraid. See… I will now be stepping off these tiles and onto the dirt floor."

He tried to keep a straight face as she, almost in slow motion, raised a leg and placed it on the ground. Then she paused as though waiting for something to pounce on her from the darkness. He tried to come up with something that would help her save face. "You're very brave. Now, why don't I walk around with you. Two sets of eyes are better than one. Besides, it's boring down here."

Relief flashed across her eyes at the same time as she lifted her chin. "If you feel you must move because you've all that sugar coursing through you and need to burn it off, then sure. But if you're doing me any favors, then you can just sit your perfe…your butt down on the stairs."

Well, wasn't that interesting? Her face was now all shades of red. She turned and began flashing the light in the opposite direction. He could tease her that she'd been eyeing his ass and that he was flattered that she deemed it perfect, but he had sympathy for her. He walked down the steps and joined her. "All right. Let's go. I assume you're leading."

She rolled her eyes. "I know how to let other people lead. I don't mind if you go first. I'll hold the flashlight."

He bit back a smile. "That light isn't going to reach far. I think the person leading should have the flashlight and the other should trail behind in the darkness."

She gave him a shove and he laughed. "Let's walk together. Not everything has to be a competition, Dean."

"Sure, Hope. Let's go," he said, yanking her hand so that both her feet were now on the dirt floor.

"So I think the light should be on the floor, directly in front of where we're stepping," she said in a shaky voice.

"Yep. One foot in front of the other," he said in his most patient voice.

"I know how to walk."

"And talk."

She poked him and then grabbed his hand. He squeezed hers and they proceeded to walk the perimeter and then the middle of the basement. Other than a few bumps in the ground, there was nothing eventful to be seen or stepped on.

And then Hope screamed and he grabbed onto her hand as he felt her fall. "Hold on," he yelled.

"It's fine, I'm fine. There's a small hole and I'm so grossed out I think I'll never sleep again and I'm never coming down here again." She clutched his arms and he held on to her waist. He'd never seen her rattled. Well, he had, but that had been with grief, and he hated thinking about that because it's not how he thought of Hope. This was panic. He could deal with panic.

"I got you. What the hell did you step in? Hold on while I see—"

"No! Don't put the light on it. After I'm back at the safety of the stairs."

He paused. "For real?"

"Dean, if you weren't the only person down here with me, I'd hurt you."

He held back his laughter. "That's really quite rude, Hope. Clearly, it's good you stay off sugar."

She drew a deep shaky breath. "I'm calm now. It was a momentary lapse but listen, don't go pointing that flashlight because if I just stepped in some warm rodent carcass, I don't want to know. I'm going to march over to the stairs and then you're going to look. And lie to me if it's bad."

"All right. I'll try to hide it in my voice if it's really nasty."

"Do you think it's nasty?"

"Of course not," he lied.

"Okay, I'll be going then." But she stood still.

"Why don't I point the flashlight?"

She nodded and then removed her hands from

his arm and took a step and yelped. He grabbed
her before she fell. "What's wrong?"

She winced, gasping. "I think I've twisted my
ankle. How is everything happening all at the
same time? What kind of dungeon, cursed basement is this?"

"Come on, I'll help you over to the stairs and
have a look."

"I'm fine." She held on to him and stood still.

"Then go," he said flatly.

"All right, I may need your help. Please and
thank you very much."

"Can you walk if I support you by the waist?"

"Yes, of course. I don't need some heroic
sweeping gesture where you pick me up and—"

She yelped when he picked her up and crossed
the room. "So far, Hope, your own sweeping
statements tonight have ended in disaster. So, this
time, I'm deciding." He stopped speaking when
his irritation gave way to awareness. The way her
body felt pressed up against his once she stopped
flailing. How soft her hair felt when he almost inhaled a strand while speaking. How good she
smelled despite the musty basement air.

He set her down gently on the tile in front of
the stairs and neither of them said anything. She
held onto him and he held her waist, not wanting
to let her go. "Sit on the step and let me have a
look at your ankle."

He slowly lowered her to the step and

crouched down, expecting her to protest. When she didn't, he paused. "You okay?"

She nodded, not making eye contact with him. "Yup. Go ahead and have a look. I'm sure it's fine."

He gently lifted her ankle and checked for any visible swelling before letting his hand do the rest of the work. Her skin was soft and he felt her tense as his hands pressed into her ankle and he didn't know if she felt the same tension he did or if she was reacting to having her hurt ankle examined. For a second, he imagined running his hand up her calf, skimming her soft skin. He was imagining things he shouldn't be imagining, he reminded himself. At least not here. He focused his attention on her ankle, methodically going over the routine check he'd give any patient. Once he was satisfied nothing was broken, he gently placed her foot back on the ground. "Probably nothing, but if it still hurts in the morning, you might want to get it x-rayed. Ice it tonight to be safe."

She rotated her ankle a few times. "I'm sure it's fine. Thanks." Her voice sounded strangled, and he didn't move just yet. This was all getting ridiculous. This basement, this unspoken tension between them, the secret he was keeping from her. All of it.

"Hope," he said, without having a plan as to what he was going to say. She looked up at him with those green eyes that were holding on to maybe as many secrets as his own. She made him want it all. She made him believe the good life was right here, even in this dingy basement. She made him believe in something his grandfather had told him—that money didn't really matter all that much if you had love.

She rubbed her hands on the front of her jeans and broke his stare. But the air that hung between them was filled with years of secrets and hurt and judgment and he wanted it blown away. "Dean, I um, thank you for everything you've done for me and Sadie. I won't ever be able to pay you back and I'm starting to feel guilty. You're working too hard, pushing it in terms of your own health, and I'm getting worried. All of this…even tonight. You're stuck in a creepy basement because of me, and I can't let this continue."

He tensed. "I'm a grown man, Hope. I know what I can handle. There's no reason for guilt, you didn't force me into this."

She stared at her hands. "Why are you doing this?"

He covered her hands with his. "Because—"

"Mom! We're home! Where are you?"

Relief transformed Hope's face and she stood abruptly. Thank God for Sadie. What the hell had he just been about to say?

He stood at the bottom of the stairs, waiting as Hope's father grabbed some tools and opened the door. The distinct feeling that he'd just avoided a disaster pummeled through him. They had to remain friends. And if he needed any reminder of why, in moments of weakness, all he had to do was think about where he came from. If Hope's father really knew the kind of family he came from, he wouldn't be thanking Dean at all for being here.

CHAPTER NINE

"Smells like heaven in here," Dean said as he walked into Hope's house.

It looked like heaven, too. Sadie had a slew of markers strewn about the coffee table and was busy coloring something. The fire was roaring. Hope was slicing what looked like some kind of freshly baked loaf. Her smile brightened the moment he walked through the door.

He had avoided coming in here after the basement debacle last week because it was becoming hellish being around Hope this much and not acting on the growing attraction between them.

"Hi, Dr. Dean! We were waiting for you to come home," Sadie said, running up to him and giving him a hug. He held her close. Waiting for him to come home. Like he belonged here, with them. He could get used to this, being the trusted family friend. It was the best welcome he'd received in his entire life, and maybe it was because, suddenly, they'd become the best part of his day.

"We've been looking out that window, hoping you'd get here in time for dinner," Hope said from behind the counter.

"I'm glad I did because it really does smell incredible," he said, hanging up his hat and coat on the pegs by the door.

"Okay, everyone have a seat," Hope said, placing a large white lidded pot on the kitchen table.

Sadie ran over and sat down. "It's my favorite. Butter chicken!"

"I thought it smelled familiar," Dean said, the rich spices adding to the warmth in the room.

"And it's all naturally gluten free," Hope said with a smug smile. Hell, what he'd give to lean forward and kiss her gorgeous mouth. She gave everyone a generous portion of white rice and a scoop of the delicious smelling sauce and chicken.

"Hooray," Dean said before Sadie launched into an epic prayer that ended up being a recounting of her day at school along with a plug for an American Girl doll.

"Sadie, honey, let's move it along," Hope said gently.

"Right. So also, thanks, God, for Dr. Dean and hopefully Mom can cure him of his itchy skin problems." Sadie turned to him, gave him a megawatt smile and then dug her fork into the rice.

He looked over at Hope whose face was bright red. "How's the itchy skin?"

Strangely enough, it hadn't been that itchy. Glancing down at his hand, he noticed his knuckles weren't red. He decided this was not something he wanted to deal with today because, if Hope was right, that would actually be worse, because it would mean giving up the very heart and soul of wheat, the very thing that made it so damn good. "It's itchy."

Her eyes narrowed on him then went to his hands. He quickly scooped up some of the rice and then dragged it through the sauce and chicken. He prayed it tasted as good as it smelled and looked. It was delicious. "This is fantastic, Hope."

She sat a little straighter and smiled. "I'm glad you like it."

"It's seriously the best thing I've had in a long time," he said, proceeding to eat as diligently as Sadie. He'd put in a long day on the property and he'd worked up a massive appetite.

"Dr. Dean, can I come and work with you around the ranch this weekend?"

"Sadie, I'm sure Dean—"

"Would love the company. If it's okay with your mom," he said, shooting Hope a glance. As if he'd say no to Sadie.

Her mouth dropped open. "Of course it is. I know you have a lot to do, and Sadie is…great at asking lots of questions. I don't want us slowing you down."

"Are you kidding? I've been needing some extra help and I think Sadie is just the kid for the job." He winked at Sadie, who beamed at him.

"I can't wait. I know lots of things about ranches, because I go to Uncle Tyler's ranch and he shows me around and he even said he'll teach me how to ride a horse this summer."

Dean didn't want to make promises Hope might not let him keep, but he spoke up nonetheless. "Well, I'd be glad to teach you to ride, too. Who knows, one day you might be running this ranch."

Her eyes widened. "That would be so cool."

When he noticed Hope starting to clear the dishes, he rose. "Let me help," he said, taking the glasses.

"Can I go to my room, since Dr. Dean is helping with dishes?" Sadie asked, clearly looking like a kid who just got out of having to help with chores.

Hope smiled. "Sure. The loaf will be ready in a couple minutes, though."

"Great! I'll be back!" Sadie yelled over her shoulder.

Hope was scraping the dishes and then running the water, not saying anything.

"I can dry," he said, coming up beside her once the table was clear.

"That's okay. You must be tired. Why don't you go home?"

"Uh, ouch," he said, leaning against the counter and staring at her until she looked at him.

"What?"

"Why don't you tell me why you're mad at me?"

"I'm not mad at you."

He didn't believe her. "I'm sorry if I should

have asked you first before saying yes to Sadie. I didn't think it through."

She let out a sigh. "It's not that. I think it's sweet you'd let her tag along. I'm appreciative of that. There are things I wish I knew how to do and, since I don't, I'm happy you're willing to teach her."

He crossed his arms. "Hope, do you want me to teach you, too?"

She rolled her eyes, but a corner of her delicious mouth turned up. "No."

"It's okay to admit you need help."

She sent a pointed glance to his hand. "How's the eczema?"

He frowned. "That wasn't me not wanting your help."

She let out a laugh. "Sure. But, really, how is the hand?"

"Remarkably better. But that doesn't mean anything. It could be a coincidence."

She sliced the loaf on a cutting board. "Sure, but just in case, this is grain-free and sugar-free. For the sake of full transparency, though, this is a new recipe. Grain-free baking is actually quite difficult. I've mastered some tried-and-true recipes but wanted to experiment with a new one." She called Sadie as she plated three pieces.

Sadie came bounding into the room. "Mom, I just remembered I need a purple shirt for school tomorrow. Can you wash mine?"

Hope let out a sigh. "I did read that in your agenda and totally forgot. Okay, I'll go throw a load in and be right back. You go ahead and start eating."

Dean watched Hope leave, the realization of how much she had on her plate striking him. It's not that he thought she had it easy, but these little things, a load of laundry late at night, school events, homecooked meals, and work…and doing it all by herself, added up.

"Dr. Dean, don't eat this," Sadie whispered, coughing.

He frowned and picked up a slice of the cake. It started crumbling. "Are you exaggerating?" he whispered.

She shook her head, her eyes wide before she downed a glass of water. "No. It's awful. Like quicksand."

He took a large bite and it was as though sandpaper was everywhere in his mouth. His eyes widened as it got stuck in his throat. He coughed and crumbs flew out. Sadie started laughing and pouring him a glass of water. He tried not to laugh.

Hope came back in the room. "Okay! Laundry's going. Sadie, time for bed, honey."

Sadie's eyes were round as the dishes as she ran out of the room. "Sure, Mom! Good night, Dr. Dean!"

"Oh, you got into the cake. How is it?" Hope

said, taking a slice.

Dean had finally managed to breathe again. "It's, uh, very different."

She narrowed her eyes at him and then picked up a piece of cake. "That doesn't sound good," she said, about to put a piece in her mouth.

He couldn't let her choke. He swatted the piece out of her hand and it went flying across the room. "Dean! Why did you do that? I just washed my floors! Do you know the amount of crumbs that is?"

"Sorry about the floor. I should probably get going. I'll get the crumbs first," he said, eyeing the paper towels on the far end of the counter. Hope crossed her arms and blocked him.

"Spill it, Dean."

He stared into her green eyes and contemplated lying. Maybe he could tell her it was so good he wanted to take the whole thing home with him. At least then her feelings would be spared. "I…it's…okay, listen. Do you want me to tell you the truth or do you want me to tell you what I want to tell you?"

"What does that mean?"

"Just answer."

"Um, okay, first I want you to tell me what you want to tell me because that I just find curious."

He leaned against the counter. "Okay, I wanted to tell you I didn't want you to eat the cake because I want to bring it home and have it all to myself, I love it so much."

She tilted her head and drummed her fingers against the counter. "Okay...now why don't you tell me the truth?"

"It almost killed me and Sadie."

"What?"

He nodded. "It was as though a thousand slivers of sandpaper were lodged in my throat. Judging by Sadie's coughing and need for water, I would say the feeling was mutual."

"I don't believe you," she snapped.

"Of course you don't. Try a piece. Just get some water. Although you don't really have to worry about choking, since I'm a doctor."

"This is getting insulting." She popped a piece in her mouth and chewed. He witnessed the moment it must have lodged itself in her throat. Her eyes widened and she reached for the water, not coughing at all.

"Cough, Hope. You can't hide the truth. You might inhale too many crumbs. It's okay to admit that this kind of baking is really not for people who like to eat and not choke."

She rolled her eyes and cleared her throat. "It's not that bad. It just takes some getting used to. I know you're so used to unhealthy food so this might come across as different—"

"Homicidal."

"Theatrical much? I wasn't trying to kill anyone. Fine, so maybe it's not one of my better recipes; I was trying something new. I know when a person first transitions to a different diet, it can be quite difficult. I was hoping to show you it is not all that bad. But clearly this one was a flop."

He paused. "You made this for me?"

She shrugged. "Well, it's no big deal."

Now he felt like an ass. "You're right, it's not that bad. I think I'll have another piece."

"Wait. Dean, don't. You might choke. It really is that bad," she said with a laugh.

He almost joined in except that he had this odd compulsion to talk to her, not leave, to make them both feel better. "When I was a kid, I'd race home from school every day and wish that my mom was there. Sometimes, when I went to other kids' houses, there'd be freshly made muffins or cookies. I would wish that one day, or on my birthday, there would be a homemade something like at all my friends' houses. That never happened. So…the fact that you thought to make this for me, uh, this is the nicest thing anyone has done for me in a really long time. Thank you."

Her mouth dropped open and his gaze went to her full mouth and he imagined what it would be like to kiss her. His desire to reach out and pull her in to him felt almost unbearable. All-consuming. So much so that he didn't even care that he'd just opened up about his childhood without even thinking twice. "That's not how I pictured your childhood," she said softly. Her eyes glistened with something that he was uncomfortable with…something like pity. He didn't do pity well.

He crossed his arms. "It's not. I'm not even sure why I brought it up. My childhood was fine. Completely normal."

"Of course. Sure," she said, shooting him a concerned look before wiping some crumbs from the counter.

He needed to shift the topic away from him. "No really, it was totally fine. I've been eating hospital food for a week so this whole thing tonight was amazing and not at all expected or required. Can I ask you something?"

Doubt flickered across her eyes. "Of course."

"What made you go into naturopathic medicine?"

She tucked a few strands of hair behind her ear and started putting things away on the already tidy counter. "Are you setting me up to mock me?"

Shit. That's what she thought of him? He'd hoped they'd moved on from that time. "No, of course not. We already made a truce. I'm curious."

She shrugged, giving him only her profile while she wiped down the counter. "All right, I'm going to admit this only once to you, but I was planning on going into traditional medicine. But it wasn't meant to be."

He was floored. That wasn't what he expected at all. He waited for her to continue and when she didn't, spoke up because he didn't want this to just drop. "Why wasn't it meant to be?"

"Uh, well, there's this weird thing that happens to me when things are going a little too perfectly, something goes wrong. I'd aced all my exams, my grades were the highest they'd ever been, I was accepted to every college, but my dad had a heart attack. We needed the money. End of story."

It wasn't the end of the story and they both knew it. It was just the beginning. She was living her story; it was in her drive to make her business succeed, in her need to heal people, it was in everything she did. And it explained so much about her to him. "But that's not the end of your story, Hope. You didn't give up."

She shrugged. "I guess. I thought it was a lost dream but it really wasn't. I mean, I love what I do now and I think I'm good at it. I like spending the time with people to figure out the root cause behind their conditions. So I guess it all worked out in the end. Unless I go out of business." She let out a laugh.

He ran his hand over his jaw, processing everything. Now he felt like a bigger ass for ever engaging in their teasing. He didn't know where to start with any of this. He was standing here, living her dream. "Your parents must be proud of you. It's obvious how close you all are. And you're clearly gifted at what you do. Instincts a lot of people don't have must help. And I don't think you'll go down that easily."

She folded a lemon-patterned dish towel, her head downturned. "Sometimes I feel tired, Dean. Like this shouldn't be this hard. Making a living. Providing for Sadie. I thought this house was my big break but so far, it's costing me a lot more than rent in town, even with all your help. I'm almost thirty. I would have thought I'd have my life together by now, but I don't. I'm still struggling. I don't know why I'm saying all this to you. I'm very grateful and I shouldn't complain—"

He took a step toward her, aware of how small the kitchen was, how intimate everything was with the lamp-lit room and the flickering glow of the fireplace. But it was more than all that. It was Hope trusting him enough with her feelings. This was a side he'd never seen. Hope had always appeared invincible.

"It's okay not to be superhuman all the time. I think an outsider would be shocked to hear you think you don't have your life together. You're the most put-together person I know. Not only are you a naturopathic doctor, you're running your own business. You just moved onto a ranch and into a house that needs a lot of work. You're a single parent and are doing such an amazing job that your little girl is basically ready to run for president. Hope, you are amazing."

She folded the dish towel and unfolded it, her eyes still downturned. "Thank you for saying that. There are days I feel like I can barely keep my head above water. Sometimes I feel like I'm failing Sadie and I never want her to see me worried about business or money or even taking on this ranch... Your opinion means a lot to me."

That admission hung in the air between them, stretching and then breaking through the uncomfortable barrier that had always existed. Hope had never let all the walls down, and he took what she was offering seriously. "So does yours."

"I should get Sadie's lunch packed for tomorrow," she said, turning from him to open the fridge. It was as though he hadn't said anything at all.

"Truth be told, Hope, I think you were onto something about the gluten thing."

She looked over at him sharply, closing the fridge door. "For real?"

Ah, hell, he was going to have to tell her. There was no way he could resist her or seeing her happy. "As much as it pains me to admit, my hands aren't feeling itchy. And a lot of the headaches I get that I usually brush off or work through have disappeared."

Her eyes were sparkling now, and he was sure it was all worth it. "I'm so happy. Let me see," she said, grabbing his hands.

He stood there, looking down at her smaller

hands holding his. She turned them, looked at them, and all the while he pretended that her touch wasn't lighting him on fire. It was a ridiculous reaction to an innocent touch. But it was real and it was Hope. "These look noticeably better."

"I think so," he said, wanting to be talking about anything other than eczema. Wanting to be doing so much more than holding her hand. She didn't drop his hands right away and he didn't want to pull them away. He didn't want to go home. He wanted to tell her everything, about the promise he'd made to Brian and that he wanted to apologize to her for keeping the secret, for letting her believe the worst in him. And then he wanted to start over with her. He wanted a real chance at a real relationship.

The pulse at the base of Hope's neck was pounding and she didn't look away from him. Her green eyes weren't guarded or scared or angry. They were open, vulnerable, soft. And hell if he didn't forget every reason he never wanted love and family and commitment. Because right now, he wanted it all. He'd even eat the damn cake to prove it.

"Are you in love?"

Hope gasped and dropped his hands at the sight of Sadie in the doorway. Sadie was…grinning, like the idea of it was something she approved of. She was standing there in pink pajamas with hearts all over them, her eyes wide and sparkling. "Sadie, honey, no. Dr. Dean and I are just good friends. Why don't you say goodnight and I'll tuck you into bed?"

Sadie ran up to him and wrapped her arms around his waist. He kissed the top of her head without thinking twice. "Goodnight, Sadie."

She pulled back and stared up at him. "I wish you'd be here in the morning."

Hope took Sadie's hand and didn't look his way. Her face was bright red. "Okay, that's enough for tonight."

"I will see you in the morning. We have our day together tomorrow," he said, calling out as Hope ushered her down the hall.

He stared at their retreating figures, his heart wedged somewhere in his chest, making it hard to breathe. He was falling for Hope. He hadn't counted on falling for Sadie. For this life. This domestic life that reminded him of his grandparents, of Morgan, and the person he used to be.

He ran his hands down his face before walking to the door, the need to leave stifling. He was not that guy anymore. He was the guy his father said he was. In the end, he would only end up hurting Hope.

CHAPTER TEN

"This is the best day of my life."

Dean grinned up at Sadie who was sitting atop the gentlest mare at his father's ranch. She hadn't shown an ounce of fear as she mounted the horse and they had spent the last hour in the corral, with Dean walking beside her. She also hadn't stopped talking for the entire time and Dean didn't mind a bit. In fact, it was even better conversation than his Saturday night bar conversation with Cade and Tyler. Sadie reminded him of Hope, but without all the walls up. She was bright and happy and fearless.

The elusive March sun had even graced them with its presence, which made the cold bearable. "This is a great day for sure, Sadie. You're a natural."

She beamed at him. "I kind of feel like I am. Did you know I always wanted horseback riding lessons?"

He shook his head. "I did not."

"It's true. But my mom said I could choose only one activity a year."

"That seems reasonable," he said, walking beside her.

"I guess," she said, looking disappointed that

he agreed with her mom.

"It's a lot of work for your mom to have to juggle school and work and then driving you different places. I'm sure she'd love to be able to say yes." He was struck again by how much Hope had on her plate.

"I heard her talking to Grandma and Grandpa about it and I think it was because it's expensive. They offered to pay for it but Mom said no. I wish she'd said yes. Everyone in my class does everything. This year, I really wanted to do dance because that's what my best friend does, but it's only okay. I like this way better, but I can't tell Mom."

Dean digested all that information, and he was angry he wasn't able to help. That he had no way to help because he and Hope were just friends. He'd left her house last night with a hollow feeling inside, like he was losing out.

And now, hearing what Sadie said, he was angry that his father had added even more to Hope's plate. "I think it's nice that your grandparents volunteered to help, but your mom probably didn't want to take the money from them in case they need it. They're retired, so they have to be careful. But you don't need horseback riding lessons. I can teach you. Look at today as lesson one," he said with a wink.

Her eyes widened. "Really? I'm going to tell my friends at school."

He chuckled. "Sure. Just don't tell them I'm giving lessons to everyone."

She nodded, her eyes sparkling. "Okay. Promise."

"You sure you're not getting cold or tired?"

She shook her head emphatically, looking like she had no plans to go anywhere without her horse soon. "Nope. Dr. Dean, I really like your ranch. I didn't think it was so big."

He followed her gaze, realizing how it must look to someone her age. Anyone who wasn't used to this, really. He'd grown up here and, because there'd been so much family drama, he hadn't appreciated it the way he should. He didn't associate any of it with happiness. There had been a time, though, when he was young and his grandfather had been alive, that it had meant more to him. When his grandfather was alive and Dean had trailed him, spending long days out on the ranch or in the mountains, he'd been proud of his heritage.

His grandfather would regale him with stories of old cattle drives he'd go on with his own father. His Grandpa Jack had been real—he hadn't let the success of the ranch change him. He still remembered when it had been a small ranch and he'd helped his father day in and day out. And Dean had sensed Grandpa Jack's disappointment in Dean's father.

Dean glanced up at Sadie who was watching

him expectantly. "It wasn't always this big. It took a few generations to get it this way. But thank you. I'm glad you like it."

"So how do you know so many things, Dr. Dean?"

He lifted a brow. He was currently feeling like he didn't know any of the right things, but he did find Sadie's admiration humbling. "I don't think I know so many things, but I guess I know a little about a lot of things, maybe. I used to help my grandpa on the ranch a lot when I was a kid. I'd follow him around and he was patient and showed me how to fix things."

Her face lit up. "That's how you know how to fix things like our porch and our barn?"

He nodded. "Exactly. My grandpa loved being outside and doing ranch work for as long as he was able."

"Grandparents are special. I love mine. Are your grandparents still alive?"

He shook his head. "Nah, they died years ago. My grandpa died when I was a teenager. I still miss them, though."

Her green eyes clouded. "Do you still remember what he looks like?"

Dean tensed, sensing this was heading somewhere delicate. "I do... I think about him often and I can still remember what his laugh sounded like. I can remember how rough his hand was, how it felt when he would hold mine when I was a kid. But I guess the thing I remember the most is how he made me feel. I always felt like I was safe and happy. He made me feel like I could do anything or be anything. He made me brave, never laughing at me when I tried something new and got it wrong the first few times. I think it's because of him I became a doctor and still wanted to be a rancher."

He stopped speaking abruptly, surprised at how much he'd revealed to Sadie. She was wise beyond her years. It was in the way she listened silently, the questions she asked. These were things he hadn't thought about in a long time, some of them never.

Sadie had leaned forward and was hanging on his every word, her eyes wide as she listened. "He sounds like a nice man. I try to remember my dad, but I can't. That makes me sad and it makes me feel bad for my mom. Like, I know she tries to help me remember, because she'll tell me stories about the times we went on picnics or the way he'd throw me up in the air and catch me and I'd laugh. I just can't remember. But I think he'd have made me feel like your grandpa made you feel."

Dean wrestled with his words, with getting the lump in his throat down, and he took Sadie's small hand in his as he looked her straight in those serious green eyes. "He loved you so much and sometimes we don't need exact memories of people, sometimes we need to know the feeling and we need to hold onto that. When someone loves us so much, it's a special gift, and nothing can ever take that away from you."

"Did you know my daddy?"

Dean squeezed her hand. "I did. That's how I know how much he loved you. He talked about you all the time. He was a great man, Sadie."

She smiled. "That's what my mom says. Sometimes she gets a sad look on her face when she stares at the family picture of the three of us. Then when she sees I'm watching her, she gives me a big smile and says how blessed she is that daddy was in our life and because of him, she got me."

Dean ruffled her hair, ignoring the slam to his gut. That was a beautiful sentiment, and of course Hope would think that way. The closer he got to Hope the more he realized it wasn't enough. He'd thought they could just be friends. He thought his feelings were just duty and obligation and attraction. But, damn, they were so much more. He cleared his throat. "She's right. You are the perfect gift, Sadie."

CHAPTER ELEVEN

"Sadie, take a sip of water."

Hope frowned with worry as Sadie shook her head weakly. Hope's parents had brought her home early because she wasn't feeling well. In the last few hours, Hope had watched her condition decline rapidly. She had a suspicion it was the flu based on her symptoms and how quickly she went down.

Placing her hand on her forehead, she decided to grab the thermometer. "I'll be right back, honey," she said, quickly going to the hall closet in search of supplies. She hadn't finished unpacking everything, but she should have known with March being a nasty month for the flu at school that she would need something. Hope hated fevers. She hated despondency. The glazed eyes. She supposed no parent liked them, but for her, they also brought up memories of when Brian was sick.

As she rummaged through the medicine bin, she cursed herself for not being more organized and having all this ready. And then she cursed herself for letting Sadie have so much sugar and junk food. But Sadie had been begging so much to be allowed to eat what everyone else was eating at school that Hope had given in. Now look what had happened. Her heart stopped when she heard the weak call from Sadie.

Racing down the narrow hallway to Sadie's room, ibuprofen in hand, she sat on the edge of her bed. Her color was whiter than the bleached sheets and her eyes had that dreaded glassy appearance. "Hi sweetie. Mama's here. I'm going to give you some medication to take your fever down and then you'll be feeling way better, okay?"

Sadie stared at the ceiling, not responding. Hope gently lifted her head. "Come on, Sadie, you have to drink this."

Thankfully, she opened her mouth and swallowed. Hope eased her back onto the pillow, pulling the light sheet over her. "You're going to be fine. This will help so much. In half an hour you'll feel way better," she said, more to herself than to Sadie, whose eyes were already shut.

Hope kept her hand on Sadie's, staring out the window, pulled back almost a decade to when she'd had no idea how to be a caregiver. No one ever understood how scared she'd been. How traumatized. Because it hadn't been about her. How could she ever compare what she'd been through when Brian was the one who died?

Hope blinked back tears as that loneliness railroaded into her without warning. This wasn't the same thing. This was just a flu. Sadie had had

the flu before. She'd had colds and strep throat
and all the common childhood illnesses, and she'd
always pulled through. But each time Hope felt
like it took a little more out of her as a mother.

She brushed a damp piece of hair off Sadie's
face, unable to take a full breath. The weight in
her chest was too heavy tonight. It was weighed
down by memories and worries and fear. She
knew on some level that her reactions were irrational. Sadie would be fine, but she needed her to
hurry up and be fine, because it was agonizing to
see her like this.

As she stared at Sadie's sweet face, she remembered her sleeping in her little bassinet,
remembering how alone Hope had been. She had
gone from caring for her husband to caring for a
newborn and somehow finding a way to make a
living. She would do it all over again—for Brian,
for Sadie, in a heartbeat. But sometimes she wondered if she was permanently damaged from the
experience. If she was brutally honest with herself, she didn't know if she even liked herself. She
was harsher than she wanted to be at times.
Colder. She didn't laugh as much as Lainey,
Sarah, and Janie. She felt older than them.

Hope glanced at her watch, surprised to see
that half an hour had already passed. She checked
Sadie's temperature again and frowned when the
reading said it was still over one hundred. Okay,
that was okay. Maybe they needed a bit more

time. Sometimes fevers could be stubborn. She frowned when she noticed that Sadie's shirt was drenched in sweat. Glancing over at the full glass of water, she tried waking her up again. "Sadie, honey, you need to drink water," she said softly. Knowing firsthand how quickly she could dehydrate, she nudged Sadie again.

Maybe she would try again in a few minutes. She stood, pacing the room and tidying things to keep herself busy. There would be no business planning tonight. There'd be no sleep tonight. She would most likely sleep on the chair in Sadie's room to be close in case she needed her. Hope was always so worried that she might miss her call during the night whenever she was sick.

For the next hour she kept herself busy by organizing Sadie's room and unpacking the last box of stuffed animals and memorabilia. She smiled as she placed a picture on Sadie's desk of her and Brian smiling. He must seem like a stranger to Sadie. Hope made a point of talking to Sadie about him with lots of description and affection whenever she would ask. But each time it filled Hope with pain, knowing she'd never know her father.

Sadie moved restlessly in her bed and Hope sat back down bedside her, determined to get her to drink water. "Hi, honey, any better than before?"

"So cold, Mama. And my throat hurts," Sadie

said, her voice raspy.

Hope glanced at the clock; it was almost midnight now. "Okay, try to drink some water. That will help with your throat." Hope held the glass to Sadie's mouth but she took only a little swallow before sinking her head back against the pillow.

"No more," she croaked.

They spent the next six hours like that and when Hope had exhausted everything to try to get the fever down, and Sadie refused to drink anything, she bundled her up and carried her out to the car. She buckled her into the back seat and took the dark country roads into Wishing River.

Until tonight, she'd been happy living out in the country. She'd been confident. But now she was scared. She hated being this far from a hospital, being alone in that house. She hated being the only parent when her child was sick. But more than all of that, she hated going to a hospital. It was the last place she'd seen Brian alive, and she did everything she possibly could to stay away from there.

Cold rain beat against the windshield as Hope drove as fast as she could safely, drowning in her memories and nightmares. She'd never wanted so desperately to get to a place she was terrified of until now. She knew she had to separate the past from the present. Sadie was strong. She was resilient. She was just sick. But she'd never been so sick that Hope hadn't been able to get her fever down or she did not drink. The last person she'd seen to spike a high fever and need medical intervention was Brian.

Sadie wasn't Brian. She wasn't dying. Sadie was going to live long past Hope. She was going to become an adult and live a full life.

Hope blinked rapidly, trying to reign in her wild emotions. There was no time for her own personal drama tonight. She needed to get to the hospital. The only good thing was the man she knew would be inside.

Hope stood in the doorway, sucked into a past that she visited only in her nightmares. The smell was the same, the powerful astringent cleaner. The sounds, the beeping, the murmuring of voices, the swooshing of doors. It was all the same. She still hated all of it. The lights were too bright, just like the memories were too real, too vivid.

And just like the night she'd brought Brian in, when his fever had spiked, there was Dean. He was older. Wiser. Stronger. But the look in his eyes, the anguish, the way he ran toward them was the same.

•••

Dean knew the second Hope walked into the ER.

Maybe it was a premonition. Or maybe it was the insane connection he had to her that he'd always had. Or maybe it was because he already adored Sadie. Maybe he'd had a protective streak for her because of what happened with Brian.

It had been a wild night in the ER but things had started winding down. He was on his way toward the reception area, an hour left on his shift, when he saw the sliding doors whoosh open and Hope stagger in, carrying a limp Sadie in her arms. Never in his life had he been more terrified. As he ran over to them, he took in Hope's red-rimmed eyes, mass of wet, tangled hair, and white face and knew the toll this was taking on her. "What happened?"

Hope shook her head and he picked Sadie up, immediately feeling the heat emanating from her small body. "She went down fast. She was fine, then this fever started and she wouldn't drink or eat and ibuprofen wouldn't bring it down. I piggy-backed it with acetaminophen and that didn't work. That's never happened before."

"It's okay. Here, follow me. I'll get her into a room and assess her," he said, trying to keep any kind of worry out of his voice. The wild look in Hope's eyes was enough to tear his insides apart. They'd both been here before. Different time. Different sick person. But it was still him and Hope. The two of them, worried about someone she loved. But Sadie was important to him, too, and he had watched Hope go through heartache once before and he wasn't going to do it again.

He would never let her suffer like that again.

He gently laid Sadie down on a hospital bed in one of the assessment rooms and was relieved when she opened her eyes and focused on him. He forced a smile. "Hello there, sunshine. I'm going to make you feel better, okay? You just tell me anything you can. Anything you feel that might help me out."

He was already taking her temperature and doing all the normal things triage would have done. Relieved that her fever was hovering around a hundred, he continued through his usual workup, carefully listening to Sadie's heart and breathing, all the while feeling the heaviness of Hope's stare as she stood at the foot of the bed. "Sadie, does anything hurt?" he asked.

She pointed to her throat. Frowning, he looked inside, hoping to find some clear telltale signs of strep. That would be simple, but that's not what he found. "Okay, good job. You rest, kiddo. I'm going to talk to your mom."

He motioned to the door once a nurse walked in, ready to do the blood work he'd ordered. "Do you know what's wrong with her? I've never seen her like this. I want you to know I didn't do this. I didn't give her anything."

He reached out and touched her arm firmly, feeling like an ass that she actually thought he would hold her responsible. "Hey, hey. Of course, I don't think you'd ever jeopardize Sadie's health.

Hope, this is me. I'm not questioning you to accuse you. I'm...I'm your friend. I care about you and Sadie. She's going to be okay."

When her eyes welled up with tears and she nodded repeatedly, he almost pulled her into his arms. But they were standing in the hospital corridor, and Hope had on her armor, and he didn't want to be the one to cause her undoing. "What's wrong with her, Dean?"

"I've ordered some blood work. My first thought was the flu, but I also ordered a swab for strep. Even though it's unlikely, you never know. We also can't rule out the flu and strep together. That would be a nasty and uncommon combo, but it's a possibility. We've seen a string of both this last week from the local schools, so it wouldn't be a huge surprise."

She drew a shaky breath. "Okay...okay. I can handle that. Strep. Of course, I'd be okay with antibiotics. I don't want you to think I wouldn't..."

He gripped her arm firmly, wanting her to stop. Seeing her fall apart like this, that tough veneer cracking, was gut-wrenching. He hated that she was doubting herself or thinking that he did. "I have never, ever questioned you as a mother or as a naturopathic doctor. I know all the people you've helped in this town, many of them my own patients. You're the most responsible, caring, smartest person I know, Hope."

Her mouth dropped open and those green

eyes that lifted to his were his undoing. He'd loved her for so long. "Dean…I thought this was it. I thought it was happening again. I was so happy. Sadie was so happy. We were finally getting what I'd always wanted. Security, a home… and things with you were going so well and now this. This always happens to me. I attract this."

His stomach tightened. "What are you talking about?"

"I let my guard down. Things were too perfect. I was too happy. The house. You. I never should've let my guard down. It's just like when Brian got sick. We were so happy."

When she stopped speaking, her voice ending on a crack, without thinking twice, he pulled her into his arms and she folded against him as though she'd done this a thousand times, as though he was a man she came to, who she trusted. His heart was breaking for her. Had she really gone around thinking that tragedy would always follow happiness? He held her against him, his lips brushing the top of her head when he spoke.

"Sadie's going to be fine, Hope. You're allowed to be happy. Life doesn't work like that. You aren't being punished for being happy. She's sick. She looks like a sick kid and that's what happens to kids. She's building up her immune system. Sometimes it looks scary and, in a day or two she'll be running around, and you'll be forcing her to sit and rest."

She scrunched the sides of his shirt, like she was holding onto him for dear life. He didn't take that lightly. It was everything. To know she trusted him. With Sadie, with herself. "I want to believe you, Dean. You know the last time I was here."

He stilled. If there was ever a justification to tell her the truth, it was now. It could give her more faith, more security. But it would also break her heart. It would make him break confidentiality. He couldn't do it. "I know, but it's not the same. These are two entirely different situations, Hope. You know that, deep down."

She sighed. "I know. You're right."

"See? Little miracles."

She let out a choked laugh. "I won't let anything happen to Sadie."

"You're so full of yourself," she mumbled against his chest.

He chuckled as he continued to hold on to her and she made no attempt to leave. "But this is where it comes in handy. Would you rather I run around flailing my arms?"

"I can't even picture you doing that."

"That's good."

"Dr. Stanton? Sorry to interrupt, but I have the rapid swab test back."

Hope jumped out of his arms and he turned to the nurse, reading the chart notes. "Thanks, Beth," he said before turning to Hope.

"She tested positive for strep. Now we need to wait for the blood work, but I can get her safely started on an antibiotic," he said.

She closed her eyes with a sigh. "Strep. Yes, of course. The sooner she gets started the sooner she'll feel better. Okay. I can deal with strep. That's great news, really, because it's easy to treat. She'll be feeling better in no time. I need to go see her." She whipped past him and back into the room to Sadie's side. Dean had no idea how she did that; she had been on the verge of collapse and was now a doting mother.

"I'm going to run down and order the antibiotics. We'll watch her a little longer until we're comfortable letting her go home. It won't be long, Hope."

Hope nodded, holding Sadie's hand as he left the room.

Dean came back ten minutes later to find Hope in the exact same spot. "She's resting so peacefully now that her fever is down. I think that's the worst. Watching them not able to sleep in that hazy fever daze," she said.

"I know, but Sadie's tough stuff, like her mom," he said, standing beside Hope.

She looked up at him and then took his hand in hers. "Thank you."

CHAPTER TWELVE

Hope opened one eye slowly, adjusting to the sunlight streaming through the windows. It took her a moment for the last two days to flash across her mind. She looked over to the other couch sharply, remembering that Dean was here.

Sure enough, he was lying there, still in his jeans and T-shirt. One arm was propped behind his head and his feet were hanging off the other end of the couch. She let her gaze linger as long as it could without seeming creepy. His features were relaxed, his face covered in stubble, his hair deliciously tousled. The strong lean lines of his body were relaxed and he looked solid and warm, and for a second, she imagined what it would be like to curl herself into his body, to share that couch with him.

A warmth spread over her that had nothing to do with the handknit throw she was lying under. The distinct memory of what it felt like to be held by him was still imprinted. Maybe that was why she'd slept so soundly. He'd made her feel safe and loved and for one night, she had loosened her unyielding grip on the world. When Sadie had been discharged, he'd come home with them and stayed. She'd trusted him with her daughter, with her world. She hadn't done that with anyone.

She'd be lying if she said she didn't want more. She wanted all of him. She wanted to kiss him, to be held by him again, and she wanted his heart. She wanted him to open up to her and trust her with those layers she sensed simmering beneath the surface. She wanted to hear him whisper her name again, because no one said her name the way he did. She wanted to feel his rough hands on her face, her body. And if she were really wishing, she'd wish for the whole deal.

But that would be scary because whenever something went too well for her, it would be followed by problems. And she'd rather have Dean as her friend than lose him completely. Sadie would be heartbroken if he wasn't around anymore…and so would she. Seeing him had become one of the best parts of her day, and jeopardizing this new happiness she'd found wasn't an option.

"I feel like I'm under a blaring light in a police interrogation room." Dean's raspy, deep voice, laden with laughter, snapped her eyes up the length of his body to meet his sparkling gaze.

Hope jumped off the couch before he could see how red her face was. "I'll brew some coffee and check on Sadie. Given that it's almost ten, I think it's a good sign she finally turned the corner."

"That is good news. And coffee sounds great." He stretched, raising one arm and folding it behind his head, the motion sending his shirt up, revealing tight abs with a smattering of dark hair. She turned away sharply, fumbling with the coffee canister and almost dropping it. What was wrong with her? It's not like he was the only man she'd ever been around. But it had been a very long time since Brian was alive and well. And there hadn't been anyone in between.

If only there had been a trial-run kind of guy to ease her back in. Someone a little soft, a little dimmer, a little…less hot. Dean was like jumping into the deep end of a pool when she could barely swim. Hoping she'd added the right amount of coffee grounds to the pot, she turned in the direction of Sadie's room. "I'm going to check on Sadie."

"Sure. I'm going to check my messages," he said, glancing up from his phone.

Phew. She was thrilled he was preoccupied and hadn't noticed her ridiculous behavior. She carefully opened Sadie's bedroom door and her heart swelled to see her sleeping so peacefully. Tiptoeing across the room, she gently laid her hand on her cheek just to make sure her temperature felt normal. Sure enough, no fever, even without any medication. With a relieved smile, she left the room and carefully shut the door. Then she ran down the hall to the bathroom. Gasping, she closed the door behind her and grabbed her brush, quickly running it through her hair, her eyes tearing as she ripped through the tangles. She had no idea how Dean could look so delectable all scruffy while she looked like an ad for a tired mom in need of a makeover.

Splashing some cold water on her face she decided against makeup because that would look like she was trying too hard. Though under-eye concealer could really come in handy. She quickly dabbed some under her eyes before brushing her teeth and was relieved to see that she looked somewhat presentable now. Straightening her shirt and sweater, she opened the door to find Dean leaning against the counter holding a cup of coffee.

"I went ahead and poured the coffee," he said, holding out a mug for her.

"Thanks." Her fingers brushed against his, and suddenly she was a teenager again with butterflies in her stomach. Noticing he looked a little gray, she frowned. "Dean, are you feeling okay?"

"Just a little tired," he said, taking a sip of coffee.

"That's understandable, but you look a little pale."

"I don't get pale."

She almost laughed. "That's ridiculous. Can I get you some breakfast? Maybe you're hungry."

He opened his mouth and then shut it, frowning. "I'm actually not…hungry," he said, staring into his cup.

She put her mug down on the counter and walked over to him, placing her hand on his forehead. "You're hot."

He grinned, but his eyes were glassy. "I'm glad you're finally being honest with how you feel about me, Hope. And just in case there were any doubts in your mind, the feeling is mutual."

Her mouth dropped open and her heart felt like it was going to run straight out of her chest. It took all her concentration to remember that he was sick. "Dean, I can't flirt with someone who's about to pass out from the flu."

"No, no, you can. I'm not sick. I never get sick. I haven't had the flu since I was a teenager," he said, placing his mug down on the counter.

"Yeah, but you've also been working yourself to the bone. You're rundown, and this is exactly what I said would happen. Then, because you're such a nice guy, you've been up with me and Sadie. Your immune system is weakened," she said, unable to help herself from squeezing his hand.

"While I'm touched by your concern, I really am fine. I don't get sick and I have no weak parts," he said, his voice thinning.

She shook her head. "Your pride is making you believe you can control that."

She gasped when instead of giving her a smart-ass retort, he slowly swayed to the side, like he was losing his balance.

Hope grabbed his arms to steady him, digging into the thick muscles of his biceps. He stood upright. "Hope, I'm liking where you're headed."

"Dean, seriously, there's no time to joke. Hold on to me. You almost fainted."

He grimaced, looking worse by the minute. "That's actually a lie. I don't faint. I don't even know how."

Hope would've laughed, but she was getting worried. She'd never seen Dean other than perfectly strong and capable. "Hold on to me. I'll get you to bed."

"I like that."

"What?" she said, as she led him toward her bedroom. He refused to lean on her so she grabbed his arm, telling herself it was wrong to notice the biceps she was gripping, when he was clearly ill. But she could feel the feverish heat radiating from his body and wanted to get him settled where he could rest comfortably.

He collapsed onto her bed, staring up at her. "Your bed."

She laughed and shook her head, picking up his legs and getting him under the covers. She did her best not to look flustered at his flirting or at his strong body taking up half her bed. It was wrong to have fantasies about him when he was practically delirious and sick with the flu. "You're very charming, Dean, and I'm sure there have been many women who've fallen for that."

"Ah, but there's been only one I've wanted. And just so you know, this morning when you were checking me out while you thought I was sleeping—"

She let out a horrified gasp. "That is not what I was doing. I'd forgotten you were even here."

He let out a choked laugh and clutched his stomach, grimacing. "Don't make me laugh. It hurts. Like I was saying, I'd also been appreciating the view. You're even more beautiful than the first time I saw you at Tilly's."

Her mouth dropped open and it was suddenly difficult to breathe as she stared into his blue eyes, reading the heat, the sincerity in them. He remembered the first time they met? "What?" she whispered.

His eyes were closing and she reached out to touch his forehead. He was burning up. "Hope? I feel like shit. I think I may have the flu."

She smoothed some hair off his forehead. "I know, Dean."

"You should watch you don't get it."

She smiled faintly. "I never get the flu. I megadose on supplements during cold and flu season and avoid sugar. But, since you eat Snickers all day as your main source of protein…"

He smiled faintly; his eyes still closed. "That's low, kicking me when I'm down and can't think of a comeback."

She let out a small laugh and squeezed his

shoulder. "Don't worry. I'll feed a bunch of supplements to you when you're too weak to protest."

His eyes opened and she thought he was going to panic. "I trust you."

She held his gaze. "Just rest. I'll be back with some water and Tylenol."

He closed his eyes and Hope watched him, the tornado of emotions tearing through her body making it impossible to move right away. He was so much more than she had even imagined. He was larger than life and strong and caring and... he remembered the first time they met at Tilly's.

He had sacrificed so much for her and Sadie, including his own well-being. He was worn-out, and it was her doing. Now she was going to make it up to him. She hated when things were out of control. She'd take care of him. She'd make homemade chicken soup and bone broth and make sure he got enough fluids. With a determined sigh, she left the room and busied herself with getting organized before Sadie woke up.

And then maybe she'd let herself sit and rest awhile and think about the man who hadn't given up on her all these years. The one who'd been right about so much. The one who wasn't scared of what the future held.

• • •

The next morning, Hope frowned as she felt Dean's sweaty forehead. She'd hoped his fever would have broken today. She stood there, holding the bottle of cold water and took in his appearance. His face was pale, his usual tan gone, and three-day-old stubble lined the face she... she'd admired for years. His dark hair was a mess and she resisted the urge to smooth it back gently in case she woke him.

She straightened the white bedsheet around him, needing to feel useful, needing to offer comfort without disturbing him. His strong shoulders were bare and her gaze trailed the lines of his muscled body to the edge of the sheet. He'd always been an attractive man. But the last few years, he'd become more so, somehow. There was less of that boyishness. Dean was all man. Not just in his looks but in how he'd come through for her and Sadie. How he'd cared for them both when Sadie was ill.

He'd been Hope's rock. All those days of teasing and cutting remarks between them had died instantly. And all those ideas, those assumptions she'd had about him, had crumbled into a pile of worthless nothings. He'd held her as though he were strong enough to solve all her problems. She'd never needed anyone to solve her problems. She'd been a single mom for so long that she'd forgotten what it was like to have another person in the house with her. To know there was someone strong and capable was...freeing, comforting. But not just anyone...Dean. This man, lying in her bed, the only man who'd ever been in this bed, meant everything. He had come to mean more to her than she ever thought possible.

Dean brought out feelings...longings she'd never experienced before. There was an electricity that hummed through her that she'd never imagined possible. And for so long that had made her feel guilty. It was one thing to want another man, to move on with her life after Brian died, but it was another thing to know that another man made her feel more...more alive, more aware, more feminine than she'd ever felt in her life. That was what made her feel guilty.

She held her breath as Dean stirred, letting out a small moan. Wincing, she opened the bottle of water and whispered his name. His eyelids flickered and then opened; the blue eyes staring at her were glazed with fever.

"Hey...I have some cold water here. You need to get some more fluids, okay?" She held the water bottle to his mouth as he managed to prop himself on his forearms. Her mouth went dry as the sheet fell to his waist, revealing the hard lines of his strong body.

He took a few long sips and then fell back on the pillow, his eyes closing. "Thanks."

She stood. "You don't have to thank me. You'll feel better soon. I have soup whenever you get your appetite back. Sleep now, Dean."

She turned to leave, wanting him to rest, and needing some space between her and all the thoughts she was having trouble controlling. He grabbed her wrist, his hand large and hot against her skin. "Hope," he whispered. His voice was raw and his eyes were still shut.

Her heart hammered in her chest, thinking the worst. "Do you need to go to the hospital? Are you feeling worse?"

He gave a small shake of his head, his eyes still shut. He grabbed her hand and brought it to his lips, and she thought her knees were going to buckle at the gesture. How was it possible this man could be this sexy when he was sick with the flu? "Your bossy pants…I like them. No one fills out bossy pants like you."

She didn't know whether to laugh or fan her face. She patted his hand and took a step back. "Dean, sleep. You need to sleep before you say something you'll regret when the fever breaks."

He grabbed her hand and she stood still. "It's always been you, Hope. I've loved you forever. Everything I did was for you. I know you hate me. I know you think I'm responsible for Brian's death, but it's not true. It's what he wanted so you wouldn't be hurt. I agreed to keep his secret. For you. I didn't want you to hurt."

The bottle of water slid from her hands onto the bed and Hope fought for a breath deep enough to fill her lungs properly. But her heart was beating so painfully, so rapidly, that she stood motionless as she watched the man who'd revealed his entire heart to her, the truth of her past, slip back into a feverish sleep.

"Dean," she strangled out, hoping he'd wake up even though she knew he was in a deep sleep. Her mind was spinning, looking for a way out of this that wasn't what he'd just claimed, because accepting that reality was too painful, was too large to accept right this very minute. Or maybe ever.

She slowly backed out of the room and closed the door with a soft click. Leaning against the door, she replayed everything he'd just said. *I've loved you forever...you think I'm responsible for Brian's death, but it's not true.*

Shame slid through her, leaving her weak, her knees wanting to give out. What had she done?

All her fear and resentment and anger had left Dean thinking she still blamed him for Brian's death. Of course, he would think that. But she'd been young and afraid and angry that Brian had died. She'd been angry at the world for her dreams being shattered. And she'd been afraid of being a single mom. But she'd been wrong about ever blaming Dean, and when he woke up, she was going to tell him.

CHAPTER THIRTEEN

A few days later, Hope opened the front door after seeing Sadie off to school to find Dean standing in the kitchen. Her breath caught in her throat at the sight of him there, drinking coffee, as though he had always lived here. He was leaning against the counter wearing a fresh shirt and jeans, his hair still wet, and looking deliciously scruffy with his unshaven face.

Remnants of the flu were still there, his eyes still a bit tired, slight hollows beneath his cheek bones. But he was still the most beautiful man she'd ever seen. And he was in her kitchen. And he loved her. Her.

"Morning. Sadie off to school?"

She pulled herself together and closed the door behind her. It was time to be honest and to face her own feelings. She owed him honesty. "That's all you have to say? You've been so sick. I'm so happy to see you're standing and looking like yourself."

He grinned. "Thanks to you. You took good care of me and you gave up your bed. Thank you. I, uh, threw the sheets in the washing machine and started a load and cleaned up your room. Thanks for bringing in my hospital bag. I showered and got into some clean clothes. I feel like a new man. Sorry for putting you out like this. First Sadie, then me. You must be wiped."

She waved a hand, barely following the conversation because she wanted to jump ahead to what he'd said. "You were an easy patient. And, yes, Sadie is off to school. She's super excited because she's going to a birthday party sleepover right after school."

A corner of his mouth curled into a smile and his eyes warmed at the mention of Sadie. Her breath caught as she realized his eyes always warmed whenever he was around Sadie or she talked about her little girl. Dean…Dean was a good man and she had kept her distance, she'd antagonized him and blamed him, and regret tore through her as she stood still, just watching him. He was here, for them. For her.

"I'm sorry I missed her this morning. I wanted to thank her for all the pictures she drew me while I was sick."

Her heart squeezed. "She felt bad she'd gotten you sick. I'll let her know you liked them. I'm so relieved your fever finally broke."

He gave her a nod and wondered at what point he'd call them on their new formality, but something had changed. He'd revealed his heart and she couldn't forget that and knew that despite what a chicken she was, she couldn't ignore it anymore. "Yeah. I feel normal again. I made enough coffee for two. Can I pour you a cup?"

She blinked back the unexpected moisture in her eyes at the innocuous gesture. But that was Dean. He took charge in a way that was practical and sensible...but also made her feel cared for. With Brian, they had been so young that neither of them really knew what they were doing half the time. Then when he'd gotten sick, she'd had to take over almost everything. She'd done it without hesitation, but it had taken its toll. Somewhere along the way, she'd gone from this carefree young woman who'd thought the world held so many possibilities and opportunities to this other version of herself. This version who was so determined to hold it all together that she couldn't risk plucking out any of the toothpicks she'd built her house on.

Everything had to be her way because it was the only way she knew to survive. But on most days, she didn't like herself. She didn't like how tightly wound she'd become. How much control she had to have over everything. Then last week, with Sadie getting sick and being unable to make her well on her own, Hope had learned that Dean would always be here for them. And he was here, standing in her kitchen, bringing out this other side of her that she didn't know. She wasn't twenty anymore. She was almost thirty and just figuring out that trusting someone, leaning on someone, didn't make her weaker. He'd told her how he felt and she needed to do the same. She cleared her throat and her pulse started racing as his blue gaze was steady on hers. "I'm glad you're feeling better. I…what you said the other day…"

His lips twitched, glancing over at her while he poured coffee. "I spoke?"

She nodded. "You are quite, um, chatty when you have a fever. You know…when you said… what I'm trying to say is that I'm sorry. I'm sorry I've been so awful to you. I don't blame you for Brian's death…"

What little color he had in his face vanished. "What are you talking about?"

She clasped her hands and suddenly felt clammy. Letting her guard down wasn't easy. Especially with the intensity of Dean's stare. "You told me. You know, everything…"

He placed his mug on the counter with a thud and ran his hands through his hair. "Hell, I'm sorry Hope. I don't even remember. I didn't mean to dump that on you. That must have been the fever, I'm sorry. What a shock. I swore to Brian I'd never say anything, and now I feel bad because I broke that patient confidentiality.

"Just know he loved you more than anything. He was so worried you wouldn't think he loved you enough to fight and go through the surgery and chemo again. He didn't want to lie to you but was worried you'd beg him to, and he knew he wouldn't be able to say no to you. Me taking the blame was my idea, pretending I missed all the signs was a lie, so don't be upset with him for that. I hate that I left you to process that while I was sick. I'm sorry."

Hope clutched the side of the counter, her ears ringing, not able to get enough air into her lungs. She couldn't process everything he was telling her. His face became blurry as she clutched the counter tighter, vaguely aware as he crossed the distance between them and held her shoulders. "Are you okay? You're not getting sick, are you?"

She fought for focus and the words that were garbled inside her head to come out of her mouth. But everything was throbbing: her ears, her eyes, her heart as she stared at him. "What are you saying? What are you talking about?"

His jaw clenched and the eyes that met hers were filled with such raw regret and honest pain that it evoked a hollow sob from deep inside. "I thought…you said I told you everything."

She leaned forward, knowing she didn't deserve him, she didn't deserve to ask more of him than she had unknowingly done for so long. But she clutched the side of his shirt. "He…Brian…he knew he was sick? You knew he was sick and he had options? It wasn't that you ignored all the signs?"

"I'm sorry," he said, his voice a ragged whisper.

"Tell me all of it," she managed, needing to hear the truth.

He ran a hand over his jaw, his eyes glittering. "He waited. Too long. Brian knew he was sick for a year. But he told me he hadn't wanted to face the reality of having cancer again. When he finally did come to see me, the cancer had metastasized, but there was still a chance. I wanted him to go to the best oncologist. I…was willing to arrange it for him, to pay for it. I begged him to include you in these decisions. I told him he could at least have a shot at five years. Long enough to have Sadie remember him. He couldn't do it, Hope. He didn't want treatment options, he just wanted to let the cancer run its course. I was going to be the fall guy. It was easier to lie and say that I had ignored and missed the signs than admit that he was unwilling to try any treatment.

"I'd never judged him. We became friends, I guess, but he was my patient. I wanted more. I wanted a different ending for you. I wanted him to change his mind, I wanted him to fight. I'm sorry. I'm sorry I caused you and Sadie that kind of pain."

Hope crumpled to the ground, the weight of Brian's lie, of Dean's sacrifice, and her own shame making it impossible to stand. Dean followed her down, placing his hands on either side of her face. "Hope, I'm sorry."

She lifted her eyes to his and wiped the tears streaking down his face. She loved him. She loved him for everything he had done. She loved him for his emotion, for his tears, for his sacrifice. But she couldn't find the words and she couldn't find the courage because, right now, she was deep in the past, and deep in a pit of shame for how she treated him. "Don't…don't apologize to me… You…you said it's always been me. That you loved me."

His jaw clenched and he pulled her hand from his face to kiss the palm of her hand, and what little strength she had left bled out of her. "Loved? Uh, well, yes, I mean, I love you and Sadie and care for you…like all of our friends. I've been attracted to you for as long as I can remember…but more than that, I wouldn't let myself go there because of Brian."

This time the sob that broke wasn't hollow, it was deep and hurt and the beginning of years of tears unleashing. Nothing made sense anymore. His answer didn't make sense, Brian's lie didn't make sense. But more than the pain was the shame that filled her. "I've been so horrible to you," she said, sobbing as he pulled her in to him. And for a second, she let him hold her and she let herself feel the comfort of his strong body. But for only a second, because she knew she didn't deserve him. The shame that engulfed her was too embarrassing to face with him. He loved her. He'd sacrificed his reputation for her. He'd helped her husband lie for her sake. And he'd endured her contempt, even in front of their friends. She'd been horrible to him, and she could never forgive herself.

"Hey, no you haven't. You didn't know. I wanted to tell you but I promised him. Hope, look at me." He squeezed her shoulders gently.

She forced her eyes to open. He was right there, his deep blue eyes staring into hers without any judgment, just concern. And love. How had she never noticed that before? But it was too late now because she'd ruined everything. Her stomach churned as she sat with the truth and Dean to witness. But there was so much there. Beyond Dean's feelings for her, beyond her own shame at how she'd gotten it all wrong, was the lie Brian had told her. She didn't know what to think of that. And she couldn't just talk about all of this now. She didn't deserve Dean. "Dean…I can't do this. Whatever all of this is. How I hurt you. I'm sorry. I…I want to be alone."

He frowned, pulling back slightly. "What? After all this, you're shutting me out?"

She leaned her head against the cupboard door and tore her gaze from his. "You just told me that everything I thought was a lie. I don't know how to deal with that. My husband lied to me."

His hands left her shoulders and she felt cold and small without them there. She looked up at him as he stood, his strong jaw clenched, that love in his eyes replaced with something else. "So, you're not going to deal with this with me. You're going to ask me to leave."

She nodded, holding back tears, because even now she was screwing things up and hurting him. She had wanted to tell him that she felt the same way about him. That maybe she'd loved him for years but had never wanted to admit it to herself because there was so much guilt there. Dean was everything she'd admired in a man, and that scared her, too. But more than anything, she needed to be alone to process all of it, and maybe because she was deeply humiliated and vulnerable and exposed.

When the door closed behind him, she gave in to the tears that threatened, the tears she hadn't cried since Brian died.

CHAPTER FOURTEEN

Hope was sitting in the middle of her open wedding album and a slew of pictures when the doorbell rang. She ignored it the first time, not wanting to see anyone, desperate to find the truth in the pieces of her past. But when she heard Lainey's voice through the door, she knew there was no way she would be able to ignore her.

Carefully stepping over the mess, she made her way to the door and opened it. Lainey was standing there with tears in her eyes and a giant piece of chocolate cake. "I thought you could use some of this."

Hope opened the door wider and her friend walked in. "How did you know?"

Lainey placed the cake on the counter and turned to her. "Dean called me. He said he thought you could use a friend right now."

Hope covered her face and she fought the urge to cry. How could he be this good to her? How had he walked out of here after the way she'd told him to leave and still be concerned about her? "God, Lainey, I'm the biggest idiot in the world. I messed up so badly."

Lainey put her arm around Hope's shoulders and led her to the couch, careful not to step on the photos. "If that were true, I don't think Dean would've called me and I don't think he would have sounded so worried about you if you'd messed things up beyond repair."

"Tell me you didn't know," she whispered.

Lainey frowned, her eyes going from Hope's to all the pictures. "Know what? All he told me was that you were pretty upset and you needed a friend."

Hope closed her eyes briefly and proceeded to tell Lainey what Dean had revealed. "All these years…wasted. I can't believe Brian lied to me. I keep looking through all these pictures, looking for something to indicate…I don't know. It's like there are two versions of my past and the one I thought existed doesn't."

"Nothing changes how much Brian loved you. The fact that he asked Dean to lie for him shows how much he cared. How much he didn't want to hurt you," Lainey said gently.

Hope nodded, picking up her favorite picture of the two of them. She'd been holding her simple bouquet of daisies and they'd been out in a field by the river. Their wedding had been small and plain but filled with love. They'd been kids. "When I look at this picture, Lainey, I don't even know who this girl is. There's like the Hope in the picture and the Hope now and I don't know who I am. Who was I? Was I someone so unapproachable that my husband couldn't tell me the truth?

Did he really think I would force him into treatment he didn't want?"

"I don't think that's it at all. This had to do with Brian more than it had to do with you. He'd had cancer as a teenager. He was afraid. Maybe he didn't want to disappoint you. Maybe he was afraid you'd think less of him for not trying. Maybe he was afraid that if he did try and then died anyway, it would have been for nothing. You'll never know and that sucks, honey. It really does."

Hope nodded slowly, processing everything Lainey was saying. "That makes me feel a little better, I guess. I still wish he would have told me. I would have supported whatever decision he made. But then again, I guess I would have been disappointed, afraid. I may have begged him. God, Lainey, I don't know. We were so young, you know? This feels like an entire lifetime ago. I didn't feel like an adult the way I do now."

"Yeah, a lot has happened in that time. Strange, isn't it? I mean sometimes I don't think I'll ever truly feel like an adult. We're parents now. Do you even feel old enough to be someone's parent? Like, all this responsibility. I love it. But sometimes I still feel like the girl behind the counter at Tilly's looking for a way out of Wishing River and fantasizing about Ty."

Hope let out a rueful laugh. "And now you're married to him."

Lainey smiled. "Yeah…life is funny that way. Bringing people together eventually. Like…maybe what's happening with you and Dean?"

Hope started gathering the photos and tossing them into the boxes, avoiding eye contact with Lainey. "I shut him down again. He poured his entire heart out, and I was so devastated by the truth that I didn't even tell him how I felt. How I feel. He thinks I'm mad at him because of this lie he told me."

"How do you feel?"

Hope took a deep breath. "I'm falling for him, Lainey. Maybe I have been for a long time but was too afraid to realize it. But I don't know if he feels the same way, because he never actually admitted he loves me more than as a friend."

"Because he doesn't want to scare you off. And if he thinks you are mad at him, you need to tell him you're not. You need to tell him how you feel."

"I don't know what I'll do if he rejects me."

Lainey shook her head, a little smile on her face. "Please. That man would never reject you, Hope. He's waited years for you. He wouldn't have called me, worried about you, if he didn't care."

Hope blinked back tears. "I could never be mad at him for what he did. He was in a horrible position. I need to tell him I understand. I…he's so different than Brian, Lainey."

Lainey nodded. "Yeah, they are very different. He's also a lot older than Brian was when he passed away. Dean is six years older than you and it's been six years since Brian died. A person changes a lot during those years. Young adult to adult. And Dean's always been more mature than most. He has a lot on his plate. He's one of the most responsible people I know. Don't compare them."

Hope shook her head. "No, it's not that I'm trying to. It's that Dean…what I feel for him is so different than what I had with Brian. And I don't know how to tell him that. Or if I should. I mean, how much can I discuss without it being weird? Ugh. I have no idea what I'm doing."

"Hey. You're overthinking everything here, Hope. Go to him. Tell him you're not mad. Tell him how you feel. That's it. Start there. I'm sure he'll have some ideas about what to do next." Lainey stood, her eyes sparkling.

Hope wasn't even going to carry the conversation in that direction because that was another point of fear and trepidation. One step at a time. "Okay. I need to find him."

"He's at River's," Lainey said flatly.

Hope let out a breath, walking to the door with Lainey. "Okay, well, I guess I'm going to River's."

Lainey reached out and gave her a hug. "I'm glad. You deserve this. You deserve Dean and so many good things, Hope. I love you."

Hope held onto her friend tightly. "I love you, too."

. . .

An hour later, Hope trudged through the wet grass to the spot she'd been visiting for almost a decade. She didn't even really need to look where she was going, she'd had the route through the various tombstones memorized until she reached Brian's simple one. His parents were buried beside him and that made her feel comforted, knowing they were all together. They had never gotten over his loss and at least now they could rest together.

But as she stopped in front of his tomb today, she was filled with so many questions. Today she was filled with Dean's voice, Dean's confession, Dean's pain. She was broken into a hundred different versions of herself.

After her conversation with Lainey, she knew she couldn't hide anymore. She was an adult now, and she was in love with Dean and had been for a long time. She needed to make things right and then move forward.

"Brian…I honestly don't know what to say today. I know I always start with how Sadie is doing because you'd want to hear about her, but I don't feel like talking about that. But I guess I should, because now I feel bad. Okay, so Sadie is awesome as usual. Our girl is a total ball of energy and light and she's growing so fast. She loves your grandparents' house and I'm happy for her, that she has the stability of a home and lots of land to run around on. She just got over the flu and strep, but you wouldn't even know it because she's back to her normal energetic self. She also wants a pony, so thanks for that."

She stopped speaking on a laugh that somehow turned into a sob. Wanting to sit, or sink into the ground, she shuffled the wet leaves and decided she'd rather be soaked than try to stand through this. She winced as the wet grass immediately soaked through her jeans.

The image of Brian's face appeared in her mind. It was strange to think that the way she remembered him, that wavy brown hair and boyish face, wouldn't be how he looked today. Then the image of Dean's face appeared and she pushed it aside, because this was about her and Brian now.

Taking a deep breath, she let her head fall back on her shoulders as she stared up at the dreary sky and opened her heart and searched for the words that might make all of this better. But all she could come up with was, "How could you do that, Bri? How could you have kept that from me? I was so angry when Dean first told me. And then I realized that maybe I'm to blame. Was I that controlling? Unapproachable? Is that why you lied? If it was…if I was, I'm sorry. I'm sorry if I did something to make you think that I wouldn't have supported whatever decision you made.

"It was your life to live, and no matter what you decided to do and how sad I would have been, I would have had your back. I guess I'm glad in the end you did it the way you wanted. But Brian, I have another problem. I've been horrible to Dean. I blamed him for years. It wasn't fair because even if you hadn't asked him to lie, I shouldn't have blamed him.

"And now things are different. I've changed. Sometimes I feel like I don't even know the girl I was when we got married. I can't get that girl back. She went through so much and she did what she could to survive. I never want to go back to that old me again. I was so afraid and hurting and was angry at the whole world. But something has changed. Brian…I have feelings for Dean. No, more than feelings. I…love him. And I think you would be okay with that. You must have trusted him in order to ask him to help you. Your instincts were right. He's an amazing man. And he's so good to Sadie, he's so sweet with her and she just adores him. I just…wanted you to know. And I also wanted you to know I'm not mad at you for lying."

She took a deep breath and stood, wiping her hands on the front of her jeans. The weight that had followed her around for almost a decade seemed a little lighter now. Making her way back to her car, she thought of the other man, the one who'd lied for a man he barely knew…for her. She needed to find him and tell him what he meant to her.

CHAPTER FIFTEEN

Dean walked through the crowd at River's Saloon not making eye contact with anyone. The loud chatter and music were exactly what he needed to drown out the noise in his head. He sat his ass down at the first empty barstool and waited for Aiden to notice him. Now that the truth was out, he also needed to talk to Aiden. But first he needed a drink.

Today had been a shit show and after everything he'd been through with Hope, it was over. Then they had their friend group. How the hell were they going to ever get together as friends. They had already made it awkward enough for everyone through the years.

"You look like you could use this. Tough night at the hospital?"

Dean looked up to see Aiden in front of him and a full glass of whiskey on the bar. He picked up the glass, took a long drink, and made eye contact with Aiden. God, it felt like a hundred years ago when he found himself on this barstool, his heart ripped out of his chest and Brian dead. Watching Hope fall apart and hate him had almost made him want to leave and never have to face the blame in her eyes. But he'd do it all over again, for her.

"You okay, man?"

Dean finished off his whiskey and looked up to meet Aiden's stare. "I'm sorry," he said flatly. This was a long time coming and even though he didn't feel like talking to anyone, he owed Aiden.

Aiden frowned, bracing his hands wide on the counter. "What are you talking about?"

"I'm sorry for the night Hope's husband died. I'm sorry for unloading like that and burdening you with that secret without giving you a choice."

Aiden refilled his glass and then poured one for himself. "You're not the first person who's sat there broken and confessing while drunk and you won't be the last. But, listen, you didn't burden me with anything. It's not my business. I know why you did what you did and, for what it's worth, I would've done the same thing."

Dean held the glass of whiskey, not drinking it, the lump in his throat making it impossible to swallow. "Thanks for saying that."

"It's the truth. I've gotten to know Hope over the years, even more now that she and Janie are good friends, and I think she's an amazing person. So I, uh, take it Hope found out the truth?"

Dean rubbed the back of his neck, the image of Hope crumpling to the ground haunting him. He'd been the cause of that pain, and that was the last thing he'd ever intended. Asking him to be alone had pretty much solidified what she thought of him. He'd done everything to protect her, and he was paying for it now. "Yeah. Apparently, I talk in my sleep when I have the flu."

"Damn. Well, I'm sure she understands. This may have been a surprise to her, but she has to know the place it came from. There aren't a lot of people who would have done what you did. In a good way. Dean, everyone can see you have feelings for each other," Aiden said.

Dean pulled his gaze from his friend's earnest one, letting it travel the room. How many years had he spent in this place? How many Saturday nights? How many women? But not one real relationship. Had he just wasted his life, his best years, wanting a woman who would always be unavailable? "It was a big lie. I lied to her for years. Every time, those early days after Brian died, I looked her in the eyes and apologized for missing Brian's symptoms. Over and over again. And the truth was, that guy was crying in my damn office. He'd tortured himself. He was a good guy who'd made a decision that gave him no shot at life. I knew a side of him that his own wife didn't and I kept it from her. I don't know that she can see past it to know that I did it for her."

"Don't count on that. She probably needs time. Hope has feelings for you, we all know it," Aiden said.

Dean scrubbed his hands down his face. This wasn't supposed to turn into another therapy session with Aiden. "I wish that was true, but I'm not so sure. I wasn't supposed to make this all about me. The other thing I wanted to tell you was that if I ever made you feel like you didn't belong in our crowd or whatever, I'm sorry. I just wasn't comfortable with how much you knew about me and that we would be keeping that secret from Hope. But it was wrong."

He caught the flash of surprise across Aiden's eyes and maybe the smallest hint of vulnerability he'd ever seen in him. "Nah, it wasn't you. But thanks for the sentiment. And I know I'm welcome. I have Janie telling me that every time she meets Hope, Lainey, and Sarah here. Things have just been busy, and I'm still working on that pony."

"I think Tyler and Cade just walked through the door," Aiden said, with a tilt of his chin in the direction of the entrance.

Dean swore under his breath. Well, he might as well get it over with. They probably already knew, because chances were that Lainey had told Tyler and then all bets were off because Tyler loved blabbing. But maybe he was happy for that because he didn't want her to carry all that alone. He felt a firm grip on his shoulder and Aiden chuckled, making eye contact with one of his idiot friends behind him.

"Hell, man, you really messed up this time." Tyler's voice, filled with grim humor, told him everything he needed to know.

Dean stared into his glass. "I know, and I'd be sitting here getting drunk except I'm on call tomorrow and can't have a hangover. Talk about bad timing."

"Let's get a table and we'll see how we can fix this for you," Cade said. The arrogance his friends had was irritating and reassuring at the same time, and he wasn't sure what that said about himself.

Dean reluctantly stood and paused, looking at Aiden. "If you want to join us, you're welcome to."

Aiden gave him a quick nod before walking to the other end of the bar and serving a new customer. Dean followed Cade and Tyler to the far end of the bar, away from their usual Saturday night table where they usually sat as a big group. He sank back in his chair and waited for the fallout.

"What the hell were you thinking, man, taking on that kind of a lie for so long?" Tyler asked, leaning forward.

Dean didn't even bother trying to lie. He stared at Tyler dispassionately. "I felt something for her from the moment I met her. Brian didn't want to fight for his life and he didn't know how to tell her. He didn't want to hurt her."

Cade shook his head. "So you let yourself be the one to hurt her."

Dean put his elbows on the table and leaned forward, not needing the entire bar to hear their conversation. "I thought it was the right thing to do. He begged me. He was…he was a good guy and he didn't think he was going to make it. The odds were stacked against him and the idea of going through all that treatment only to die was something he didn't want to face. I got him in with the best oncologists for second opinions. He had a chance, it wasn't a good one, but it was a chance." Dean stopped talking abruptly because he didn't want to sound judgmental, and he didn't want to get into what really pissed him off about Brian, because he'd never walked in Brian's shoes. And Brian was young. He'd never had to face what Brian had to face, so he'd take his own feelings about that to the grave.

Dean cleared his throat and tried to redirect. "Long story short, he decided there was no way he could beat it for long, but he didn't have the heart to tell Hope."

"So you were the fall guy. Hell, man," Tyler said, taking a long drink of beer.

"I'd do it all over again except this wasn't the way Hope was supposed to find out. I never wanted her to find out. This is all so stupid. What the hell, if I didn't catch that stupid flu none of this would have happened."

"No, it needed to happen. It's about time you got this out there. You can't hold on to shit like that. And give Hope some credit, she must know your intentions were good. There's no way she's going to just let this go," Cade said, his gaze suddenly going to the door.

"Doesn't really matter. I'm sure she understands my intentions but that doesn't mean she can forgive being lied to that long. And I don't think this ever had to do with me. I don't think she's ever gotten over Brian. I'm not sure she ever will, and I can't compete with a ghost. It's not a fair fight."

Tyler shook his head. "That's not it. Everyone sees it, the way she looks at you. Even Cade can see it."

Cade tried to knock Tyler's beer from his hand. "Even though Ty is a moron, it's true. And that's probably what she's going to tell you." Cade stopped speaking abruptly, his gaze traveling to the door.

"Either that or she's going to kill you," Tyler said, following his gaze.

Dean turned around, shocked to see Hope weaving her way through the crowded bar, around the tables of boisterous people. Hell. His stomach twisted. He stood slowly, ready to take whatever it was she was going to throw at him.

"Brave man," Cade said in a strangled voice as Dean stood there.

Hope made eye contact with him, and every muscle in his body tensed like they were ready to snap. The look in her eyes was desperate, fiery, filled with something he'd only ever gotten hints of. Her long hair was loose and wavy, flowing, bouncing as she walked to him, eyes locked on his.

He let his gaze trail over her, aware that this may be the last time in a long time he'd be able to appreciate the woman he'd been in love with for almost a decade. He'd risked too much, wasted too much time, to lose her. Her red sweater showed off her flawless ivory complexion, the gentle curves of her body and her dark jeans hugged her long legs as she walked…marched… toward him like he was the only person in the bar.

He was vaguely aware of his friends pushing their chairs back from the table and Aiden placing beers down in front of them. Only vaguely aware because Hope had his undivided attention and, when she was finally standing in front of him, he could see now that her eyes were glittering with tears.

"Dean." She said his name in a choked whisper that sounded as though she'd pulled it out from deep inside, like she'd never said his name before.

He wanted to reach out and pull her into him, but he stood still. He'd laid it all out there earlier. He had exposed his heart, his feelings, everything.

It was her turn now. If she wasn't going to hit him, then she had to come through with something. He met her gaze. "Yeah?"

She took a step in to him, raising her head to meet his stare head on. The look in her eyes was almost his undoing. It was filled with desire. Blood started racing through his veins, but he waited. God, he'd waited this long for her, he could wait a few more seconds. He glanced from her eyes to her mouth, her lipstick accentuating her full lips, an exact match to the red of her sweater. He was pretty sure he was dying a slow death.

She closed the distance between them, standing on her tiptoes, curling her hand around the nape of his neck and pulled him down to her. And every fantasy he'd ever had about kissing her came true, and he realized that waiting was overrated.

He wrapped her in his arms, lifting her off the ground, and kissed her with everything he had. Hope tasted like every dream, every promise he'd ever wanted to make. The world, the saloon, their past, shrank to nothing as she held on to him. He kissed her, completely unable not to, because as he'd known for a long time, she was the woman he'd never get enough of. She was the woman worth waiting a lifetime for.

"I'm sorry. I'm so sorry for everything," she whispered against his mouth.

He pulled back slightly, his hands on either side of her face, not wanting to ever let her go again. "Don't. Let's get out of here."

She nodded and he grabbed her hand. "Later," he remembered to say to Tyler, Cade, and Aiden, who were getting an eyeful.

He was vaguely aware of Cade handing a twenty-dollar bill to Tyler who chuckled and tucked it into his breast pocket. "Told you she wasn't going to hit him."

• • •

Hope held on to Dean's hand like it was her lifeline. Maybe it was. The walk to the door of River's felt like it was miles but, finally, Dean was opening it and the crisp cold night air hit her flushed cheeks. She couldn't believe she had done something so...*not her.*

When she had walked through that bar and saw him sitting there with Tyler and Cade she had almost backed down and walked out. But she knew she couldn't. She owed him everything, and just the thought he believed she still blamed him was enough to make her move forward. And then when he'd stood, his handsome features drawn but his eyes filled with pain, she knew it was time for her to be bold and claim the man who'd been by her side for years.

But he'd claimed her with his kiss, with the desire that had coursed through her and made her forget everything but him. She wasn't a widow, she wasn't a mom, she was just Hope when he'd kissed her. But she was the Hope that she could be when she was with Dean.

They ran over to Dean's truck but instead of opening the passenger door, he turned to her and cupped her face. "Do you have any idea how much I want you? How many times I've thought of this, of you, in my arms?" Just his words alone, the rawness in his voice, was enough to make her knees weak, to make her forget the person she usually was and become the woman he saw in her.

This time when he kissed her there was an urgency there, a ferocity that matched his words, a desperation she felt deep in her core. Her back to the truck, Dean's strong body covered hers, and she didn't think she'd ever be able to stand again. He was everything she knew he'd be. He was everything she'd ever fantasized about, and kissing him was all-consuming. Her hands curled into the thick hair at the nape of his neck. "I didn't expect you to come here tonight," he said, pulling back slightly.

"I'm sorry. I sent you away because I was humiliated and ashamed of how I treated you, not because I was mad at you. I needed to process everything. Never in a million years was that what I expected you to say. I mean, for over five years, I've been thinking one thing. One way. I had to wrap my mind around Brian's lie, yours, and how I've treated you. I understand what you did. What you did for me. I'm so sorry."

"Don't apologize. I never wanted you to find out like you did. I didn't want you to be hurt, and Brian didn't either."

Her eyes filled with tears. "I know. And you were there for him. And me."

He leaned down to kiss her. "I tried, Hope. I will always be there for you and Sadie. I don't want to rush anything between us."

She stood on her tiptoes to kiss him again. "There's nothing rushed about us. This is years in the making. Dean, I denied my feelings for you for so long because yes, I felt guilty because of Brian for a long time, but it goes beyond that. You bring out this other side of me that terrifies me. You make me feel alive and special and safe, and I've never felt that way before. I'm ready to move forward. I have been for a while."

It felt right. Each time she said it felt more and more natural. This—he—was what she wanted, and she'd been a chicken for trying to deny her feelings for so long. This feeling, this rush that was Dean was impossible to contain anymore.

"I don't want to take you home and I don't want to go to my place." He leaned down to give her a slow kiss that made her drop what was left of her defenses.

She squeezed his waist. "Come back to my place. Sadie's at my parents."

CHAPTER SIXTEEN

Dean wasn't a complete ass to know that Hope's invitation may have sounded like everything he'd ever wanted, but wasn't. But there was nothing more that he wanted than to just be with her, in any way, shape, or form. Yet he did still drive the streets back to her house with an urgency that he felt was reciprocated.

That was confirmed when she unlocked the door to her house and kissed him again. He kicked the door shut behind him and kissed her back. He'd never been so consumed by a woman before. It was like Hope was everything. He wanted more of her. More of her scent, her taste, her mouth, her body. She shoved his jacket off his shoulders, and they scrambled over to the couch and he followed her down, covering her body with his. Hope felt like she was made for him, like she had always belonged with him. He ran a hand under her sweater, her soft, warm skin a balm against everything wrong.

She clutched the hair on the nape of his neck and said his name in a way that he was pretty damn sure he'd heard in quite a few dreams. She pulled back slightly. "Just so you know, I may be a little out of practice."

He lowered his head to her mouth again, much preferring a conversation that could also keep him close to her. "Are you kidding me?"

"No, seriously. Brian was the only one and it's been…like almost seven years since I've…so…"

When her voice trailed off and her face went red, he knew he had to tell her. "I kind of figured. But if it's any consolation, it's been two years for me."

Her mouth dropped open.

"You don't have to look so shocked."

"It's just, I kind of assumed…"

"Two years ago, I drove you home from Lainey's welcome-home party. That was the first time I felt you were aware of me, attracted to me. That was when I knew you and I were inevitable and I didn't want anything or anyone to get in the way of us."

Her eyes filled with tears and her head dropped to his shoulder. "I've thought so many things about you. So many things I wish I could take back. But if someone had ever told me that, I wouldn't have believed them. I was so wrong about you for so long. Maybe because I didn't want to believe it because it scared me. Because that pull…that attraction was always there for me too, Dean. I knew the physical…" She placed her hand over his heart and looked up at him. "But I didn't know about this. So many wasted years. I have so many regrets, so many things and feelings

I kept from you and from myself. You…what I feel when you look at me, when you touch me, terrified me for a long time."

He searched her eyes and waited, not knowing where she was going with this.

But she reached up and held her lips a whisper from his. "No one has ever made me forget how to breathe, made me weak in the knees, made me forget everything and that made me feel guilty for so long. But I don't want to feel guilty anymore. I don't want to deny what that means, what you mean to me. I just want to finally let go and give in to everything you make me feel."

Her honesty hit him deep inside and he didn't want to answer her with words anymore. All they had ever had between them were words and secrets and never this. They had never had each other.

She'd laid it all out there tonight, and he knew he'd never get the image of her walking toward him at River's out of his head. But she'd trusted him enough to come to him, and now she was trusting him with the truth of what she'd been battling. It was humbling and enlightening all at once, and he wasn't about to disappoint her.

She was here. Her heart in his hand, and he would never take that for granted, everything she was giving him. He leaned down to kiss her, because a second was a lifetime now, and he'd already waited a lifetime for her. When he lifted his head, his hands filled with the curves he'd admired and fantasized about forever, his eyes went to the picture of Sadie smiling at him.

He shut his eyes and kissed Hope again, telling himself that he wasn't doing anything wrong. They were both adults. She unbuttoned the front of his shirt and ran her hands over him. "I like this," she said with a smile that almost made him forget the little girl who was staring at him in the picture frame.

He ignored Sadie's toothless smile and focused on Hope, keeping his head down so that the pictures wouldn't be in his sight line anymore.

And then he heard his dad's voice. *You've always had a thing for trash, haven't you, Dean? Go and get your fill… You think you're so different from me? So much better than me? You and your friends, going to River's every weekend? I know how many women you've had at that cabin. We're the same, Dean. You think you can just decide one day to be monogamous for the rest of your life? Good luck with that, you naïve, pathetic boy.*

Dammit. His mouth stopped working and his conscience took over…and his insecurities. He wasn't like his father. He knew that. But for some reason, that comment plagued him.

"Dean?" Hope whispered.

Her back was arched, and he was pulling away like a guy who believed in self-torture.

He slowly lowered his head and kissed her

before sitting up. "I think we should stop here."

Anger and regret battled it out in his mind. He ran his hands through his hair and stared at the ceiling so he wouldn't have to look at her covering up her beautiful body from him. "Is everything okay?"

What did he even say to that? No, nothing was okay right now, because he was sitting beside her on the couch and she was now fully clothed. How would he explain this one without mentioning his father? He'd have to tell her the part about his conscience. The part that didn't have to do with his dad.

"I've waited years for you to trust me. I've waited years for all of it. For you, here, with me. I could wait forever for you, to make this right, to make this whatever you need it to be. But there's not just you. There's Sadie. You were married to her father and…I think that's important to you and I don't want any regrets between us. There's already been so much between us. I don't want there to be any doubt in your mind about what I want. I think we should take this slow."

Her gorgeous mouth dropped open and then she threw her arms around him. He held her close, the soft curves of her body fitting against him perfectly. "I don't want you to think I don't want to be with you. I do. More than anything, and I have zero self-control when it comes to you, I think. And I don't know what took me so long to get here," she said, pulling back slightly.

He lay down on the couch, pulling her with him. She tucked her head into his shoulder. "For the record, I have zero self-control also. But then I saw Sadie's picture, and I don't want to mess this up."

She propped her chin on his chest and her eyes were glistening. "I've been such a fool. I didn't want to see who you really were. You're more than I ever dreamed, Dean. And for the record," she said, her mouth tilting up in an irresistible, sexy smile as her hands drifted over his shoulders. "For the record, you're even better than all those fantasies I had about you."

Desire slammed into him again at her words and he pulled her up to him, kissing her. His hands were lost in her hair, her mouth the sweetest thing he'd ever tasted. He kept his hands at the nape of her neck, a desperate attempt to keep his hands in one place instead of touching her body that was pressed against him. "So much wasted time," he said against her lips. "Think of how many nights like this we could have had. But they would have had a more…satisfying ending."

She laughed against his mouth. "I can't wait."

"Yeah. It might be the slowest, most delicious form of torture," he said as she pulled back. She was staring at him like her thoughts had shifted.

"Can I ask you something?"

He kissed the top of her head. "Anything."

"Can you tell me more about your family? I feel like I know nothing about them. Your mom. Morgan."

He tensed slightly, almost regretting saying she could ask him anything. He never talked about his family to anyone, but she had a right to know things. He knew so much about her, and it wasn't fair for him to keep things from her. But there were reasons he didn't talk about them. There were wounds there that were thick and jagged and deep, and so many hadn't closed up yet. He met her stare, those green eyes filled with faith in him, with a gentleness he'd never had directed toward him from any relationship he'd had, knowing he'd open up the vault for her. "What do you want to know?"

"What was your mom like? I think I must've seen her a few times around town."

He stared at the ceiling and searched for the words that could fairly articulate what was a complicated relationship. "She...loved my dad, very much. She tried hard to make their marriage work."

She pulled back to look up at him, her brows drawn. "I didn't think they were divorced."

Damn. Dumb phrasing on his part. "Yeah, they were. I mean, they never divorced or anything, but uh, it wasn't a good marriage."

"Oh. I'm sorry to hear that."

He didn't say anything for a long moment and

then when she still didn't speak, he knew he had to reveal more. "My father cheated on her repeatedly."

Hope let out a small gasp. "Oh, Dean, that's horrible. And she knew?"

He gave a terse nod. It was strange, sharing like this. It's not like he hadn't expected to have to talk about his family or feelings, but it was still unsettling. He surmised it the trade-off for being in a real relationship. If Hope wanted to hear about his family, then he would have to tell her, no matter how uncomfortable it was.

She was staring at him like she was waiting for more. He didn't say anything. "Did you know? Like, when you were growing up?"

His instincts were to stand up and put some distance between them, thinking it might help make him feel less exposed. But the image of his father walking out of rooms, giving them his back, whenever they demanded some kind of answer, some kind of emotion from him, plagued him. He wasn't like him. He'd never be like him.

So instead, he fought the urge to disconnect and took her hand in his. He stared at their fingers intertwined and then slowly raised her hand to his mouth and kissed it. She sighed and he knew, in his mind, in his gut, that he'd made the right decision. "Maybe on some level. I knew more the older I got, of course. He never could love anyone as much as he loved himself. My father can justify bad behavior like it's no one's business. It's never his fault."

She squeezed his hand gently. "That's hurtful."

He shrugged. "I think at one point my mother started believing him. Like, that it was her fault for not being appealing enough for him. As though that was why he was having affairs. The most disgusting part of it all was then running into these women around town. My mom knew. And she pretended to not care or not notice, but it was slowly killing her. All her self-confidence, her self-respect died, little by little. He didn't care enough to stop; he didn't even care enough to try to hide it. He humiliated her. I could never understand how she could have so little self-respect. As I got older, I realized it wasn't that simple. That for her to think she deserved so little, he must've destroyed her self-esteem.

"She had no interest in things. In me or Morgan. All those things you do for Sadie? She couldn't be bothered because she was obsessed with my dad. I think the only reason she had us was, again, to try to win his love." He stopped speaking abruptly, because talking about his mother was hard. He never talked about her. She'd always been at arm's length, her preoccupation with his father always overriding her interest in him and Morgan. She was there but not really there.

When Hope didn't say anything, he glanced

down at her, wondering at the expression in her eyes. On some level, he was concerned that his father's disgusting lack of morals would be reflected on him, that she would be worried that he was the same. He felt like he had to go the extra mile to prove he was nothing like him.

Hope leaned down to kiss him. "I'm sorry. That must've been confusing as a child and heartbreaking as you got older. I'm sure she loved you both. I can't imagine not loving my kids."

He shrugged, not sure what to do with the emotion coursing through him. This was proving a much more difficult conversation than the ones he had with Tyler and Cade. She was asking him things he tried to avoid thinking about, but he knew this was what real relationships were built on—opening up. It was the stuff that people held deep inside that needed to be shared, even if it meant being vulnerable. "Maybe in her own way. She was preoccupied with my father. Looking good, acting a certain way to please him, that kind of thing. They spent a few nights at the country club, attended social functions, and then those nights that he was out by himself, she was pacing the living room window, looking for signs of him coming home. But he didn't. So, the next morning she'd be a wreck, not having slept, and he'd come in looking like he didn't have a care in the world. Morgan and I would be relieved to get out of there and go to school."

"How did that affect your relationship with your father?"

"What relationship? When we were younger, we didn't really know there was something wrong with him. We thought it was us. So we tried hard to meet the impossible moving target of pleasing him. But nothing we ever did was good enough. And then when we were older and had figured him out, we despised him for the way he treated our mother, for the way he treated us. He was so full of himself. He belittled us every chance he got and then to the world projected the image of this perfect family. We wanted to stand up for our mother, but she didn't want us to. It was like the more we mentioned, the angrier she got. It's like we were reality, and she didn't want to be in reality."

She squeezed his hand. "That is awful. I think so many people believed you had this perfect life. All that wealth and power. And your family really did look perfect."

"Yeah. It's tough to complain about because, big deal, we didn't have it all. So many had it worse. It's not like he's the first spouse to cheat. Or we're the first kids to deal with parents who didn't really care."

"While that's true, it doesn't make it hurt any less."

He ran a hand through his hair. "It doesn't hurt."

She tilted her head. "Of course it does. You don't have to pretend with me, Dean. How could that possibly not hurt? You're watching your dad with all these other women, repeatedly hurting your mom. And then she's so preoccupied with your dad she can't even enjoy her time with her sons?"

He let out a short laugh. "Well, when you put it like that."

"Seriously. This is awful. How did I not know any of this? Or Lainey. Wait. Do Tyler and Cade even know?"

He shrugged and avoided eye contact.

She jabbed him in the shoulder. "Dean."

"Maybe some. Not all."

"How could you carry this around all these years?" she said softly.

He met her gaze. "I told you. No one wants to hear that from me. I refuse to be the poor little rich boy. Everyone has problems. They had their own crap to deal with. I had mine. Done."

"I don't think you give them enough credit. They'd never think that about you. And is it? Done? Where's Morgan?"

He pushed past the frustration and his urge to change the subject, in order to be an open book for her. He hadn't waited this long to be with Hope only to shut down because he hated talking about feelings. "Don't say I didn't warn you. My family is different from your family. This one is going to be gross. Morgan left because he found my dad…with his girlfriend."

Hope scrambled into a sitting position, her face stark white, her eyes wide, as she stared at him. He'd never felt more disgusted by his father than right now. He also felt like he was on a talk show. "What?"

"Yeah. You heard that right, even though it's almost impossible to imagine."

Something flashed across her eyes that he wasn't sure about. But it was gone so quickly he wondered if he'd imagined it. "That's awful. What…did your dad do? Did he care?"

Dean shook his head. "I think he got off on it. It was a way of proving he had something over on Morgan. He was still in his prime. He was threatened by me, by Morgan. So, he needed to prove to Morgan that he was still on top."

"I'm so sorry. That's why Morgan left?"

Dean nodded. "Yeah. I think he hit rock bottom when he realized he wanted to kill him, so he left."

Hope stared at him, her eyebrows up and her mouth open. "Dean."

Dean shrugged. "I can't say I blame him. I mean, I think I'd feel the same way."

Her eyes were stormy and he wondered what she was thinking. Had he just scared her off? Like, what kind of a family was this? And she probably wasn't taking the whole killing-their-father thing lightly. Who would? She also had her own run-in with his father, and maybe it was too much. Brian's family had been simple and uncomplicated. Brian had been a normal, nice guy. Dean and his family were neither. "Well, feeling and doing are two different things," she said finally.

He nodded. "Of course."

She let out a sigh. "And what about Morgan? Are you in touch with him?'

God, how he wanted this conversation to end. It was like she was plucking out all the painful quills in his body he'd tried desperately to keep intact all these years. It was more comfortable to walk around with them than have them yanked out. "No."

"What? Why?"

He shrugged. "He needed to leave, so he left."

"But you were close."

"Yeah. And now we're not."

She poked him in the stomach. "Have you tried to reach out to him?"

"I'm kind of pissed off at him, Hope. Like I was pissed at Tyler for leaving. Being the one left behind, holding all the crap, is not fun. I know why he left and I'm not judging him, because I do believe he made the only decision he could at the time, but I was still in high school. I couldn't take off without any money. I already knew at that point I wanted to be a doctor. So, I stuck it out in that house without him, and the longer he was gone without a word, the more I grew to resent him. I'd also promised my grandparents I'd stay. I regret it sometimes, I guess. Sometimes I wish I had left with him, but I love Wishing River. I love the life I've built here, and I'm glad I kept my promise to my grandparents. But if I'm being completely honest, I wish he were in my life again."

She drummed her fingers against his chest. "You need to call him."

He stared at the ceiling and tried his best to be patient. She wasn't asking him unreasonable requests, but he still didn't want to deal. "I'm happy. He's happy. He's living his own life and I'm not going to barge in and disrupt things. If he wanted a relationship, he'd have contacted me. Maybe he's pissed I never went with him; he could think I betrayed him and I wouldn't blame him. I don't know. It's been too long. And what's the point? He'll never move back here."

She frowned at him and he was oddly touched by her irritation with him. "Dean, you guys loved each other. You were more than just brothers, you were good friends. He left because he was hurt and angry and really because of your father. I'm sure he understands why you didn't go with him. You don't actually feel like you betrayed him, do you?"

He let out a groan. "Hope, are you trying to make me depressed?"

She placed her hand on his chest. "Of course not. I'm trying to help. I'm sorry if this is bringing up uncomfortable feelings for you."

"I'm not uncomfortable." He tried to soften his response by placing his hand over hers.

She winced. "You look like you've got food poisoning."

He almost laughed. "I think that's a little dramatic. I don't like thinking about this. If he wanted to come back or have a relationship, then why hasn't he contacted me?"

"Maybe for the same reasons you listed. Maybe he thinks you're mad at him for leaving. Maybe he's scared."

"He's not scared. And I am mad at him."

She patted his shoulder. "But not *that* mad. Look, you made up with Tyler. And now the three of you are the three musketeers again."

He reached out to kiss her while laughing. "You're purposely trying to irritate me. We didn't make up. We weren't broken up. And do not refer to us as the three musketeers."

She laughed against his lips. "But it's so fun."

He smiled. "I don't know, Hope. Part of me wonders if too much time has passed. He might be married, have kids. I don't want to disrupt whatever he has going on."

"Or maybe it won't be seen as a disruption. Maybe he's been waiting for you to make the first move and he misses you and regrets leaving you behind. Maybe he wonders if you and your dad are close and that you've taken your dad's side. Maybe he thinks he wouldn't be welcome."

He shrugged, not wanting to offend her but not wanting to talk about this anymore. His mind went to that argument with his father, of his dad's assessment of Dean not reaching out to Morgan. He was wrong. He'd rather think that Hope was right. "Maybe it's something I'll deal with one day. Just not now. If he contacted me and came back into my life, then I'd deal with it. If I'm completely honest, you are right: I would be happy to have Morgan back in my life. We were close and he's a good guy. He's nothing like our dad. Right now, I'd rather think about you. This place we're trying to build."

Her eyes softened. "I like that. I like that you're part of this. Can I tell you something else I like about you?"

"Sure. I rarely hear the things you like about me."

She laughed. "Well, then I guess I should change that. And, in all seriousness, that makes me feel bad. There's a lot I've liked about you for years. I was just too stubborn or scared to ever do anything about it. But one of the things I like most about you is that you never acted different than the rest of us. You never let your background…your wealth change you. I was kind of embarrassed when you suggested wanting to work here because what I was offering was nothing for you and this place is also…not much to someone like you. But you seem so at home here, like this house and everything in it is good enough for you."

He framed her face with his hands, looking deep into her eyes, wanting her to feel his sincerity. "I'd give it all up in a second if it meant having you and Sadie in my life. This place is you, which means it's everything to me, it's perfect. It's sweet and warm, just like you. Your happiness, Sadie's, is everything to me. This has always been about you, Hope."

Her eyes filled with tears. "I wasted so much time when we could've been like this. I could have had you like this, so agreeable and charming. I don't think I'll ever get used to that, Dean. You…you make me feel so alive. I regret every single day I wasted being afraid. Will you spend the night here?"

He clenched his jaw, his head filling with thousands of contradicting thoughts, only some of which were appropriate to share. Because the most important things were showing Hope that he could be trusted. That he wasn't like his father. He'd let his guard down earlier when speaking about his father, and it didn't sit well that he might be compared to him. That Dean could be a risk. A part of him knew that he had to prove himself, because it wasn't just about Hope, it was about Sadie, too. "Of course I'll stay here. But I don't want you to feel rushed into anything."

She tilted her head to the side, eyeing him in that way that almost made him squirm. "Right. And then there's Sadie. I'm not sure what to tell her about us."

He stilled. Did she consider him father material? Had her opinion of him changed after what she'd learned about his father? And then she was probably thinking how his dad was definitely not grandfather material. Like, who the hell would want him around their daughter? This was why it was better to keep feelings shoved down and repressed. Now he had to worry about how much she trusted his intentions…and his ability to be monogamous. He cleared his throat. "What do you want to tell her?"

"I don't want to confuse her. I mean…there was Brian and now there's you. There hasn't been anyone in between. She doesn't remember Brian, which is heartbreaking, but she knows him through pictures and videos. And she knows you now. She's always adored you, Dean. But I guess…since we don't really know where this is going, maybe we shouldn't say anything. We can just be friends in front of her."

He ignored the stab of disappointment and dismissed it as irrational. "You're her mom, so you call the shots. Whatever makes things easier for you. Whatever you think is best for her."

"I value your opinion, though. I don't want you to think that I'm not taking our relationship seriously. I think the reason I haven't been with anyone else hasn't been because of Brian, but because of you. My heart knew I wanted you."

And right there was everything he'd ever wanted to hear. "Me too, Hope. I haven't been with anyone since that night I drove you home from Lainey's."

"I can't believe you did that," she said softly.

"Is that so hard to believe?"

Her face turned red. "No…well, yes, you and I were nothing until a few weeks ago. And…that's a long time. I thought you had a slew of…" When her voice trailed off and her cheeks were the same color as her red sweater, he knew he had to set the record straight. He wasn't his father. He wasn't.

"I think I have enough self-control to wait for the woman I really want. I just needed you to hurry up and figure things out. And I'm not my father. I can be monogamous. I can be in love with one person and wait for that person," he said, sitting up.

She squeezed his knee. "Hey, hey, I know you're not him. I would never think that. I guess I'm shocked. And touched. But speaking of your dad… I don't think he'll be happy about the two of us together. Do you want to not…say anything?"

"I'm not afraid of my father and I'm not hiding anything from him."

She broke his stare, and unease sliced through his chest at the thought of his father, his threats, and just how far he would go to keep Hope out of Dean's life. But he was willing to gamble that his father was all talk at this point. Dean was the only son still speaking to him; there was no way he'd cut him out of the will. He had to make himself clear. Then he could have the family he wanted and he could keep his promise to his grandfather. But none of this was Hope's concern. It had taken them this long to finally get together, he wasn't about to let his father come between them.

"Trust me," he said softly. He raised his hand to grasp the nape of her neck, gently, loving the soft sigh that escaped her mouth. Loving the way her body seemed to melt onto his, the way she tasted, the way she just was.

If life could stay like this forever, if this moment with her could last forever, he'd never want anything more.

CHAPTER SEVENTEEN

"This porch looks brand new."

Dean looked up to see Hope's father standing there, admiring the completed porch. Dean was putting his equipment back in the toolbox. He'd just completed the finishing touches on the handrail. Dusk had settled and the warm glow from inside the house had an oddly comforting effect on him. He was content. Not the boring kind of content, but the kind that came from knowing life was exactly how he wanted it to be. He'd never experienced that before.

He could see Hope and her mom and Sadie in the house. Sadie was doing her homework and Hope was helping her. After this they were planning on heading out to River's to meet their friends. "Thanks. I guess a porch railing and posts aren't that different from a fence. I've fixed one too many of those," he said with a laugh.

"I bet you have."

"Once the weather warms up, I'll be able to paint it and then it'll be complete."

"I think Sadie has already decided she's going to paint it with you," Jeff said, his deep voice filled with warmth and affection.

Dean gave a small chuckle. "I don't doubt that.

She helped sand the railing and was basically ready to take over the entire restoration."

"She would've done a fine job, too," he said, pride in his voice.

Dean cracked a smile. "No doubt."

"I'm glad you're here, actually. I've been meaning to talk to you," Jeff said, his voice growing serious.

Dean stood, shoving his hands in the front pockets of his jeans. He ignored the irrational tingling of nervousness. He wasn't a teenager anymore, waiting to be lectured by his girlfriend's father. But it wasn't really that. Part of him wanted to earn Jeff's approval. He was a genuinely good human being and a great father. It was early days yet, but where Dean's father saw their family name as a blessing, Dean saw it as a curse. Anyone who knew anything about his father would be worried if their daughter was getting involved in their family. Dean couldn't even blame Hope's parents for being concerned for her.

And then there was the whole Brian thing. Had they blamed him for their son-in-law's death, too? Had Hope told them the truth? "Sure, what's on your mind?" Dean said, as a damp March wind drifted around them.

"I've been meaning to thank you for the way you took care of Sadie not that long ago. She and Hope couldn't stop singing your praises. Of course, I'm not surprised. I've heard for years what a good doctor you are."

Dean held his gaze, surprise making him at a momentary loss for words. "Jeff, you don't have to thank me. I was just doing my job and Sadie… well, she's like family. You all are."

Jeff broke into a smile, lines appearing everywhere, signs of laughter and a life well-lived. "That's good to hear, son. We feel the same way about you. Which leads me into the next awkward topic—we never blamed you for what happened to Brian. I would hate for you to think we had. I probably should have said something years ago. But Hope told us what you did. The sacrifices you made. I don't know that I could have stood the idea of people thinking that I had been so wrong. But I could have done that for my wife. I know I would have done that for her, like I know I would do anything for the women in my life. I'm glad you feel so much for Hope."

Dean drew in a shaky breath, emotion coursing through him as he stared at Jeff's watering eyes. This man was not afraid to love. To show love. To put his loved one's needs above his own. And this man would never be friends with his father. He'd never understand the world Dean had lived in for so long. Hell, Dean didn't even understand. And now, more than ever, he wanted out. He wanted to escape like Morgan had. But Morgan's break was clean, because he could leave town. Morgan hadn't promised their grandfather anything. Now, with Hope and Sadie, leaving town wasn't an option. Wishing River was their home.

But ever since his conversation with Hope the other night when she'd asked some hard questions about Morgan, he'd been thinking more and more about his brother. It had been easier to just try to forget him day to day. Now that Hope had brought it up, he'd started remembering their time together. He remembered late night talks in Morgan's room. He remembered tagging along with Morgan on the ranch. What Morgan had learned from the ranch hands, he'd taught Dean. Then he'd gotten to wondering where Morgan was. A ranch? Had he pursued his instincts and dived into the crypto currency world? Was he married? Did he have kids?

Dean met Jeff's gaze. "I've…I've had feelings for Hope for years. I've been waiting for her to be ready…to move on. I don't want to pressure her into anything she isn't ready for."

Jeff gave him a nod, not breaking his stare. "I don't think you have to worry about that, the way Hope talks about you. It's brought us a lot of relief, hearing such joy in her voice."

Dean stood a little straighter. "Thank you. The feeling is mutual. I'd do anything to keep them happy and safe."

"That makes me feel even better. This is quite the piece of land out here. Hope was filling us in on the plans you both came up with. I'm excited to see her business expand and see what you can do here."

Dean rubbed the back of his neck. "She's worked hard for her business. It would be great to see her dreams come true. There's enough space for it, that's for sure."

Jeff braced his arms against the railing, his gaze going out to the mountains. "I was worried there for a while when I heard about her rent going up."

Dean swallowed hard. He assumed Jeff knew that his father owned the building. He didn't want to lie, but if he told Jeff the truth, he'd tell Hope, and that would blow everything. And the last thing he wanted was to do anything to jeopardize their relationship. He hadn't exactly figured out how he was going to fix that situation. "I'm glad that was taken care of."

Jeff gave him a long stare. "Me too. You're a good man, Dean. Your father must be very proud of you."

Dean gave him a nod and tipped the brim of his hat a little lower. He swallowed past the lump in his throat. "Thank you, Jeff."

• • •

"Dean, why are they clapping?" Hope whispered in his ear and squeezed his hand. He followed her gaze as they made their way through a packed River's to their usual table.

"Dear God, they are clapping at us. For us."

"That's so sweet," she said, smiling up at him as they approached the table.

"What? It's not sweet, just look at Tyler and Cade's faces. It's a trap of some sort," he said, reluctantly continuing forward.

"Congratulations! We've all been waiting years to see the two of you walking toward us, together, holding hands!" Lainey said, standing.

Much to his horror, everyone at the table stood: Tyler and Lainey, Cade and Sarah, and Aiden and Janie. Worse, they were each holding a glass of champagne. Even worse than this show of...whatever it was, were the expressions on the guys' faces. Tyler looked like he was going to explode in uncontrollable laughter at any moment. Cade, about to keel over from repressed glee. They were, of course, laughing at Dean and his obvious discomfort.

Dean slapped on his most apathetic face and handed Hope one of the two champagne glasses waiting for them at the edge of the table. Dean tried to fight the heat rising up his neck when it was his turn to order. Hopefully, no one was listening. "I'll have the River burger and fries. Uh, make the bun gluten free," he said, lowering his voice to just be audible.

Everyone stilled. Hope was sweetly rubbing

his back so he couldn't even make assholish remarks to his friends because he didn't want to
hurt her feelings.

"Sure," the waitress said.

"And a beer."

Hope gave him a small nudge and he resisted
the urge to swear under his breath. Was wheat in
everything? "Uh, no beer. I'll have a whiskey."

"What the hell is even happening? What year
is this?" Tyler chortled.

"I would have hoped fatherhood would have
matured you, Ty," Dean said dryly.

"Not a chance. But seriously, Dean, I'm happy
you're dealing with whatever issues you have.
Hope helped me. No more gut issues for me,"
Lainey said.

"Yeah, I'm pretty sure Dean's gut was leak-
ing," Cade said, choking on his own laughter.

Dean tried to tip his chair over but Cade held
onto the table, barely.

"You guys are children," Sarah said.

"Speaking of," Cade said, leaning to the side
and whispering something in Sarah's ear. Her
eyes were sparkling while she nodded and kissed
him.

Cade tapped his fork against the table in a
totally obnoxious manner. "We have an an-
nouncement."

Dean felt Hope tense beside him and he shot
her a look, but she wouldn't make eye contact

with him. "You're getting a pony," Dean said flatly.

Cade grinned. A grin Dean had seen not that long ago—on Tyler's less than appealing face. "Better. We're having a baby. Sarah is. We're going to be parents."

Laughter and cheers erupted around the table, and it was almost surreal to witness the change that was taking place among all of them. Even Aiden had a kid. And though Janie wasn't his biological mom, she had raised him, so she was a mother. Dean was the only one at the table who wasn't a parent.

The rest of the night passed in a blur and soon Lainey and Tyler were saying goodbye and then they all decided it was time to leave. That again, all of them leaving before midnight, another reminder of how time was passing, how they were all changing.

"I'm so happy for Sarah and Cade," Hope said when they were back in the truck.

He stared out into the darkness, concentrating on the road the headlights were illuminating. "Me too. Honestly, Hope if you'd told me two years ago that Cade was going to get married and have a kid and be running his own ranch, I would have laughed."

"That's mean."

He let out a laugh. "I didn't mean it like that. I just meant he was a different guy. Things change. People change."

"I don't know. I don't think anyone has really changed that much. I think they've become the people who were already there. Does it bother you that your two best friends are married and fathers?"

He slowed the truck as they approached her street and he thought about how to answer that. He knew what he wanted, but hell if he knew whether they were the same things she wanted, and he couldn't scare her away. Because it wasn't that simple for him. He wanted all those things when he was with Hope. But late at night, he was still plagued by the idea that he wasn't the right man. He wasn't his grandfather. He was still his father's son. "Of course not. I am genuinely happy for them. They both deserve happiness, and I've never seen them like this. They're good guys. We've all been through a lot together."

She didn't say anything for a moment. "Do you want kids one day?"

"Sure. How about you? Do you want more?" he said, not missing a beat as he pulled into her driveway. He didn't want to add anything else; he didn't want to talk about his father or his insecurities.

"I don't know. I always thought I did. But now I'm not so sure. Sadie's getting older, and it seems so strange to start over again. Maybe that ship has sailed in my life. It would be like starting a whole new family."

He shifted the truck into park, not letting his disappointment show. Hell, he didn't even know when he'd decided he wanted a kid. It was Hope. He had never thought about kids before her. So he shouldn't be disappointed by her answer. He didn't know if it was that she was scared or if she really meant it. "Or maybe you need to think about it differently."

She looked down into her lap. "Or maybe there's just too much going on right now. With the house, the land, and my business slowly tanking, who can even think about kids?"

"Well, that's true. But your business isn't tanking, Hope. It just needs to change with the new circumstances. You've worked too hard to give up now. You need a night out, and I want to take *you* out, not with our friends. A real night. You and me."

CHAPTER EIGHTEEN

Hope took a deep breath and stole a quick glance at herself in the rearview mirror. She tried not to let her horror show, because Sadie was sitting in the back seat staring at her. "You look fine, Mom. Let's go in and surprise Dr. Dean."

They were sitting in the hospital parking lot and Hope had a plate of homemade chocolate chip cookies on the passenger seat. Tonight was their big date night, and she had no idea where he was taking her. But she wanted him to know she was thinking about him. It was her attempt at redeeming her baking skills.

When he'd come over to her house the other night, he'd been an open book. A slightly bearish, wounded, open book, but an open book, nonetheless. She knew opening up was hard for him and so she was even more touched that he'd come to her after a hard day. She knew that wasn't the type of thing he'd do with his friends. Or his father. Dean was the entire package. He was smart and hard-working and just about as hot as any man could be. And he was hers.

But, unfortunately for her, she was a bit of a mess, because when she'd gone to pick up Sadie at school, Sadie had begged her to go to the park with a friend. So, Hope and another mom braved the miserable March drizzle while the girls had played at the local park. Now, all the effort she'd made to blow-dry her hair and curl it were for nothing. Her mascara had smudged. The rosy glow she'd carefully constructed was now replaced by splotches of redness from the wind. Even the bottoms of her jeans were covered in mud.

She inhaled slowly. She almost hoped they wouldn't run into Dean and she could leave the plate of cookies for him, because while Dean managed to make disheveled look hot, she knew she did not.

"Are you going to marry Dr. Dean?"

Hope stilled at the innocent question. The excitement in Sadie's voice was obvious, and Hope slowly turned around to look at her. "Sadie, marriage is a really big deal and not something that we can jump into."

Sadie nodded wisely. "So, are you going to marry him?"

The moment might have been funny if there weren't so many other things to address, which she had no idea how Sadie would process. "Dean and I have known each other a long time, but we've never actually…dated each other. So, this is new to us. And I also have to consider you in all this."

"Me?"

She nodded. "How would you feel if Dean and
I were serious?"

"And got married?"

Hope sighed. Clearly that was the focus.
"Okay, sure. But just so we're clear, this is way
too soon to be talking about marriage. How
would you feel to have Dean as your dad?"

Sadie broke out into a wide grin. "I love him."

Hope's heart swelled in her chest and she
blinked back tears. How she had let the conversation go in this direction was beyond her—and
dangerous—but at least now she knew where
Sadie stood. Dean had won her little girl over.
And her. Hope cleared her throat and smiled
gently. "He's a very good man, isn't he?"

Sadie nodded. "Yeah, he is. So can we go see
him now?"

Hope laughed, picking up the plate of cookies
and grabbing her purse. "Yes, let's go."

The made their way across the parking lot,
hand in hand, and Hope let her mind get carried
away. Could this be their life one day? Dropping
off some food for Dean or meeting up with him
for lunch after work? It was scary to wish for this.
But all she knew was that right now, with Sadie
holding her hand, and the anticipation of seeing
Dean soon, she felt like she was floating. Like, she
hadn't remembered a time she'd been so happy,
so excited about life.

The Emergency Room doors swooshed open

and Hope guided Sadie over to the main reception area. Dean had mentioned he'd be finishing around this time so she asked the woman behind the counter if he had come out yet.

"Oh, Dr. Stanton was called into an emergency. You can leave those with me if you'd like. I promise I won't eat them," the older lady said with a laugh.

Hope smiled, trying not to let her disappointment show. "I'd appreciate that. Thanks so much. You can tell him they're from Hope and Sadie."

The woman jotted their names down on a sticky note and placed them on the plastic wrap over the plate. "Will do."

Hope turned to head out the doors when she noticed a beautiful woman smiling and approaching them.

"Sorry, I didn't mean to eavesdrop but are you Hope Roberts?"

Hope nodded, trying to place the woman, hoping she wasn't a patient or someone she couldn't remember. "I am."

The woman extended her hand. "I'm Celeste Wellington. I'm a good friend of Dean's. We met for lunch. He's told me so much about you and your daughter."

Insecurity and surprise coursed through Hope as she scrambled to come up with a polite reply. Celeste. The woman Dean's father wanted him to marry. The woman in front of her was very much the type who'd run in Dean's circles. She was so elegant, even though she was dressed casually. Her brown hair had lighter, stunning shades of blond highlights that fell in perfect shiny, loose waves that framed her flawless face. Her makeup was dewy and not overdone, perfectly coordinated to highlight her already perfect features. Her camel-colored, what looked liked cashmere, sweater draped beautifully over her slender frame and dark skinny jeans. Her tall riding boots complemented the brown tote on her shoulder—and Hope was pretty sure it was a soft, buttery leather and came from some designer. But the worst part of this entire exchange was how nice Celeste seemed. Her pale-blue eyes were sparkling with kindness and she was smiling at her and Sadie as though they were all friends.

The only problem was Hope. An insecurity she'd never felt before crept in, making her hyperconscious of herself. Of the way she looked right now...and the way she always was. While she did enjoy getting dressed up and doing her hair and makeup—it wasn't like Celeste. It was whatever brand of clean makeup she could get on sale somewhere, and if it wasn't in the right shade, she'd go without. There wasn't one designer thing in her closet and there never had been. She'd never had to even think about those things, because the life she lived was a practical one. Her friends, while some of them were better off were still nothing like Celeste. Or Dean. The last time Hope's skin had ever looked that dewy was when she was running a bath for Sadie.

As Hope stood there, her mind wandered to the two of them grabbing lunch together. And she wondered if they'd ever been together. All those years Hope had brushed him off, had been angry with him, he could have had this whole other life.

Sadie yanked her hand gently, her eyes wide. Hope took a deep breath and forced a smile as she met Celeste's friendly gaze. "It's so great to meet you, too. This was an unplanned drop-off."

What did that even mean? An unplanned drop-off?

Celeste smiled at her and then Sadie. "Well, I'm sure Dean will love them. He has a major sweet tooth. Today at the Club he ordered two desserts. I'm not sure where the man puts it all," she said, with a laugh.

Sadie joined in as though she were nine going on nineteen and knew what Celeste was referring to. "He does. That's one of the things I love most about Dr. Dean."

Hope's throat tightened as she stared at the top of Sadie's head. Her daughter was so sweet and so attached to Dean. She'd always known that, but now it had evolved even more. By "the Club," Hope knew she must have been referring to the country club. It wasn't in Wishing River but close to Billings. They probably both belonged.

"I think Dean is smitten with you as well. Anyway, it was so great meeting you both. I've got to run. I hope we'll meet up again one day," Celeste said, giving them both a glance and a little wave.

Hope stood there and nodded, keeping her smile fixed until the woman had disappeared out the sliding doors. Only then did she let out the breath she hadn't realized she'd been holding.

"Wow, she looks like she should be on one of those hair commercials," Sadie said, tossing her own heap of damp, tangled hair over her shoulder. But Sadie was smiling and looking up at her as though she had no idea what Hope was thinking, which was a good thing. There was no way she'd let her irrational insecurities infiltrate Sadie.

"Yeah, she does," Hope said, forcing a casual note to her voice. She wasn't too sure she was passing.

"So, what do we do now?"

Hope shrugged. She knew exactly what she was going to do—she was going to race home and spend the rest of the afternoon getting ready for her date tonight with Dean. Just like a teenager. But she mentally went through all the items in her small closet, trying to come up with some outfit that Dean had never seen her in. What if he was taking her somewhere special? Somewhere elegant? What if he planned on taking her to the country club, too? She didn't know the first thing about that kind of place. And what if his father was there?

She tried to take a deep breath but it wasn't happening. She couldn't go in her usual jeans and a sweater or blouse tonight. When was the last time she ate at anywhere but River's or Tilly's? Oh, and that meant he certainly wouldn't be picking her up in his truck. She'd spotted his shiny BMW sedan out in the parking lot. She wasn't the type of woman he normally went out with; his father had made that clear.

She suddenly felt uncomfortable in her own skin.

"Mom? Are you okay? You look a little green."

Oh, the irony was not lost at all, but that wasn't the impression she wanted to give Sadie. And really, she had never experienced this level of insecurity before. But it was one of the things that had always separated Dean from the rest of them.

She forced her eyes shut. This had nothing to do with Dean. She knew who he was, deep inside. He was a good man. He'd never made her feel less than for what she didn't have. He'd always made her feel good enough. This was her projecting. She opened her eyes and smiled down at Sadie. "I'm totally fine. I guess it's good Dean wasn't available right now or he'd be eating even more dessert."

Sadie giggled as they made their way through

the Emergency Room doors. Rain drizzled down and they walked past his car in the Doctors Only parking spots until they reached her old SUV. As they drove away, Hope tried to regain her excitement for tonight and shake off the insecurity that was now looming over her.

CHAPTER NINETEEN

Dean stood on Hope's front porch, piling up the last of the gifts he had for Sadie. He'd been waiting for tonight, but an uncharacteristic wave of insecurity hit him as he realized how enormous the stack of boxes was.

He should've asked her if it was okay. But he'd gotten carried away and before he knew it, with Celeste's help, he'd one-clicked everything on that American Girl website. The image of Sadie's face telling him about her friends all having these dolls had done him in. He knew Hope was struggling far more than she was letting on.

There were other images, the ones that had haunted him for years, the ones that he knew deep down would never go away just because he could afford to buy expensive gifts and fill a barn with ponies. The images, the memories of Hope holding Sadie in the hospital as they visited Brian. The image of Brian holding Sadie in the hospital bed. The image of Hope holding Sadie at Brian's funeral. He wasn't sure, despite Hope knowing the truth, that he'd ever be able to truly look at Sadie and not feel guilty.

Pushing those thoughts aside, he knocked on the door and seconds later Sadie whipped it open.

She gave him a big hug and he held onto her for a second, letting himself feel the love she unabashedly threw at him. "How you doing, Sadie?"

She beamed up at him. "Wait until you see Mom. She looks amazing. Like your friend."

His curiosity was piqued as he tried to figure out who Sadie was referring to, but his attention was drawn to Hope. She gave him a small wave, standing beside the couch. She did look incredible wearing a formfitting black dress that accentuated every perfect curve of her body and strappy black heels that made her legs seem endless. Her hair was loose and framed her face in soft waves. Her full lips were slightly glossy and her eyes seemed greener than usual, and if it weren't for that flicker of insecurity in her eyes as she stared at him, he might've just stood there gawking. He cleared his throat. "Sadie's right. You look beautiful, Hope. But you always look beautiful," he said.

Her cheeks colored slightly, and her gaze flickered over him. Only then did it hit him that she was quite dressed up. While he wasn't wearing his working jeans, he was in jeans. A button-down shirt, but nothing formal. Hell, he hadn't said they were going somewhere out of town for dinner, had he? He hadn't thought they'd be able to, since her parents were babysitting and they'd need to be back at a decent hour. And there was no way in hell he'd want to go to the country club and run into his father and have him ruin Hope's night.

He shrugged off the unease and reached for a bunch of the gift-wrapped boxes on the porch. "Sadie, I have a few things you might like."

He piled them all in the house and Sadie stood there, her mouth hanging open, staring at the gifts but not moving. "These are all for me?"

He nodded, jamming his hands in the front pockets of his jeans. "You bet."

"Dean," Hope said softly, her eyes filled with questions.

He shrugged. "I thought Sadie might be needing some things for her new room."

"Can I open them?" Sadie said, her gaze going back and forth between the two of them.

"Fine with me, if it's okay with your mom," Dean said.

Hope nodded, giving Sadie a strained smile. Hell, he hoped he hadn't overstepped. "Of course. I can't wait to see what Dean's been up to," she said, shooting him a quizzical look. He was relieved to see that the sparkle had returned to her eyes.

Soon the room was filled with Sadie's audible gasps, gift wrap flying in the air as she opened the gifts in record time. He stood there awkwardly, his attention going between Sadie and Hope. When Sadie opened the last one, she looked up at him with tears in her eyes. She scrambled, almost tripping over the boxes and nosediving into the coffee table if he hadn't caught her. She threw her arms around his neck and held onto him with a grip that went way beyond gratitude for a bunch of dolls and toys. "Thank you, Dr. Dean. You made all my dreams come true."

He almost laughed at the comment, but instead found himself choked up as she clung to him. He hugged her back with the same ferocity, never expecting this kind of emotion to course through him. Sadie was a kid who was easy to love. It was easy to want to make her happy. Before he could say anything, or look at Hope, the doorbell rang.

He stood as Sadie raced to the door. When he glanced at Hope she quickly turned away to greet her parents whom Sadie was ushering through the door and toward her pile of American Girl dolls and paraphernalia. He was greeted warmly by Hope's parents.

"Well, I can see you're going to be person of the year in Sadie's life," Hope's father said with a chuckle and a warm smile.

Dean grinned as Sadie ran through each item for her grandparents. "Will you help me set all this up tonight?" she asked them.

"Of course," Hope's mom said, as Sadie shoved the barn in front of them.

"Sorry about that. But I can always help assemble when we get back," he said.

Jeff waved him off. "I love doing this stuff. It'll be fun. You kids go out and have a nice evening."

"Hope, you look so lovely," her mom said.

Hope smiled. "Thanks, Mom."

He walked over to the door and held it open, noticing Hope still seemed stiff. "We won't be back too late. I know you have that early morning," he said.

"Have fun!" Sadie said, barely looking up from the box she was ripping open.

"We will," he said, hoping like hell it was true.

Hope stopped when they reached the bottom step, glancing at her feet. "I feel like I chose the wrong footwear for tonight."

He cringed at the mud leading to his truck. He took her hand. "Here, let me lead and hopefully you won't get any mud on you."

When they reached his truck, he opened the door. "Do you need help getting in?"

She shot him a look that he couldn't entirely decipher. "I'm okay. I've been getting into trucks like this my whole life, Dean."

As he rounded the front of his truck, he couldn't quite shake the feeling that something was off. Like they were operating on different wave lengths, and that usually didn't happen. He hopped in and turned on the ignition, aware how cold it was. The March night air, especially out in the open country, could be especially frigid.

"Uh, here. I sat on your cell phone and wallet

by accident," Hope said, handing him both.

He winced as he accepted them. "Sorry. The truck's a bit of a mess. I'm just running behind this week."

She gave him a strained smile. "No problem. Dean, thank you for all that stuff for Sadie. She's been really wanting American Girl for the last few years, and I've tried making it work, but there's always something she needs more than that. I, um, that was sweet of you."

He pulled the truck out onto the main road. "I'm happy to do it. I feel like you're not entirely happy with me. I should've asked but I got carried away."

She didn't say anything for a moment, and he stole a glance. She was staring out the passenger window and he knew there was nothing that interesting, since it was pitch-black country roads. "Of course not. It really was the nicest thing. And you did too much. It really was too much, but how can I be mad at that? You've given Sadie things I never would have been able to. Sometimes I think a little indulgence is good. I guess in this case it was a lot of indulgence, but she hasn't had the easiest of childhoods."

He reached across the seat and took her hand in his. "I'd give her the entire world if you'd let me. I think you both deserve a lot of indulgence, and I'd do anything to be the one to give it to you."

She squeezed his hand. "You're too good to us. Even tonight, I know you've been burning the candle at both ends and you went ahead and planned all this. You didn't have to."

His stomach clenched as he turned down the road that would lead them to downtown Wishing River. He kept his eyes peeled for a spot outside Tilly's Diner and pulled into a spot right in front of the diner. He put the truck in park and faced Hope. Her profile was to him, but he already knew this was bad. "I…I didn't think there would enough time to go out of town for dinner. And I knew it was…lasagna night and…"

Who the hell had he become? Had he suddenly turned forty? Hope was the woman he'd wanted for years and they were finally together and he thought that bringing her to her best friend's diner on lasagna night was an acceptable answer? He looked around his truck, noticing the dust on the dash and the mud on the hood. And Hope was dressed like a million bucks. Shit. He'd screwed it all up.

She turned to him and offered him a cheery smile. "Lasagna night is my favorite."

As they walked into the crowded diner and found a booth near the back, he was already rehearsing what he was going to say to her. This was a shitty date, and it was all his fault. He was supposed to make her feel special, not like they were two friends going to the local diner. Once they sat down, he leaned forward to take her hand in his, when Mrs. Busby, Martin Donnelly's good friend and resident busybody zoomed over to them as though she'd just received an APB that they had walked into the restaurant. "How wonderful to see you both here together!"

Hope offered her a wan but warm smile. "Hi, Mrs. Busby. It is lasagna night, after all."

Mrs. Busby nodded. "Exactly why we're here. Nice to see you, too, Dr. Stanton. I'll have you know I'm keeping an eye on Martin. He thinks he's Tyler's age again! Been out there every day on horseback and in this weather too," she said with a huff.

Dean forced a smile. "Well, I think the best medicine for Martin is doing what he loves. Once a rancher, always a rancher."

She nodded. "You're right. I'm a worrier, I guess. But he is smitten over that grandbaby of his, not that I'm not. She's the apple of everyone's eye!"

Dean grinned. "She is that."

She glanced back and forth between them as though a lightbulb had just gone off. "Well…I'll leave the two of you to enjoy lasagna night. It really is wonderful. Sally in the kitchen has mastered Lainey's recipe. I should get back to my own friend. Poor Mrs. Collins," she said with a dramatic sigh.

Dean shifted in his booth, trying his damndest

to look like he was interested in whether or not Sally was doing a good job with Lainey's recipe or what was wrong with "poor, Mrs. Collins."

"Is she all right?" Hope asked. To her credit, she looked as though she actually cared.

"She's recently widowed. For the third time." She said it in a theatrical sort of whisper-yell and then she proceeded to make three very exaggerated signs of the cross. One, he was assuming, for each of her dead husbands.

He glanced over at Hope, whose face had turned white as the napkin in front of her. Hell. This date was going from bad to worse. "That's tragic. And thankfully *rare*," he said, trying to keep the irritation from his voice.

Mrs. Busby's eyes widened. "Of course! Oh, of course it is. But it's such a tragedy. There she was, each time thinking she was going to get her happily-ever-after, only to end up burying another husband. Yes, yes, I should get back to her," she said, before turning faster than she usually moved.

Dean let out a rough sigh and faced Hope. He hated seeing how pale she was. God knows, she was probably thinking about Brian now. And then probably about how she never wanted to take that kind of risk again. And who could blame her at this point? Hell, they were sitting in a diner. That was the best time he'd shown her. Hell.

"This was not how tonight was supposed to go."

. . .

Hope glanced over at Dean when he didn't turn onto her street. Their date had gone from bad to worse. From the moment he'd arrived at her house with all those American Girl toys for Sadie, she had been wary. It'd been kind, sweet. Extremely generous.

And if it hadn't been for her own insecurities, she would've been completely excited for Sadie. Except all she could think of was how it had taken her almost five years to try to save some extra money to buy Sadie one doll and Dean had come in with half the store.

But there was more. Celeste. He had taken Celeste to the country club in his "nice" car and he had taken Hope to the diner in his muddy truck. If she hadn't ever met Celeste, she wouldn't be thinking any of this. It was that he had chosen all those elegant things for Celeste and for Hope, he'd picked the usual. Like…she wasn't that special. And how could she compare to Celeste? There was no comparison.

She glanced down at her nails, painted a glossy pale pink Sadie had picked out. But they were short. And Sadie had begged to do at least one nail, so Hope's pinky now had a giant clump of nail polish on the end. Her *only* nail polish because her organic nail polishes were ridiculously expensive. But even though she thought she did a pretty decent manicure; it was nothing compared to Celeste's professional one. And, lastly, she worried maybe Dean hadn't taken her to any of those places because...he thought she wouldn't fit in. That maybe she would embarrass him. And that broke her heart. She was embarrassed. And where could they ever go from here?

"You, uh, don't have to be back anytime soon, do you?"

Dean's gruff voice broke though the silent air and she realized they were turning onto his family's property. Estate was more like it. She broke out in a cold sweat at the idea of seeing his father again.

She glanced over at him, wondering at the hard expression of his profile. "No, I guess not. I didn't think we'd be coming to your...house," she said, even though they drove right by the enormous house that was lit up like Vegas. Everything was lit. The water features. The garages. The landscaping. But Dean passed by all those things until they reached a dirt road and he picked up speed.

"Good," was the only reply.

"Should I be concerned you're taking me into the mountains where no one knows where I am?" She didn't do surprises well.

He let out a low laugh. He took her hand in his and squeezed it. "You're always safe with me, Hope."

Her heart raced at the sincerity and thickness in his deep voice. At the way he reached across for her hand. At the way his hand felt in hers. She shrugged off her disappointment at their date, telling herself that none of that mattered, and just tried to guess where he was taking her.

He slowed the truck and, in the distance, she could see the twinkling lights coming from what looked like a small cabin. A minute later Dean parked the truck and hopped out. He opened her door and instead of letting her climb out, he picked her up.

She yelped with surprise as he carried her over to the covered porch. "What is this? What are you doing?"

"You've got these gorgeous shoes on and I already made you walk across the mud once."

He set her down and pulled out his keys, unlocking the front door. "Come on in."

She walked through the open door and he followed her in. Her gaze roamed the small cabin, with its log walls and rustic wood floor. There was a utilitarian kitchen, round table, two couches with a coffee table sitting in front of a stone, wood-burning fireplace. There were two doors, one she assumed was a bedroom and the other maybe a bathroom. She had no idea what this was. Or whose it was. Until she saw Dean's battered cowboy hat on the coatrack and his work boots. And the duffel bag he brought to the hospital.

She turned to him, where he was in front of the fireplace. "This is *your* house?"

He fiddled with the fire he'd started and then stood, cramming his hands into the front of his jean pockets. "It is. It was my grandparents'. I moved here after my grandfather died. He left it to me in his will."

Her mouth dropped open. "I…I wouldn't have guessed."

"My best childhood memories were with him. And Morgan and my grandmother. They worked themselves to the bone. They were simple people, good people. Morgan and I would learn everything about ranching by my grandfather's side. My grandmother was a doctor. On the days she wasn't working, she'd cook these incredible meals. They were true partners. It wasn't one thing they did; it was everything. It was the heart they did everything with. There was this deep, deep love that was felt from the moment we walked through the door. The kind that made you feel like, just for a moment, you could forget every problem in the outside world and sink into this abyss of acceptance and comfort. I remember the smell of homemade biscuits, stew, and freshly baked apple pie. I remember the look in her eyes, the smile on her face, when we walked through the door. Like we were her whole heart. And maybe we were. They were ours."

His hands went to her face, his thumbs gently swiping the tears from her cheeks. She stared into his eyes, into the moisture there, and wondered how she could have ever underestimated him. She raised her hands to frame his face, the stubble there prickling against the palms of her hands. "You…you've blown me away, Dean. You have this heart I never could have imagined. This soul that's so beautiful."

His jaw clenched beneath her hands, his eyes glittering. "You give me too much credit. But you've drawn this from me. These are things I hated thinking about, memories I pushed aside for so long, thinking that I could never feel that way again. But, at your house…when I walk through the door…God, I feel the love there. Between you and Sadie. And me. The way you look at me when I walk through your front door is a thing of dreams. You are. You are all my dreams come true." He leaned forward and kissed her with an intensity that made her knees incapable of standing on their own. He held her to him like he knew, like he'd never let her fall.

"I realized something tonight. I screwed up. It occurred to me I made it look like I didn't care where I took you. You got all dressed up and you look even more beautiful than usual and I'm not sure how that's even possible, since you're the most gorgeous woman I've ever met. The last thing I ever want you to think is that I've taken you for granted or wouldn't want to give you the best of everything."

She blinked furiously past the moisture in her eyes because she wanted to focus on him, on what he was saying, on the look on his handsome face. But he'd already said more than she'd ever dreamed, and she was pretty sure she was going to be crossing that room in seconds. "Dean…it's not. That's not it at all. I'm not high-maintenance and I don't expect candlelight meals and—"

"You should. You deserve all that. I didn't want to run into people I know at those places. My father. I…wanted tonight to be about us. The first time I saw you…really saw you as a woman, was at Tilly's. So many memories of you there. And, frankly, Lainey's lasagna really is the best lasagna I've had outside of Italy."

Hope laughed through her tears. "That's why you chose Tilly's? Because you remember me there?"

He crossed the room slowly, his gaze steady on hers. She stopped breathing when he stood directly in front of her and took her hand in his. "I still remember the look in your eyes. The way your mouth curled up and smiled at me. I was done. But I'm also more than someone with a lot of money. None of that is important to me. This is me," he said, spreading his arms wide.

"Dean...I'm so sorry," she began before he shook his head.

"Don't be. There's nothing to be sorry about. But this is me, Hope. I'd trade all that in a heartbeat for the right people. I know what's important in life and, while I appreciate my heritage and am proud of what my great-grandparents and my grandparents built here, it's not the same with my father in charge. Money has given me a lot. I like that I have security, that I can help people, that I can buy Sadie almost anything she wants, but it's not everything. I'd take my truck over that BMW any day. My father gave me that car with so many damn strings attached, with a backhanded insult, and I hate driving it. I didn't want anything negative attached to tonight. I wanted it to be just about us. But I gave you the wrong impression and I'm sorry. I'll take you anywhere you want to go next time."

She covered her face with her hands and groaned. "Dean, I'm so embarrassed. I feel like I was a total brat. The only reason I even acted disappointed was because I ran into Celeste and became so insecure, so I borrowed this dress and these shoes from Sarah and—"

"Hold on. You ran into Celeste?"

She dropped her hands and nodded. "At the hospital, when we dropped off those cookies."

"But I talked to you and thanked you. You

never mentioned anything."

She cringed. "I can't believe how petty I acted. I just...ugh. I don't know. She's just so beautiful and poised and elegant and—"

"Who?"

She frowned. "Celeste." She crossed her arms. "Come on, Dean, you can't tell me you haven't noticed."

He ran a hand over his jaw. "All I know is when I see her, I picture her with olives stuffed up her nose."

"Pardon?"

He nodded, as though there was nothing abnormal about his response at all. "Celeste and I have known each other since we were babies. She's like my sister. She comes from an equally wealthy and dysfunctional family. We hung out together at all the parties when we were supposed to attend but not really be seen. That's when the olive situation happened. We were five. I got the olives out with tweezers. It was my first surgery."

Hope burst out laughing.

He grinned at her and her stomach flipped over a few times at the sight. How he could be incredibly sexy and handsome and all man, and yet there was still a hint of that boy inside. She wondered at that, at him, when he was little. She wondered if that sadness when he spoke of his regrets was there when he was little. She wondered if he had been lonely, confused at all the turmoil in his house. She touched one side of his face, her eyes on him, as his stubble pricked the palm of her hand.

He met her gaze, took her hand and kissed the inside, her knees wobbling at the touch, at the look in his eyes. She almost forgot what they were talking about until he started speaking. "It's true. She had a crush on Morgan but, since he was four years older than us, he ignored us when he turned thirteen, because as an official teenager he couldn't hang out with us anymore. But, anyway, she also used to cart around this American Girl doll wherever she went. Pretty sad, actually, because she'd pretend it was her younger sister. What was even worse was when I tried to perform open heart surgery on her doll."

Hope inhaled sharply, completely mesmerized by his storytelling, at the warmth and humor in his deep voice. "You didn't."

Dean nodded grimly. "She didn't make it."

Hope laughed, falling for him a little more. How was that even possible? But she could listen to him all day, to his stories, to these pieces of his past, to the boy he was. "That's awful."

He kissed her hand and pulled her into him. She was torn between melting against his hard body and listening to more of his stories. "It is. I was a horrible doctor back then. But I bought her a new one when she expressed horror at the sight of my stiches in her doll's chest. So, when Sadie was talking and talking about American Girl, that reminded me of Celeste. I asked her to meet me for lunch to help me choose a bunch of stuff for Sadie. I wanted it to be a surprise."

Hope shut her eyes as regret stormed her body. She lowered her forehead to Dean's shoulder. "Ugh, I'm so embarrassed."

"I should have told you."

"Never in a million years did I think that would be your explanation. I thought maybe you were embarrassed by me. And I was too embarrassed to tell you I've been scrimping and saving just to get Sadie one American Girl doll and you came in with like the entire store. You had taken her to the country club, in your car, and me…"

She stopped speaking when he placed his hands on either side of her face, looking deep in her eyes. His hands were rough, but his touch soft, tender. His eyes, the expression there, told her everything. Everything about what kind of man he was, what she'd always known on some level but never admitted. She'd been afraid of everything he had to offer. "You are everything to me, Hope. I'd give you everything. I'm sorry. I'm sorry this night was a failure, but I'll try to make it up to you right now." He leaned down and kissed her.

She pulled back only slightly, because she couldn't make herself leave the connection to

him, to his body. "You never have to make everything up to me. This is one of the best nights of
my life. I loved hearing about you, your grandparents, Celeste. I wish I knew you back then. I wish
I could meet that boy with all that mischief inside.
I wish I could meet Morgan."

He clenched his jaw, his thumb slowly grazing
her cheekbone as his hand rested on the side of
her face. "You would like Morgan. He would like
you. As for the kid I was…I like to think I had
some of that spunk Sadie does."

Her heart melted a little more at the affection
in his tone when he said Sadie's name. "You're so
sweet to her. She's always adored you. But everything you've done…the time you spent with her,
teaching her to ride, eating dinner with us, taking
care of her, and now even the American Girl
gifts…Dean, you've become so important to her."

His eyes glittered with emotion. "She uh…I…
she's always had a piece of my heart. And if I'm
laying it all out there, Hope, I live with this guilt."
He stopped speaking abruptly, his voice hoarse as
he squeezed his eyes shut for a moment.

Her heart was pounding as she waited for him
to continue. He ran a hand over his jaw. "Hey,
what are you talking about?" she said gently
when he didn't speak.

The blue eyes that stared at her were filled
with heart-wrenching guilt that made her stomach turn. "I should have tried harder with Brian. I

should have done more to convince him. If I had, then maybe Sadie would have her dad here."

Hope stopped breathing as emotion coursed through her, through every part of her. She felt her love for him deep in her veins, in her heart that felt as though it was going to burst from the ache. "Oh God, Dean. Don't do that to yourself. No one blames you. It wasn't your decision to make. Brian was an adult. Sadie's dad is gone and one day I'll tell her about what a great friend you were to him, because you were. You were there for him in a way that I couldn't be. He'd made his decision before he ever came to you. And you've been there for me, for us, even when I was so mean to you."

He leaned down to kiss her, this time with a fervor and emotion she'd never experienced, and she kissed him back with all of the same. "I want to have it all with you. I want to give you everything."

This time when her knees went weak, he held her up, capturing everything she wanted to say with his mouth. His powerful body against hers, the reassurance, the promise that he was strong enough to face whatever came their way. His hands delved into the hair at her nape, kissing her with an intensity that made it impossible for her to think anymore. As his hands traveled the length of her body, she knew that he'd made her new. He'd given her back her dreams, her faith, her passion.

But more than anything, he'd shown her a side of herself she hadn't known existed. He'd shown her a love that wasn't easy or slow or delicate. He'd shown her a love that was wild and all-consuming. She never wanted to go back to who she was before she loved him.

CHAPTER TWENTY

"I'm sorry to see business hasn't been going well."

Hope gasped at the sound of Dean's father in her office. She spun around quickly, holding a stack of files she was about to place in a box. She'd spent the morning packing, trying not to cry and feel like her dream was dying.

While she knew Dean's plan was a solid one, she couldn't help but feel like a failure. With a new naturopath in town, charging half her rates, there was no way she'd be able to afford rent. She met Dean's father stare and saw none of the warmth she always saw in his son's eyes. He was dressed impeccably, looking less like a rancher, not like a man who got his hands dirty.

She lifted her chin, refusing to be intimidated by him again. She was going to answer and defend herself but it struck her as odd that he would know anything about her business. A trickle of doubt crept through her. "How do you know my business isn't going well?"

He smirked, taking a step forward. Her little office felt far too small suddenly and she forced herself to take a deep breath. "You do have a relationship with my son; it shouldn't be that surprising I would know."

Hope clutched the stack of files to her chest, not believing him. Everything Dean had told her about him made it very easy to see he was up to something. "I've already informed your property manager I'm leaving. Since we're month to month, I've fulfilled the amount of notice required."

"I'm not interested in whether you've fulfilled the terms of your tenancy here. I am interested in that offer I made you a while ago."

Her stomach turned painfully and she forced herself to remain calm, even as he walked toward her. So it hadn't been her imagination last time.

He stood uncomfortably close for a casual conversation and her heart raced, sensing danger. He wouldn't do anything. He was intimidating her. Nonetheless, she scanned her desk and empty shelves for an object she could use to defend herself if needed. There was pepper spray in her purse but that was all the way by the door.

You're overreacting, Hope. Just calm down. He wouldn't hurt you. He's just trying to scare you.

"I'm not interested in your offer, and I made that clear last time. Now, if you'll excuse me, I'm trying to finish packing. Dean will be here any minute to pick me up." She added that last bit hoping it would scare him off.

"Dean isn't coming here now. He was just called into the hospital."

Dread pooled in her stomach, but she refused to let him see her fear. "I wonder what Dean will think of your offer?"

"I think he'd probably laugh at it and not believe you. Listen, sugar, I'm going to get to the point; you're not good enough for my son. He has a bright future ahead of him and I don't want you ruining it. Do you not even care that the woman he was almost engaged to is the heiress to a corporation even larger than ours? You're ruining his chances at a different life."

She wasn't going to let his dad throw her off; she could worry about that later. "Dean is a grown man. He can decide for himself."

"Clearly you have a hold on him. He was always the type to go after the sparkly new object. I can see why you appeal to him. I can offer you money. I can get you an office double this size for free. I can make sure that other business leaves town and I can make you very happy in ways that my son can't."

Hope didn't know if she wanted to throw up or yell at him. She knew he was toying with her and she knew hands down that Dean would believe her. She couldn't process what all this was going to mean for them, though, or how she was impacting Dean's life, or how it would feel to know his father thought so little of her. She'd deal with that later. Right now she needed to get him out of here. "You're disgusting. You don't know your son at all. I don't need you to help my business, I don't need you for anything."

"Right, because you've got my son running around your place like a pathetic lap dog, doing whatever you want, paying your rent increase. What exactly are you giving him in return?"

Her heart stopped for a moment. "What?"

"Stop pretending you don't know my son has been paying the property management company the difference in your rent each month. What are you going to beg him to do next? Run that new business out of town? So, he's doing that, he's fixing up your shack, he's playing daddy to a child that isn't his…yes, you're a real prize, Ms. Roberts. You've really done a lot for his career."

Hope forced herself to keep her chin up even though she felt like crawling under her desk and trying to sort out everything he was telling her. He made it all sound ugly and dirty. And Dean paying her rent…she had no idea how he could have done that without telling her. She forced herself to speak and not show him how he was quickly gaining the upper hand. "I had no idea he was paying my rent. As for the rest, you'd never understand. Your son loves us. He is nothing like you. I never forced him to do anything. And that business that happened to appear in a town this small? I know you're behind it."

"I gave you a chance with me. None of this had to be this way. Stay out of Dean's life. I have plans for him. You stay out of his life and nothing will happen to you."

She tried to cross the room, determined to get away from him if he wouldn't leave. When he grabbed her arm, she stopped breathing. His grip was powerful, his strength as obvious as the anger in his eyes. "Let go of me."

He tugged her over to him. "I made you an offer before you were with him. You should have taken it."

"How could you think I would have any kind of...relationship with you? That's disgusting. You're disgusting. He is your son. Is this what you said to Morgan's girlfriend? Maybe she was too young and too naïve to see you for what you really are. Anyone who would do this to their sons can't love them."

"You know nothing about my sons, about our life. You don't know who Dean really is. I know. He's like me, that's why he's stayed with me all these years."

"He's nothing like you."

"Wrong answer," he snarled, twisting her arm.

Hope managed to kick him in the kneecap, catching him by surprise. He cursed, releasing her arm as his knees buckled to the ground. "Get out. Get out of here and you'll be lucky if I never tell Dean about your offers, or you showing up here."

He slowly stood, smoothing his jacket before he set a deadly gaze on her. "This isn't over. Not by a long shot."

Only when she heard the downstairs door shut did she let out a ragged breath. She ran to the window, peeking through the blinds to make sure he had left. Her eyes blurred with tears as she watched him get into his shiny black Mercedes sedan and pull away from the curb. She started shaking uncontrollably, letting go of the files and slumping into the desk chair. What had just happened? How could he be Dean's father?

As much as she hated him, doubt did trickle in. Was she complicating Dean's life? How could she let him give up everything for them? She would have to tell him about the first time his dad had given her his offer, and he would wonder why she hadn't told him before. But he'd believe her. Dean was nothing like his father. He was a thousand times a better man than his father. Just because Dean had stayed behind didn't mean he was like his dad.

She stared at her small office, everything she'd ever worked for. For Dean's family this place was nothing. It was the size of a closet, but for her it had been a symbol of her hard work paying off. And what did Dean have now? Because of her, he was stuck working three jobs. He was repairing old structures and helping her plan a business. He was an important person. She could have hired a handyman to do what he was doing. Maybe she was holding him back from living the best life he could.

She needed to tell him everything.

· · ·

Dean hopped up the front steps of Hope's house, a sense of optimism he hadn't felt in ages humming through him. Even though he'd worked all day at the hospital, and he needed to just go home and crash, he wanted to see Hope. It was past Sadie's bedtime, but it was too early for Hope to be asleep.

Just as he was about to lightly knock, the door opened and Hope flung herself into his arms. He held on tightly, feeling a tremor run through her. "I think I could get used to this," he said, pulling back to kiss her.

He frowned when he caught sight of her red-rimmed eyes. "Hey, what's wrong? Is Sadie okay?"

She nodded, closing the door behind him. "I just tucked her in. You look tired. Do you want to crash here? Have you eaten? I have leftovers." She'd already moved away from him and was opening the fridge, her movements jerky and her voice coming out fast.

He joined her at the fridge, closing it and reaching for her hand. "I already ate. Hey, what's going on?"

She took a shaky breath and picked up a glass

of wine that was sitting on the counter. "Do you want wine? Actually, this wine is cheap, never mind."

He frowned. Why was she saying that? She put the bottle down, her face pale. Her hand was shaking, and then he noticed a red mark on her forearm. A sliver of dread ran down his spine. "Hope, what happened to your arm?"

She rolled her sleeve down. "It looks worse than it is."

He tore his gaze from her white face to her arm, gently reaching for it. He clenched his teeth hard and tried not to jump to conclusions, but his mind was already flashing through the possibilities and the women he'd seen in his ER with similar markings. But that didn't make sense. Maybe an angry or unstable patient? "Tell me what happened," he said. Hope was as stubborn as he was, and he knew if she didn't want to tell him something she probably wouldn't.

Her chin wobbled and she raised her green eyes to his and everything inside him went numb. "You have to promise me this stays between us. You can't tell anyone."

He ran a hand over his jaw, trying to hide the alarm and anger coursing through him. She was hiding something. Someone had done this to her and he had to pretend to be calm enough that she would tell him. It wasn't the time for him to say that when he found out who'd touched her like that, he'd find him and make sure he never came near her again. "Why would I have to promise that?"

"Dean," she choked.

He'd say anything to get her to speak right now, because this was torture. Seeing her hurt, physically, emotionally, was unbearable. "I'm sorry. You know you can tell me anything."

"I…I haven't been completely honest with you about your dad…there was something I left out. That night after you drove me home, he um, he sort of implied that if I had nothing to do with you…he and I could, uh…it wasn't really overt and I tried to brush it off, thinking that maybe I was imagining things. But then this morning…he came into my office."

He gripped the edge of the counter so tightly his fingers felt like they were going to split in two. This wasn't what he expected. His dad. Hell. Morgan's words about wanting to kill him pushed into his thoughts. Now he knew.

This was all his fault. He should've shut this down years ago. He should have walked out like Morgan. But he knew better than Hope and he knew that nothing his father did was by accident. He forced himself to take a breath. *Get it together, Dean. Don't lose your shit.* "What did he want?"

"He…came in and made me a similar offer. He blames me for ruining your life. He told me he'd get me a new office, for free, the same offer to be with him, to leave you so that you could get back together with Celeste…"

Dean knew there wasn't much more he could handle without smashing something, and that was the last thing he was going to do in this house. "When did he touch you?"

She folded her arms across her chest and his heart felt like it was going to explode in his chest. She looked scared and vulnerable and that was the opposite of who this woman was. Hope was invincible and his dad had taken that away from her. "When did he touch you?" He repeated.

Her gaze darted around the room and rested somewhere over his shoulder. "I wanted him to leave. I told him none of that would happen. He reached out and grabbed me and I kicked him in the kneecap."

"He touched you."

She nodded.

"In anger."

Her eyes filled with tears and he gripped his rage and shoved it away for a moment, for her. "I'm sorry," he said, his voice sounding harsh to his ears. "I'm so damn sorry, Hope. He had no right. This is my fault."

"It's not your fault, I just want to forget about it," she said, reaching for the wine again.

"Forget about it? Hope, we can't forget about this. I'm going over there right now. I never want him near you again."

She poured a glass of wine but didn't pick it up. "Dean, I'm fine. I can defend myself."

He shoved his hands in his pockets, trying to be in two places at once. He needed to be here for Hope, but his mind was on his father. "You shouldn't have to. Especially from my father. Hope, this isn't okay. You should have called me."

She frowned. "I wasn't going to call you at work."

"Why? Yes, call me. Anytime, wherever I am. You call me. That's what people in relationships do. Don't minimize his behavior. This ends today," he said, walking away from her, the anger for his father rising like a tidal wave, and he needed to get out of here before it spilled out of him. He needed to leave before Sadie woke up and saw him like this.

"Wait, where are you going?" Hope said, following him to the door.

"To see my dad," he said, yanking the door open.

Hope followed him onto the porch. "What? No. You promised you wouldn't."

"That was before I knew what you were going to say. Hope, we're not teenagers, pinky swearing secrets. I'm ending all of this. My relationship with him. Everything."

"No, no you're not. He's your dad and I'm not going to be the one to come between you. You will lose everything, Dean. He has so much power. He will cut you off and you will lose your rightful inheritance."

"Inheritance? That's what he's telling you? Hope, I don't give a shit about any of that. This was over a long time ago. He's my father in name only, and I am nothing like him. I'm not going to live my life following his rules."

"What about the promise you made to your grandfather?"

He ran his hands down his face. "My grandfather would tell me to do what I'm doing. There's no way he would have condoned this kind of behavior. He was repulsed by my father. He would understand what I'm doing. I should have realized that sooner."

"What about Celeste? You were in a relationship?"

He paused, frowning as the insecurity in her voice registered. "Not a real one. There's no one I want. Celeste has her own life. I told you, we're like brother and sister. I couldn't care less about money or who my father thinks I should be with."

"But, Dean, that's your inheritance. That's generations of your family. It's your grandfather, and now I'm in the middle of this. You can't go to him. This is my situation to deal with."

"Wrong. It's mine. You wouldn't be in this situation if it weren't for me. Do you actually think I'm going to let him go around town threatening you? What if he shows up here? What if Sadie is here? He cornered you. You were alone and he touched you. That's it. We're done," he said, marching down the porch, his rage fueling him as he pictured Hope in that office alone with his father.

"Dean! Stop it. You don't get to make decisions for me. He told me you were paying the difference in my rent. You should've told me. I was humiliated."

Dammit. "This is all irrelevant now. Would you have accepted my help?"

"Of course not, but I'd have had my pride. He stood there and called me white trash and he started listing all this stuff...you being a handyman here, raising Brian's kid...I don't want to be that woman who takes you away from your family legacy. You'd lose it all. What about your grandparents? And their house?"

"My choice to make."

"I would feel guilty forever, Dean, knowing you gave all that up...how could I live with myself? That is not just a family business. That's legacy."

He scrubbed his hands down his face, itching to move on, to confront his father. "I know what I want, and what I want is you and Sadie. I haven't been with anyone in over two years because of you. If that's not a sign of my faithfulness and my decision, then I don't know what is. I'm not standing here anymore defending my actions. I'm going to go and defend you now, to the man who hurt you."

"I'm asking you not to."

He stilled. "What?"

"I'm asking you not to say anything, just like you promised. I don't want to start a life like that with you. With you leaving your family for me. You breaking your promise to your grandfather for me. With all that hate. And you promised me you wouldn't say anything."

"Yeah, well, that was before I knew who was involved."

"Just leave it alone."

"No. I'm mad as hell, I'm pissed off."

"Just calm down."

"No. I won't calm down. You've got to stop telling me what to do. I know my dad. I know what this is all about."

"What? I'm not telling you what to do."

He ran a hand over his jaw, his mind on his dad, on the truth behind what he'd tried with Hope. "You are, Hope. You think I'm going to what? Sit down and have a glass of wine and ignore the bruise forming on your arm put there by my father? No way in hell."

"You're breaking a promise to me and letting your anger control you."

He tried to see it from her perspective, he tried to tone it down and give her what she needed. But all he saw when he looked at her was his father entering her office, alone, and grabbing her. "My dad threatened you. He hurt you. There's a line that always has to be drawn, Hope. *He* crossed. Now I deal with it."

"This is getting way too out of hand. I'm a grown woman, I've been on my own long before you."

His stomach churned as the futility of this argument hit him like a train. He was being held to a standard he'd never meet. A man who was long gone. "I will never be Brian."

Her face went white and she took a step back. "What are you talking about?"

He ran a hand over his jaw, the tension in his body ready to burst. But he couldn't hold it in anymore and he didn't know where the hell all this was going, but it needed to be said. "I'm not a twenty-four-year-old man. I'm thirty-four years old. I've seen things, I've lived through things, I've had people die in front of me. I've had to tell family their child or spouse is dead. I've held strangers in my arms as they fall apart after the loss of the only person in their lives. I was raised in a house without love. I get pissed off.

"I'm the farthest thing from perfect, but damn it, Hope, I'm not going to hide who I am.

"I want to build it all, from scratch, with you, and I will defend everything we're creating. So, if someone comes in and threatens that, you can be damn sure I'm not going to stand around and play nice. If that bothers you, if my anger right now is offensive to you, then there's no place to go from here. I won't ever be the man you really want, and I'm going to walk out that door and never come back. My dad touched you in anger. I won't stand for that. If that makes me a backward barbarian to you, then we were never meant to be."

Tears fell from her eyes, and he turned toward the door because he couldn't stand to watch her cry. But everything, all the emotions coursing through him, were jumbled. His father's actions. His father's own assessment of him, of Dean's inability to love, were forcing him to leave. He didn't know what was wrong with him, but his first issue was protecting Hope and Sadie.

"What are you even saying?" she said in a choked whisper.

If he were like his grandfather, he wouldn't have said that to her. He would have told her he loved her and would be back. But he couldn't. Because he didn't know anything about himself anymore. He didn't know if he was what she needed. If he could give her the love she needed, if he could give Sadie the love she needed. Right now, he was so far from being the family man Hope wanted him to be. He cleared his throat and opened the door, his back still to her. "I need to go."

CHAPTER TWENTY-ONE

"What were you thinking?" Dean stood in the doorway of his father's home office. He dug his fingers into the doorjamb to divert some of his anger.

His father looked up, his face relaxed as he put his pen down. "What are you so upset about, Dean? You're not my hotheaded kid. Pour yourself a drink and sit down."

Dean braced his hands on either side of the door, watching his father through a seedy haze of rage and a trickling of clarity. As a kid, he'd come in here searching for a father who didn't exist. He didn't know how many times he'd try and be disappointed. Nothing had ever been good enough—perfect grades, awards, graduating at the top of his class, nothing. Nothing had ever been good enough. At some point, before he was a teenager, he'd stopped trying.

"I will never sit down with you again, ever share a drink with you again. What did you do to Hope?"

He shrugged one shoulder. "The truth. You don't belong with her."

"But you do?"

"It was a test. She's not my type."

"I think your type is whoever your sons are with. The only reason you slept with Morgan's fiancé was because you wanted to show him that you could. It's always about power with you.

"Except the only difference is that Hope didn't fall for it like Morgan's girlfriend did. Hope recognizes you for the scum that you are, and you couldn't stand that. So, because she said no to you, you tried to make her life miserable. You tried to ruin her business. You tried to ruin us. Our relationship. All of it is a sick game for you."

"You always wanted to assume the worst about me, thinking you're so perfect. You're taking her word over mine. What would you say if I told you she came on to me?"

"I'd say you're full of shit. I'd say you're desperate now because you know you crossed so many damn lines. I don't care about any of it, but I want to know the part about you grabbing her."

His father squared his shoulders. It took everything in Dean to keep still, to keep control of his anger. "It wasn't that big of a deal. What, did she come whining to you and now you're playing the hero?"

Dean cut him off and pinned him to the wall. He stared deep into his father's eyes, knowing this would be the last time. His father was everything Dean never wanted to be. "You stay away from her. Away from her daughter. I will make your life a living hell if you ever go near Hope again, if you ever talk to her again. You think you have all the power? I've made my own friends in this town. I've earned respect, too. I'll expose you for the abusive, misogynistic animal that you are. I will humiliate you. You may think you still have all the power but you don't. I am thirty-five years younger than you, and you don't intimidate me. Ever again," he said, leaning in with his forearm to make his point clear. His father's face had finally gone white.

"You actually think you'd be anything without me?"

Dean loosened his grip slightly, knowing his father was partially right. Maybe. But he had an answer to that too. This would all be over today. What had kept him here? Duty. Loyalty. Guilt because of the promise he'd made to his grandfather. "The only reason I'm here is because of the promise I made to Grandpa. He knew you were trouble. You want to talk about shame? He was ashamed of his son for his lack of character, his lack of morals. He asked me to watch over you. But I'm done. You crossed too many lines. Hurting Hope was the last one. You cost me so much already. A mother. A brother."

He scoffed. "Your mother didn't want you or Morgan. She did it to please me. And my father was a pathetic sap."

Dean refused to be sidetracked. "He wasn't. You were just jealous of any man around you who was better than you. As for Mom, you are to blame. You threw all that love back in her face. All that devotion and love she had for you. You didn't deserve her. You don't deserve any of us. And as for what you think you did for me? I don't think you were the one who went through med school."

"But I'm the one who paid the bills."

Dean had already anticipated this. He'd already known walking in here what he was going to do. This was years in the making, and he'd planned for it. He released his arm and took a step back, watching with grim satisfaction as his father rubbed his neck. He pulled out the check he'd already prepared and slapped it down on the table. "There's the cost of medical school and college."

His father's face went white then red.

Dean belatedly remembered his BMW had been given as a gift when he'd graduated medical school and the truck he was driving belonged to the ranch. He pulled his keys out of his pocket and dropped them on the table without thinking twice. "And now I think we're even."

His father stood there with that stony expression Dean knew so well. He'd seen it with every accomplishment Dean had ever had. His father was proud of him when others were around. He was proud to boast about him publicly, but privately Dean would never be good enough. And if he'd gotten it all wrong, if somehow he'd misinterpreted his father for thirty plus years, then he'd find out right now.

He knew his father would cash that check, because spite and money had always meant more than family. "What about your grandfather? I thought you promised him you'd stay and claim your legacy? What a disloyal shit you are, Dean. Going back on a promise to your grandfather for a woman."

Dean gripped the back of his neck. His promise was the only thing that hurt about him leaving. He turned to his dad, one last time. "Grandfather would have understood. Even he couldn't have imagined how low you could sink. There is no way he'd expect me to stay after this. I know that now. He loved Grandma. He understood what that meant. He would have gone to hell and back for Grandma and there's no way he'd ever put up with another man hurting her. So right now, I think if he's watching over me, he'd be clapping. So this is goodbye," Dean said, walking out of the office, out of the monster of a house, and into the cold March night.

He walked down that long driveway, March rain hitting him in the face, bitter wind stealing the rest of the heat from his body, yet he'd never felt freer. But as he walked and walked, he realized he had nowhere to go. He had no car to get into. And he'd walked out on Hope and broken her heart.

He stopped for a moment, just one, and stared in the direction of his grandparents' cabin, leaving their memories behind, the only thing keeping him from feeling completely at peace. "I'm sorry, Grandfather," he said under his breath, before he walked away.

CHAPTER TWENTY-TWO

"Thanks, man," Dean said as he hopped into the passenger seat of Cade's truck half an hour later. He was chilled to the bone but at least it was warm in the truck. He wasn't sure what he was going to say. The last thing he felt like doing was talking.

"So should I ask why you have no car or truck?" Cade said, once they were on the road again.

"Maybe after I've had a drink," Dean said flatly.

Cade let out a short laugh. "Fair enough."

Dean let out a frustrated breath, turning to look out at the mountains in the distance. For a second, he let his gaze linger on the side mirror and his family home slowly shrinking into the background. A strange feeling he couldn't quite pinpoint, couldn't quite feel comfortable with, sat in his gut. He'd thought he'd be filled with relief. This day had been coming in his mind for years, but he never thought he'd actually go through with it.

Family was something he thought would trump everything else. He had tried, God, he'd tried to keep his grandfather happy. But too many lines had been crossed, the ultimate one being Hope's well-being.

He'd hoped people could change. That was why he'd put up with the bullshit for so long. He had seen how Tyler had walked away from his father and how he'd suffered for it. He'd witnessed Tyler's dad fall apart without his son and his wife. He knew Cade didn't have any family to speak of.

So Dean had always put up with this, thinking that because he'd been given everything his friends hadn't—that he'd been given every material thing he could ever want, that he was going to inherit a lucrative ranching business, more millions than he knew what to do with—that he couldn't complain. But Hope... He'd learned what love was. As cheesy as it sounded, watching her raise Sadie on her own, giving that little girl the very best of herself, without all the material things, brought to light the shitty stuff he'd kept buried.

He'd never complained to his friends about his home life. It had made him uncomfortable. Not that any of the three of them were great with sharing feelings, but it was different. He felt almost ashamed of everything he'd been given. How could he complain when he'd grown up in a mansion while Cade hadn't had a home at all?

"Dean. Where are we going?"

Dean ran his hands down his face. "I have no

damn clue. I can sleep at the hospital."

Cade shot him a look. "Do you really think I'm going to let you sleep at the hospital? You're coming to my place, man. We have rooms to spare."

Dean slouched down in his seat. "Not that I don't love Sarah, but I don't think I have an ounce of civility in me. I can't sit around shooting the shit and being polite."

"I get it. But you know Ty and I won't let you blow this. Whatever it is that's happened, we'll help you out. You've always been there for us, Dean. And just because you somehow managed to become a doctor doesn't mean you're smart in the real world."

Dean almost laughed. He would've liked a biting retort but he didn't even have it in him, because all he could think about was Hope's face when he stupidly ranted about not being like Brian. "Great. Just what I needed to hear right now. Thanks a lot."

Cade grinned as he pulled into the driveway that led to his house. "That's what I'm here for. Listen, let's go inside. I'll invite Ty over and we can figure out what the hell you're going to do."

Dean stared despondently out the windshield. "I've lost everything, Cade. Hope, Sadie, my family, my money, my house, my inheritance. And I broke my word to my grandfather. All of it. And the only damn things I care about are Hope and

Sadie, and I don't think I'll get them back."

His friend cast a worried gaze in his direction. Cade was never worried. "You will. At least you know what matters. Let's go inside. I've got a bottle of whiskey with your name on it."

Dean followed him through the front door of the large home. He forced a polite smile as the long-time housekeeper came rushing toward them. Edna Casey was both beloved drill sergeant and matriarch and usually she brought a smile to Dean's face with her stiff, but well-intended remarks. "My goodness, I can tell trouble is afoot. Dearest Doctor Stanton, come in and let this home be your sanctuary."

Cade could barely hold onto his laughter as he crossed the large room to the liquor cabinet. "Yes, Dean. This sanctuary also has whiskey so sit your sorry as—yourself down on the couch and I'll pour you a glass."

"Mrs. Casey, thank you for your hospitality. I'll stay for a little while. Please, though, call me Dean," he said, sitting on the couch opposite Cade and reaching for the glass that was already waiting for him. Good friends.

"Oh, I could never be so informal," she said, her thin hand going to her cheek.

He almost smiled. "Please."

She reached out for the glass of whiskey Cade was holding for her. Edna was known for being able to drink any cowboy under the table and walk a straight line. "Then you must call me Edna."

"Then call me Dean."

"How about Dr. Dean?"

Ah hell. A lump formed in his throat and he thought of little Sadie, the only person in the world who called him Dr. Dean. He stared at the whiskey in his glass and wished for things as if he were a kid again.

"I'm sorry, I didn't mean to upset you. I knew that was too informal," Mrs. Casey clucked as she hurried about and unfolded a large, red knit blanket.

Cade scowled at him. "What the hell, Dean?"

"Not at all, Edna. You'll just have to call me Dean," he said with a nod, worriedly looking at the blanket as she approached him.

She gave him a nod and downed her whiskey. "I will try my hardest. But you look chilled to the bone. Here, bundle yourself up in this blanket."

Dean sat still as she proceeded to place the blanket on him. He eyed Cade, whose eyes were dripping with tears of laughter. "Edna, I'm fine. Thank you."

She straightened, her cheeks turning red. "Of course. Now, I'm going to give you men some privacy. I'll bring out some snacks, though. I have just the type of reinforcements for you men," she said as she marched out of the room.

The doorbell rang before Dean could make a remark.

Cade stood. "I've got it. That's Tyler," he said, crossing the room.

Tyler took one look at him and shook his head as he sat down next to Cade. "I knew it was bad, but not this bad. Why are you wrapped up like a sausage?"

Dean untangled himself from the blanket, even though it had been warm. But then again, that's what whiskey was for. "I was trying to be polite. Anyway, has Hope reached out to Lainey?"

Tyler poured a glass of whiskey and shook his head. "Nope. Are you going to fill us in?"

"My dad made a pass at Hope," he said flatly, staring at his empty glass. Then the image of the marks on her arm floated before him and he re-filled his glass and downed it.

Tyler choked on his whiskey just as Edna walked in making the sign of the cross with one hand and laying out a massive charcuterie platter on the coffee table. He had no idea who could even eat at a time like this. Both his friends filled their plates like it was the last supper.

"Pretend I was never here, Doctor," Edna whispered theatrically as she bustled out of the room.

"Are you kidding me? What did Hope do?" Tyler asked.

Dean dragged his hands down his face and leaned back in the sofa. "She told him to get out. Then he grabbed her, left marks," he managed to say through clenched teeth.

When he looked over at his friends, both their faces were taut and their eyes flashing. "What the hell," Cade bit out.

"Welcome to my wonderful family. And then, to make things worse, instead of being supportive or understanding I got pissed off. We ended up in a huge argument and I brought up Brian and how I'll never be like him. And, honestly, I don't think she'll ever be over him. I think I've wasted the last few years loving a woman who is unreachable."

There was a long pause, and he knew things were even worse than he thought when neither of them ate anything on their plates. "What were you doing at your dad's when I picked you up?" Cade asked.

"What do you think? I ended it. This relationship lasted way too many years."

"You knew he was like this?" Tyler asked.

Dean shrugged. "He's always been a cheat. He's the reason Morgan left town. He screwed his girlfriend and Morgan found out."

"What the hell, Dean? Have you been living a double life?" Cade said, refilling his glass of whiskey.

Dean shrugged. "Like anyone needed to hear about my problems. Poor little rich boy, right?"

The silence in the room was uncomfortable and the three of them sat there with their dumb feelings. They all reached for the bottle at the same time. Since he was the loser today, he won and poured himself a glass first. "You can stop staring now."

"Of course we would have made fun of you for being the poor little rich boy, but we would have also had your back. You could have given us a chance, man," Tyler said roughly.

Dammit. "This is all getting turned around. This isn't supposed to be about me and things I've held back. This is supposed to be about me starting over and finding a place to live."

"With Hope. You two haven't tortured all of us for the last few years only to end up single. No one wants to sit at a table with you two at River's after this. Find a way to fix this, Dean," Cade snapped.

So much for friends who sympathized. "I walked out on her."

Tyler leaned forward. "So, walk back in. Explain and apologize. How do you know she's not waiting for you right now?"

Dean propped his feet on the coffee table. His gut told him she wasn't. "I know things. Lots of things."

"Right. It's just us who know nothing because you've basically been living a double life. Are you even a doctor? I did doubt that right from the start," Tyler said, barely hiding his smile as he lifted his glass to his lips.

Idiots. "Funny. But yes, I'm a doctor and it's a damn good thing or not only would I not have a house or a car, I also wouldn't have a job."

"You should call Morgan."

Dean groaned and leaned his head against the couch. "I have enough problems right now."

"You need to go back to Hope and explain why you acted like such a dick," Cade said, starting to eat from the heaping plate of food.

"I told you. Even if I did, she has Sadie to consider. I'm pretty sure after all this shit with my dad, she's thinking that we are hardly the type of people she wants around her little girl."

"Whoa. Those are a hell of a lot of assumptions you're making," Tyler said.

"Yeah, well, I…I don't think I can give her what she wants. Look at my family. I'm my father's son. My father came on to her and then manhandled her. I think she can do a helluva lot better than me right now."

"Oh, so glad you explained. Well, this is a great plan. So, you're going to do what exactly? Start seeing other people?" Cade said with a disgusted snort. Dean eyed his plate and was tempted to send those perfect cheese cubes flying across the room. But knowing that would send Edna into a frenzy, he sat back on the couch.

"No. I'll go to work and find a place to live. No women. Done with women. And my dad."

"Yeah? You really think Hope, whom I haven't

seen even look at another guy in the last five years, is just going to start dating? You really think you're not the man she wants? Maybe you should let her decide who she wants."

There hasn't been anyone since Brian. Hell. That image. The sound of her voice. The way she felt in his arms plagued him to the point that he needed to squeeze his eyes shut. He'd never, in all his thirty-four years, wanted anyone like he wanted her. They'd both deprived themselves…to be with each other. And he was going to walk away from all of it?

"Dean, you're fooling yourself if you think you can just end things with her.. Lainey has told me, right from the beginning, that you and Hope were meant for each other. You are the man she needs. You are not your father. Don't sell yourself short like that. So go there and lay it all on the line and tell her how much you love her. If she shuts the door in your face, then at least you'll know. Then try again the next day," Tyler said.

Dean held out his empty glass of whiskey, his stomach roiling at the idea of talking about all of this out loud. What had become of his life? He was getting advice from Cade and Tyler. But in all fairness, they were both married. Happily. He took a deep breath. "I haven't actually told her I love her."

Cade frowned. "What are you waiting for?"

Dean shifted his gaze into the bottom of the

glass. "I've never been in love or thought myself capable. Hell, certainly not the kind of love Hope deserves."

"That's bullshit. You've been in love with her for years. You kept a lie for her husband so that you wouldn't hurt her. You let her think the worst of you to protect her. You're fixing up her ranch for no money, working yourself to the bone. You walked away from a legacy, from millions, and you don't think you're capable of love? You don't think that's the kind of love she deserves? Hell, you gave up gluten because she told you to. All of that is the definition of love. What the hell?" Tyler said.

Dean stared at Tyler, focusing on his words, pushing aside the words his father had said about him his entire life. Tyler and Cade knew him. Hope and Sadie knew him. Not his dad. He had no idea that loving someone would bring out these insecurities. "You think she'll shut the door in my face?"

"Depends on how much she likes that face. But in all seriousness, I know we come from very different places, Dean, but in some ways it was the same. I know what it feels like to be told you're a piece of shit. I know what it's like to be raised by people who don't care. It's easy to carry that into adulthood, but if you're not careful, you'll be left with nothing. Having been on the other side, I know that I wasn't living a life before

Sarah. It was sort of half living. This…Sarah, a baby on the way, this is living. They are worth the risk. Don't miss out on all that because of your family, because of your insecurities. You are who Hope needs. Flaws and all, man. Take the chance."

The three of them sat in silence for a long time. Maybe five minutes. He let his friends' words sink in along with the whiskey.

Dean stared at both of them. "I'm going to crash here tonight. Tomorrow, I need to find the best damn pony around."

CHAPTER TWENTY-THREE

Hope sat cross-legged in the corner of Sadie's room and cried like a baby. She'd ruined everything. In her attempt to show Sadie how to be strong and independent she had inadvertently showed her the opposite. Because love was scary and required strength. Being alone and calling all the shots was easier. But allowing herself to be vulnerable, to be loved, to be happy…that was a hell of a lot harder.

Right now, if she could start over with Dean she would. She'd take it right back to that very first day. But she wasn't that same girl. She wasn't a girl anymore. As much as he'd made it clear he was very much a man. Not that she'd needed the reminder; she was a woman. A changed woman. She'd had her world crumble, and she'd had to find the strength to pick herself up again, to make a life for herself and her daughter. And somewhere along the way she'd forgotten how to be brave. She'd forgotten that love was worth the risk. She'd forgotten that she was worth that risk. That she deserved love. She should have told him she was in love with him. She should have told him she trusted him to handle his father.

She should have told Dean it wasn't him, that

it was her, she was the one who was afraid she wasn't enough. She was the single mom making ends meet. She was the mom who thought Target shopping was a splurge and who'd never entered a country club. When his father had shown up… he'd tugged all those insecurities out and exposed them, and a part of her had wanted to hide them again before Dean could decide she really wasn't good enough. She didn't want to be the source of family tension. She…wasn't worth it.

But this was wrong, too. He had left thinking she was mad at him or he wasn't good enough and that she'd been comparing him to Brian. Maybe she had, subconsciously. But not the way he thought. Guilt had been preventing her from going all in. Guilt because her love for Dean was larger than life, larger than she'd ever experienced with Brian, and that made her feel guilty. Dean made the giddy, weak in the knees, kind of happy. Dean made her feel safe, loved. He made her feel like she didn't have to have it all together all the time. He'd shown her he could be her rock. And she'd never experienced that before in her life. It had always been her. She'd been the rock in her relationship with Brian and she had to be the rock for her daughter.

Dean made her want to believe in happily ever after. He was larger than life. He filled their house with something that had been missing, and he was brave and hardworking and…

"Mom? I'm home!"

Hope gasped, swiping at the tears on her face and standing. "Coming, honey!"

But Sadie was already in the room and staring at her. "Are you crying?"

Hope shook her head, frantically trying to come up with a lie. Sadie had never seen her cry. She never wanted her to see her cry. She wanted to be strong for her and never have her think they had things to cry about. But maybe that was silly. What did she know anyway? She'd sent Dean away. She cleared her throat. "No, no. I was just dusting and started sneezing."

Sadie crossed her arms, narrowing her eyes on Hope. "It's okay if you're crying. I cry a lot. Is it Daddy? Do you miss Daddy?"

Hope sighed and sat on the bed. She should have known. Sadie was getting too old to be told simple white lies and half-truths. "This isn't really about Daddy. It's hard to explain, I guess. I'm so used to dealing with stuff on my own, you know?"

Sadie nodded and sat down beside her. "Is it Dr. Dean? He's not here."

Hope picked at some fluff on the front of her jeans. "It's kind of about Dean."

"Do you love him?"

Hope sucked in a breath and stared at Sadie, who was staring back at her with a wisdom way beyond her years. "Would you be okay if I do?"

Sadie smiled and nodded. "I love him, too.

When I was little, I wished he could be my dad. Not because I don't love Daddy, but I didn't remember him. I still don't. And Dr. Dean was always so nice to me. And I liked the way he looked at you."

Hope's heart ached until she thought it was going to burst open. Her throat hurt and she forced herself to speak. "The way he looked at me?"

She nodded. "Like I look at you, like you're the best person in the whole world."

"What?" Hope whispered.

Sadie smiled at her. "Yeah. When you're not looking or when you're saying something, he smiles, too. And he knows you're the best person in the world, like I do. And you are. You're the best mom in the whole world and I want you to be happy with Dr. Dean."

Hope pulled her onto her lap and held her close. How many times had she held her little girl like this? Sadie had been her anchor in the storm without even knowing it. She'd kept her here; she had made her strong. "I love you, Sadie. You've always made me happy. I am happy. But I do love Dean and I'm so happy that you love him, too."

"Remember that awful blueberry loaf you made?" Sadie said, scrambling off her lap and sitting beside her.

Hope wasn't sure whether she should laugh or cry, remembering that night.

"You know, the one that tasted like sandpaper and Dr. Dean choked on it because it just wouldn't go down his throat?"

"Thanks, Sadie. Yes, I remember."

Sadie gave her a nod of approval and crossed one leg over the other, looking years older. "Well, when I was trying to throw mine out without you catching me, and I offered Dr. Dean a way out, too, he refused. He ate it. He said you worked so hard. He didn't want to hurt your feelings. Mom, he kept coughing and drinking water to try to get it down his throat. I'm going to marry a man who'll eat any kind of awful food I make and I'll do the same for him if he's a horrible cook."

Tears were rolling down Hope's face and she couldn't control her laughter. Everything was in that statement. Her whole heart. Sadie and Dean. They were everything to her.

She was going to need to get it together. But how? How was she going to prove to him she loved him? How was she going to show him he was the man she'd always wanted? That she trusted him with her heart and with Sadie's? That she wanted to go all in, just like him?

She could sing. At River's. Just like last year, when she and Sara had started. But then life had gotten in the way and Hope didn't have regular babysitting and it was just easier to give up altogether. And then there was the fact that she'd sung her and Brian's song there, in front of Dean.

And the look on his face that night, before he'd walked out, had kept her awake many nights. It had encompassed everything she'd come to love about him—everything she'd been afraid of until now. He had a passion in him, a passion for life, for work…for her. And at one time, that had scared her. Not anymore.

She needed to do something special for him. Something that wasn't tied to Brian's memory. His birthday was next week. What had he said about his childhood birthdays? There had never been anything personal. Never a handwritten card, or a homemade cake, or banners. Everything had just been perfect all the time. What had been the one thing he'd wanted? Love from his parents.

Maybe she and Sadie could do that for him. Maybe she could find a way to get him over here, if he ever agreed to see her again. But that's what friends were for. She'd invite them all over and she would give him the birthday party he'd never had. And she would have faith that everything would work out. That Dean did love her. And she wasn't going to hide her love from anyone anymore. And maybe she could show Dean how much she loved him. Maybe she could reunite him with Morgan. She hugged Sadie. "Why don't you go have your snack? It's on the counter. I just need to um, make a couple phone calls. And then after that, would you like to help me plan a surprise party for Dean's birthday?"

Sadie gasped. "I love planning parties! We must make it amazing," she said before running out of the room.

• • •

Two hours later, with a little help from Tyler and Lainey, she was calling Morgan Stanton. Instead of trying to hide this and do it on her own, she'd reached out to Tyler and told him everything. He and Lainey had raced over and the three of them had tracked Morgan down. It had been an easy search—apparently Morgan had made a name for himself in the crypto world. She wished she could reach out to Dean and tell him. He would be so proud of his brother.

Tyler and Lainey were now sitting in the family room with Sadie while she told them what she was planning for Dean's birthday. Hope smiled as she heard Sadie saying something about sprinkles and icing.

Hope's heart raced as the phone continued to ring without an answer, as she waited for Morgan to answer. She paced her bedroom and tried not to panic as it kept ringing. Her gaze went to her bed where she remembered Dean lying there, telling her the secret he'd been holding on to. And the way she'd trembled when he kissed her hand. What she'd give to have him here right now.

"Hello?"

Panic shot through her at the sound of Morgan's deep voice. He sounded like Dean. What if he yelled at her and told her he wanted nothing to do with Dean? What if she was about to make everything worse for Dean? "Um, hi, is this Morgan Stanton?"

"It is. Who's this?"

She took a deep breath. "I'm Hope Roberts… from Wishing River. I'm Dean's…I'm a good friend of Dean's and…I'm wondering if you can help me."

CHAPTER TWENTY-FOUR

Hope stared in horror as the top layer of the chocolate cake she and Sadie were making kept sliding to the side.

What was wrong with her?

She couldn't even bake with regular ingredients. It was a disaster. The first layer wasn't straight and the second was worse, and the third was just downright sad. Hope forced a wobbly smile for Sadie's benefit, as her daughter continued to slather the chocolate icing like the cake was a work of art. "I'm happy Dr. Dean's favorite cake is chocolate."

Hope picked up her spatula and gently tried pressing the cake in the opposite direction, but it was no use. "Why, sweetie?"

"Because it's my favorite, too. Do you think he'll like sprinkles?"

Hope didn't even have time to answer before Sadie started dumping the sprinkles like confetti all over the cake. Really, at this point, how much worse could the cake get? Between this lopsided nightmare and her own nerves about whether or not Dean would actually show up, and when and if he showed up, whether or not he'd forgive her, she was a mess. "We'd better hurry and set the table."

Sadie nodded. "Agreed. At least the cake is done."

Hope glanced out the window, her stomach in knots. It was going to be okay. Morgan would make it in time. He'd promised. When she'd tracked him down in Colorado, she'd hesitated, worried she was about to make a huge mistake. But just as she'd suspected, Morgan had been worried that Dean hadn't forgiven him for leaving. She hadn't even had to persuade him to come out here for the surprise party. Hope gave the cake, which now also contained an entire jar of rainbow-colored sprinkles, one last glance and shuddered. She had no idea how she could have messed this up so badly. It was Lainey's grandmother's famous chocolate cake recipe, and it was Dean's favorite. Whatever. She turned and set her sights on the banner Sadie had decorated for him. She blinked back tears as she stared at it, hanging over the dining room table. Sadie had spent an entire day perfecting the letters and coloring it and adding all the hearts. She knew that even if he couldn't forgive Hope, he'd never reject Sadie, and that might buy her some time to talk and explain.

Hope adjusted the groups of balloons and then walked to the windows. "Everyone should be getting here any minute now."

Sadie ran up to the window. "I can't wait! We've never had a surprise party before. He's going to be so shocked. Are Auntie Lainey and Uncle Tyler bringing the baby?"

"I'm pretty sure."

"I can't wait to see her again. I love babies. I wish I had a baby brother or sister."

Hope wanted to groan out loud or go and cry in a corner. She had wanted more children. But this was the first time Sadie had mentioned wanting a sibling, and it broke her heart to think that maybe her daughter had kept that from her. "That would be really nice, Sadie," she choked out. She couldn't let herself think about Dean and marriage and babies. It was foolish. Dreams that belonged to a younger version of herself. She may have blown all of this. She didn't even know that if Dean forgave her, he'd want the future she wanted. It could be too late for her.

"They're here!" Sadie said, jumping up and down.

Hope recognized Cade and Sarah's truck and seconds later it was followed by Tyler and Lainey. But there was no sign of Dean. She walked over to the door and Sadie had already opened it and was standing on the porch. Soon enough, everyone had filled up the small living room and dining room and were all fawning over the baby.

Hope couldn't take it anymore. She hadn't seen or heard from Dean in days. There was no indication he would ever forgive her. She pulled Lainey over to a quiet corner in the kitchen. She managed to whisper to Lainey. "Do you think he'll come?"

"He'll be here," Tyler said, coming up behind Lainey. There was a sparkle in his eye that she was going to take as a good sign.

Hope bit her lower lip, looking up at Tyler. "Really?"

Tyler grinned. "Hope, you have no idea... Dean, he'll be here. Definitely. And Morgan?"

Hope smiled, wringing her hands. "He promised he'd be here tonight. Thanks again for helping me."

"My pleasure. Dean deserves this, and I'm glad Morgan agreed. You had a great idea. I think that might be Dean right now with Aiden and Janie," he said, his gaze going to the window.

Hope frowned and she followed Tyler's gaze. Sure enough, there was Aiden's truck with a horse trailer attached. What in the world? "Oh no, Morgan's not here yet," she moaned.

"Well, one surprise at a time. Poor Dean, he has no idea what's coming," Lainey said with a laugh.

"He's here! Everyone, turn off the lights! We have to surprise Dr. Dean!" Sadie yelled, loud enough that Hope wondered if Dean could hear from inside the truck.

Everyone obeyed, and soon they were all sitting in the dark, barely making a noise. The sound of footsteps on the porch had Hope's heart pounding in her chest, and she placed her hand on the knob. This was it. This was her believing that good things could come to her and that they would stay with her. This was her believing in Dean and letting him know it. This was her saying to hell with her old ideology that whenever something good came into her life, something bad would happen. This was her believing Dean was her good. There was barely a knock before she whipped open the door. Sadie turned on the lights and everyone yelled surprise.

Dean was standing there, the expression on his face something she'd never seen. For a second, she wondered if this had been all wrong, if she'd gambled and lost. His face had turned ashen and his jaw was tight. No one said anything for a moment, but then Sadie jumped into his arms and he lifted her up and, as he made eye contact with Hope over her little girl's shoulder, she saw it. They had his heart. It was in the sheen of his blue eyes, in the way he held onto her, the way he wouldn't break Hope's gaze.

He slowly placed Sadie down and reached for Hope. The second he wrapped her in his arms, she felt the tremor that ran down his strong body. He buried his face in her neck and she held onto him. "Happy birthday," she whispered.

He held her closer. "I love you."

She held onto him tighter as those powerful words sank in, suddenly making everything right again.

"Dr. Dean, you have to have cake! We spent the whole day making it!" Sadie said, excitement lining her voice.

Dean pulled away, a thousand words unspoken as he turned from Hope to Sadie who was pointing at their cake. Hope shaded her eyes. "It's slightly lopsided, but it has cups of real sugar and all the gluten and sprinkles and chocolate a person could ever ask for."

He held out his hand and Sadie clasped it. "That's the best-looking cake I've ever seen."

Sadie beamed up at him, her expression brighter than all the sprinkles on the cake. "I think so, too. The only problem is that I don't think we'll have enough room to put that many candles on one cake."

Dean choked out a laugh as he walked with Sadie to the cake. After they sang a very loud and very off-tune version of "Happy Birthday" and cake was cut and served.

Dean motioned for Hope toward the porch. She gladly followed and stepped out into the cool spring night. "Hey," he said, gruffly, holding his hand out.

The thrill of holding his hand, of having him here, made her giddy and excited and so grateful. "Hey, yourself. I wasn't sure we'd be able to pull this off...or that you'd want to come here. Dean, I'm sorry. I'm sorry for not trusting you enough."

He shook his head. "I was going to come over

here to tell you how sorry I am. I know I lost it and I didn't explain everything that was going through my head. But I never expected this. What you've done for me tonight…it was the best birthday I've ever had. It was the best birthday cake I've ever had. The only homemade anything I've ever had. So, thank you. Thank you for caring about me enough to do that."

Hope blinked back tears at his words, at the emotion etched in every line of his handsome face. She reached up to touch the side of his face. "Love you. I love you so much. Dean…something you don't know, something I should have said, but you…you bring out this side of me that I didn't know existed. You make me feel things I've never felt before. And it scared me." He took her hand and turned it over, kissing her palm.

"Never be scared of me."

"Not of you…of how you make me feel."

"How do I make you feel?"

"Like I'm alive. Like I was never alive before. I never felt this deeply before, and it terrifies me, because you are too perfect. This life that could be ours is too perfect, and it scares me to wish for it. When Brian was dying, I prayed and I had faith and then I was bitter because it felt like it was all for nothing. But maybe it's what kept me going. Maybe it was what brought me here. I'm going to stop looking over my shoulder, I'm going to stop worrying about tomorrow and just trust that we're going to be okay. That is…if you're here for good."

A slow grin that had her heart racing took over his face. He leaned down to kiss her, slowly, deeply, deliciously answering her without words. Dean wasn't a man who would ever give up on her, on Sadie, on whatever problems they had. When he finally pulled back, he held on to her hands, the sheen in his eyes, the emotion in them telling her who he was in his core, who he'd always been. Had that always been there? How could she have missed this? How could she have missed the depth and the love in this man? But she knew how—she'd been so afraid. "I'm here for good. For bad. For all of it. I'm here, forever, sweetheart, if you'll have me. I want to build a lifetime, an empire, a legacy with you, Hope. I want to give you everything you've ever wanted."

She reached out to him, throwing her arms around his neck and holding onto him for dear life. "You are all I need. I love you so much."

"Me too. Also, I should warn you that there's a pony in Aiden's horse trailer."

She pulled back to look him in the eyes. "I should be surprised. But, since we're still confessing secrets, I have one, too. I have something to give you," she said, her eyes on the truck that had slowed and turned up her driveway.

He pulled back, staring at her quizzically. "What are you talking about?"

He slowly turned around, following her gaze. The truck door opened and an older, slightly rougher, more disheveled version of Dean hopped out. Dean swore under his breath and squeezed Hope's hand. "Are you kidding me, Hope?"

"I think I owe you almost a decade of happy birthdays," Morgan called out, his voice hoarse. Hope trailed behind, wanting to give the brothers their space, as Dean walked over to him.

They stood there, the two of them tall and strong and stoic. Hope couldn't breathe as she waited for one of them to do something.

A second later, Morgan brought Dean into a fierce hug that melted Hope's heart. Goose bumps broke out over her arms, and she trembled with emotion at the sight of them. At what this meant for Dean.

Morgan made eye contact with her over Dean's shoulder, the gratitude shining in his eyes making tears fall from hers. "I missed you, man. So much."

"Me too," Dean said hoarsely.

"Hold on. There's someone I want you to meet," Morgan said, pulling away and opening the back door of his truck.

Dean held his hand out to Hope who joined his side as they waited. A moment later, Morgan pulled out a sleepy baby girl who rested on his shoulder. "Meet Sofia. Your niece."

Hope knew at that moment, when both brothers were swiping away the tears that were falling down their faces, fawning over Sofia, that she was witnessing a miracle. And as Sadie joined them, Dean picking her up like she was his family, she knew that second chances didn't get better than this. And when the rest of their friends surrounded them, welcoming Morgan and his little girl back home, Hope held on to Dean and Sadie tightly, desperately cherishing the love that surrounded her. It was this kind of love—the love of friends and family who would do anything for one another, who sincerely wanted the best for one another—that was the greatest gift she would ever receive.

Dean turned to her, amid the laughter and chaos and conversation, and kissed her. "I love you. More than I ever knew possible. You showed me what was possible. You believed in me and who I was before I even knew what I was capable of. Hope, I walked away from everything I ever knew and I would do it all over again in a heartbeat. It was the right thing to do, because letting go of all that hatred, all that resentment, means I can be whole for you. For Sadie. I want it all with you. If you'll have me."

Hope kissed him, not caring that everyone was around. She was done with the days of hiding from her feelings, from love. Dean kissed her back with the passion she'd dreamed about and the love she'd yearned for. He pulled back slightly, his eyes misty, his hand cupping one side of her face. "I was supposed to give you the world, but you've given it to me. You've given me your faith, your love, and family."

"Dr. Dean! Aiden says there's something in that trailer for me!"

Dean looked down at Sadie, and the love shining in his eyes made Hope's heart feel as though it had become new again.

He held out his hand for her and she grasped onto it with all the faith in the world. As Hope stood there, surrounded by family, she watched Dean walk with her daughter. Sadie skipped around him instead of walking, and the sound of his deep laughter made her smile.

Hope didn't take her eyes off the two people she loved more than anything in the world, and grasped onto that faith her daughter was filled with. With the sun tucking in behind the mountains, on this land she'd been so intimidated by months ago, she believed that everything was the way it should be. Past and present coming together. She knew their best days were to come.

EPILOGUE

Hope stared at the two pink lines on the home pregnancy test indicator in disbelief. A flurry of emotions rushed through her. This wasn't planned. Six months ago, when they'd gotten married, with their friends and family by their sides, they'd said they would wait a year.

They'd wanted to use this year to continue building Hope's business, but also their plans for the ranch, which had turned out to be far bigger and better than any of them had imagined. This land was a new beginning for all of them. Morgan had built a home for him and Sofia on the property, closer to the mountains, and the brothers had worked tirelessly on starting a ranch. And Dean had somehow found the energy to put in his hours at the hospital while Hope worked hard to save her business.

The brothers had rebuilt their relationship as though no time had been lost. Forgiveness and hard feelings were easily given because their love and respect for each other was so profound. Their father had reached out only to tell them they were both dead to him and wishing them failure. But that had only motivated them even more.

And somewhere along the way, this tiny miracle

had happened. Months too soon, but right on time. The old Hope would have been so busy looking for problems she would never had expected a blessing. But this was a blessing; late or early, planned or unplanned, this baby was a blessing.

She scrambled to the front door, glancing at the clock. Half an hour before Sadie's bus would be here. Dean and Morgan were probably on their way back from working on the line of fences that needed repairing. She flew out of the front door and ran as fast as she could, hoping she'd be able to catch sight of him.

"Hey, beautiful, where's the fire?"

She stopped abruptly at the sound of Dean's teasing voice. He was standing in the door of the barn, dusty, dirty, and the most handsome man she'd ever seen. Without giving it a second thought, she ran straight for him, knowing he'd catch her. "I missed you, too. Do we have time for me to show you how much? Those bossy pants are looking especially fine on you today."

She laughed. She couldn't believe that not that long ago she'd been ready to throw in the towel, to trade skinny jeans for flannel. "You're a charmer, but I have something to tell you."

"Should I be worried?"

She shook her head, deciding she needed to tell him something else first. "I'm so proud of you."

"Proud of me?"

She nodded. "Everything you've done, everything you've built this year. The way you love me and Sadie. The way you rebuilt your relationship with Morgan, the way you forgave him. You made all this time for all of us—you are building a life for all of us. And after all that, you became chief of staff at the hospital. Dean, I've never known anyone like you. I'm so proud of you. So proud to be your wife."

"I don't know what to say. You've made me the happiest I've ever been, happier than I thought possible. And you've given me everything I ever wanted. A real family. No one has ever loved me like you do. And you gave me back my brother and a niece. And then this ranch—what's happened here is something I imagined possible only in my wildest dreams. Joining this ranch with Tyler and his dad…I get to work beside my best friend and brother every day, and that's all because of you."

She blinked back tears. "I didn't have anything to do with that."

"Don't be modest. This is because of you. Morgan had the money, and combined with mine, we were able to make a fair partnership with Ty and Martin. This is all you," he said roughly.

"I might have something else for you," she said, barely containing her smile.

"I'm all ears," he said, leaning down for a kiss.

She pulled back slightly, wanting to see his

face when she told him. "A baby. I'm pregnant."

His mouth dropped open and he blinked rapidly. "What?"

She nodded repeatedly, watching as he processed the news. When he didn't say anything after a few seconds, she felt the sting of insecurity hit her. "I know things are crazy and we totally didn't plan—"

"Are you happy?" he whispered hoarsely, his eyes watering.

She nodded repeatedly, her heart ready to burst. "So happy."

He framed her face with his hands, leaning down and looking at her squarely in the eyes. "You've given me everything. You've given me your whole heart. I said it before, but you were worth waiting for, Hope. I'd have waited a lifetime for you if I had to. For your heart, your body, your soul. You are the woman I will be forever in love with. Thank you for making all my dreams come true."

"You've done the same for me, Dean. A few months ago, I kept looking over my shoulder, waiting for something catastrophic to happen. I kept thinking that if I was ever truly happy again, something would happen and it would all be taken away from me. You made me brave again. You made me excited for the future, not afraid of it."

As he leaned down to kiss her, Hope knew that this new chapter in her life would be the best one yet. There'd be ups and downs but she was strong enough to face whatever came her way, because she was whole again, when she never thought that possible. She was a different person, accepting each day and being grateful for it, not worrying about tomorrow.

Her daughter was happy and thriving and *Dr. Dean* was an endearing name, a wonderful memory of days gone by, for the man who had become her father. Hope's biggest lesson, the one she'd teach Sadie when she was older, was to never push love away, to always fight for it, and to never lose hope for a happy ending.

ACKNOWLEDGMENTS

To Liz Pelletier...Thank you for continuing to bring the Wishing River stories to my readers!

To Louise Fury...Thank you for always believing in me and being a champion of my work.

To Alethea Spiridon...Thank you for joining me in Wishing River and your dedication!

To Lydia Sharp...Thank you for coming back to Wishing River and your insightful comments.

To Elizabeth Turner Stokes...Thank you for this dream of a cover and capturing the chemistry between Hope and Dean.

To Curtis Svehlak...Thank you for always being so prompt and cheerful and for everything you do.

To Nancy Cantor...Thank you for the liveliest set of copy edits I've ever received! :)

To everyone at Entangled and Macmillan for believing in my books and giving me the opportunity to write these cowboy stories. You have made my dreams come true. Thank you to the countless talented people who made this book possible!

Thank you to my readers for your loyalty, support, and kindness. I treasure all of you.

Victoria
xo

Mail Order Cowboy is a heartwarming story of finding love and the true meaning of family, which ends with a satisfying happily ever after. However, the story includes some elements that might not be suitable for every reader. Cancer and death of a spouse are mentioned in character backstory. Additionally, the story includes: infidelity from a minor character, not from the romance couple; attempted sexual assault; psychological abuse; and father/son feuding. Readers who may be sensitive to these elements, please take note.

Return to Blossom Glen, where two opposites must put their differences aside to help the small town they both love...

the
SWEETHEART
FIX

MIRANDA
LIASSON

Juliet Montgomery absolutely loves her small town of Blossom Glen, Indiana, and everyone loves her. Except for the fact that she's a couples counselor who suffered a *very* public breakup that *no one* can forget. And now her boss asks her to take a step back... which is exactly when the town's good-lookin' and unusually gruff mayor offers her an unexpected job.

Jack Monroe absolutely loves being the mayor of his small town. Except when he actually has to talk to people. Can't he just fix the community problems in peace? Like right now, he's mediating the silliest dispute two neighbors could possibly have. When the town sweetheart steps up and solves everyone's problems in five minutes flat, Jack realizes what this town really needs...is a therapist.

Juliet is able to soothe anyone — other than the surly mayor, it seems. But there's a reason they say opposites attract, because all of their verbal sparring leads to some serious attraction. Only, just like with fireworks, the view might appear beautiful — but she's already had one public explosion that's nearly ruined everything...how can she risk her heart again?

Find something luckier than catching the bouquet in this delightful small-town romance perfect for fans of Virgin River…

The
MATCHMAKER
and the
COWBOY

ROBIN
USA TODAY BESTSELLING AUTHOR
BIELMAN

Callie Carmichael has a gift for making bridesmaid dresses—some even call them *magical*. Somehow, every person who's worn one of her dresses has found love. *Real* love. And as long as that happily-ever-after is for someone else, Callie is happy. Because she's fully over getting her heart broken…which is why her new roommate is *definitely* going to be a problem.

After being overseas for six months, Callie's only choice is to stay with her best friend's ridiculously hot brother, Hunter Owens. Cowboy, troublemaker, and right now, the town's most coveted bachelor. Only, Hunter isn't *quite* the player she thought. And if it weren't for her whole "no more love" thing, their setup could get confusing *really* fast.

Now, Hunter wants Callie to make him a best man suit—a "lucky for love" kind of suit. But what happens if she makes the suit and he finds true love…and it isn't her?

A shy woman. Her outdoorsy crush. And the bet that could bring them together...or implode spectacularly.

first
Bride
to fall

NEW YORK TIMES BESTSELLING AUTHOR

GINNY BAIRD

Nell Delaney will do almost anything for her parents and her two sisters. But enter a marriage of convenience to save the family's coffee shop? *Too* far. So Nell and her sisters strike a deal: whoever hasn't found love in thirty days has to step up to take one for the team. The good news? Nell knows the perfect guy to fall in love with. The bad news? She's going to have to pretend she likes the outdoors...a lot.

Adventure guide Grant Williams knows immediately that Nell is not exactly Little Miss Outdoorsy. She's a walking natural disaster—an amazingly *adorable* disaster. And whoa, their chemistry is unbelievable. Everything between them is so perfect, he's not even a little bit shocked when he starts thinking of forever...

Right up until he catches the town gossiping about the Delaney sisters' bargain and realizes she's just using him to win a bet. Unfortunately, his family's unreliable reputation means he can't just dump one of the town's sweethearts. No, she needs to dump him. If she's going to pretend to be the perfect doting bride, well, he'll just pretend to be the worst bachelor on the market.

Let the games begin...

AMARA

an imprint of Entangled Publishing LLC